# THE GIRL IN THE CLOSET

EVA RAE THOMAS MYSTERY - BOOK 18

# WILLOW ROSE

# Prologue

SHE SLIPPED the key into the lock with the practiced ease of someone who had opened the same door countless times. The house greeted her with its familiar silence—the steady hum of the air conditioner as it battled Florida's unyielding heat. Everything appeared in place, yet a subtle disturbance hung in the air, an unnamed sensation that her body recognized instantly.

She placed her purse on the entry table and put the car keys next to it. The grocery bags were carried directly to the kitchen, where she methodically emptied them, placing each item in its proper place. Order had always been paramount.

After putting away the groceries, she retrieved the laundry basket left by the sofa earlier that morning. The clothes, still slightly warm from the dryer and redolent with the clean scent of detergent, were folded with precision. Neat stacks formed on the coffee table—shirts, pants, undergarments—and, last of all, a set of T-shirts.

The house remained quiet apart from the persistent hum of the air conditioner and the distant, rhythmic crash of ocean waves beyond the back windows. Ten years by the beach had not dulled the dual effect of the sounds—both soothing and ominous, constant reminders of forces beyond control.

Carrying the folded laundry toward the bedroom, her footsteps echoed on the hardwood floors. The hallway seemed unusually long as she paused at the thermostat, frowning at its low setting. Had it been left this way? She adjusted it upward, yet the chill that had wrapped around her felt sourced from something else entirely.

Something was not right.

A persistent thought, unwelcome as it was, slithered into her mind—a product of decades spent honing an instinct that sensed shifts in familiar patterns. She carried over six decades of survival instinct.

With her pace slowing, she advanced down the hallway as the air grew heavier. Her hand brushed along the wall, not out of physical unsteadiness but from a need for reassurance. Her breathing quickened before she caught herself and slowed it intentionally.

"You're being ridiculous," she murmured to herself, a self-address reminiscent of a long-forgotten admonition from childhood.

Yet the prickling on the back of her neck persisted.

Standing before the bedroom doorway, she noted that the room was arranged as it had been that morning—bed neatly made with hospital corners, reading glasses resting beside a well-worn mystery novel, curtains drawn halfway to balance light and privacy. And yet, subtle differences betrayed a disturbance: the antique silver hairbrush lay at an unfamiliar angle on the dresser, and the bedside table's drawer was completely closed when it was always left ajar to avoid sticking. Her eyes swept the room, cataloging every minor anomaly that others might overlook.

Inside, she placed the laundry basket on the bench at the foot of the bed. The floor creaked beneath her—a familiar sound now seeming louder and oddly deliberate. Moving toward the dresser, she gently touched the hairbrush, repositioning it as it should have been. Her fingertips gathered a thin film of dust, except for one clean streak where another hand had clearly gripped it.

Her heart pounded within her ribs; she was not mistaken.

Slowly, she turned and surveyed the room once again. The closet door immediately drew her attention—it stood slightly ajar, revealing an inch of darkness in its gap. It was never left open, not after everything that had happened in the past.

A tightening in her throat recalled painful memories she dreaded to revisit. Still, she forced herself to focus. Calculating the distance between the room's door and the open closet, she hesitated briefly—should she leave, or call for help? Explaining that the closet door was open or that the hairbrush had been moved would only invite worry and analysis, creating doubts about her grip on reality.

No. She needed answers.

Approaching the closet with the caution reserved for a predator's lair, she felt the coolness of the wooden floor through her thin socks. Her breathing echoed in her ears as she took six steps toward the closet, then five, four…. Her neatly arranged conservative dresses and blouses were visible through the gap, hung in color-coordinated sections—dark hues on one side, lighter tones on the other. Nothing stirred; not even a whisper of movement.

Three steps. Two.

A bead of sweat began to trickle down her spine, leaving an icy trail despite the warmth of the day.

One.

Her hand trembled as it reached for the handle, but she forced steadiness. After all she had survived, she would not be undone by an open closet door in her own home. Gripping the cool metal knob firmly, she pulled it open.

Dark eyes met hers through the narrow slits of a black mask. In that frozen heartbeat, the world contracted to a scene of predator and prey, suspended in the dim light of the bedroom. Every detail was arrayed with unsettling clarity: the gleam of leather gloves, the dark clothing, and the subtle rise and fall of breath beneath the mask. Then, with no warning, the silence shattered as the figure lunged.

A primal, desperate scream burst forth as gloved hands reached for her. She staggered back, her hip colliding brutally with the edge of a dresser. Sharp pain flared, and the intruder's momentum sent them both crashing against the wall. A framed photograph tumbled to the floor, its glass shattering in a harsh, resounding clink that sparked a surge of survival instinct over fear.

She fought back furiously.

Fingernails raked across the attacker's forearm where the sleeve had ridden up, drawing forth a hiss of pain and a thin streak of blood on pale skin. That sight kindled her determination: at seventy-three, she was not ready to surrender.

"Get out!" she snarled, her voice hoarse and stripped of all hesitation.

The assailant reached for her throat with ruthless efficiency. Twisting apart, she entangled her feet with the laundry basket, and together they tumbled, colliding with the nightstand. The lamp wavered before falling, its bulb shattering on the hardwood with a sound that echoed like a gunshot.

Her elbow struck something solid—a stomach or ribs—and a brief moment of freedom emerged. Scrambling toward the far side of the bed, she gasped for breath, her heart pounding wildly.

"Help!" she screamed, though the sound would be lost in the isolation. The nearest neighbor was distant and unlikely to hear over the ceaseless murmur of the ocean and the drone of the air conditioner.

The attacker recovered swiftly, vaulting across the bed with unforeseen agility. A gloved hand seized her shoulder, spinning her around. A flash of those merciless, dark eyes passed her vision before a fist crashed into her cheekbone.

Pain exploded across her face as her vision blurred, darkness threatening its edges. Staggering back, her shoulders slammed against the dresser, sending perfume bottles and other trinkets crashing. The mingling scents of shattered glass and cloying perfume intermingled with the metallic tang of her blood.

The assailant pressed forward again, the hands making another lunge for her throat. Desperate, her fingers fumbled across the dresser until they closed around the heavy silver hairbrush—a cherished gift from years past. With every ounce of strength, she swung it, and it struck the assailant's head with a dull thud. Though not enough to halt the attacker entirely, it granted her precious seconds.

Disoriented, the attacker shook their head once before charging anew with furious determination. Their body slammed into hers, forcing her back against the wall. The impact roared the air from her lungs as the weight pinned her, and the hands found her throat, fingers digging in relentlessly.

In the grip of panic, she lashed out, her knee rising in a wild attempt to strike a vulnerable spot. Though she only connected with a thigh, the hold loosened just enough for her to twist sideways, sending them both off balance.

They crashed into the nightstand, its contents—reading glasses, a water glass, a phone—scattering across the floor. The phone, its screen aglow, lay within tantalizing reach.

She lunged forward, stretching her fingers, when the assailant grabbed her ankle, yanking her backward. Her chin struck the floor, teeth clattering as she tasted coppery blood. The phone drifted just out of reach.

"No," she gasped, kicking backward with her free foot. Her heel found its mark—a hit to a nose or mouth—and the attacker grunted in pain.

Crawling on her hands and knees, she reached for the phone and gripped it tightly. Before she could unlock it, a heavy weight crashed down onto her back, pinning her to the floor as the phone skittered beneath the bed.

"Get off me!" she cried, bucking and rolling until she found herself on her back once again. The attacker's weight settled over her hips, the gloved hands returning to her throat with murderous intent. Claws raked at the wrists and arms, and her nails caught the edge of the mask, tilting it just enough for a fleeting glimpse of the face.

As her vision began to darken at the edges from oxygen deprivation, she refused to succumb in her own bedroom. With a strength born of desperation, she thrust both hands between the attacker's arms and struck out, breaking the hold on her throat.

The sudden release allowed precious air to rush back into her lungs, painful yet life-affirming. Without hesitation, she slapped her hands against the assailant's ears—a move from long ago. Disoriented by the pressure shift, the attacker reeled backward.

Twisting free, she half-crawled and half-stumbled toward the bedroom door. Freedom beckoned in the hallway and beyond the front door, where help might be found. Though her legs wavered and her throat burned, she persevered.

Reaching the doorway, she forced herself upright against the frame and propelled into the hallway.

The hallway stretched before her like a runway to salvation. Staggering forward with trembling hands pressed against the wall, she left crimson streaks on the pale paint. Her breaths came in ragged gasps—a mere ten, perhaps twelve, steps to the front door. She had to make it. Behind her, the bedroom door frame splintered as the attacker burst through, the pursuit as relentless as an incoming tide.

"Help!" she screamed once more, her voice raw and trembling with fear. The cry echoed off the empty walls, returned in a mocking refrain. No one was coming; no one could hear her. She was utterly alone with the intruder in the secluded home she had chosen as her sanctuary.

Lunging forward, her fingertips grazed a decorative table where mail and keys were kept. The front door glimmered at the hall's end, its small window framing a rectangle of late-afternoon sunlight. So close.

Then, without warning, a firm, unyielding hand wrapped around her ankle—a vise-like grip that yanked her back with brutal force. Her chin struck the hardwood floor, her teeth slicing into her tongue as blood flooded her mouth. She clawed desperately at the smooth floor, nails breaking under the strain of fighting the pull.

A pained, garbled "No!" escaped her lips through blood and fear.

Dragged backward, she slid across freshly polished floors—a bitter irony to the meticulous care taken to keep her home a sanctuary. Hips scraped against the floor, her dress sliding up as her skin burned from friction, every movement a battle. Her foot connected with something—perhaps a knee, maybe a thigh—and she kicked again with all the strength she could muster.

That kick connected solidly. The assailant staggered back, clutching the knee. She pushed herself to stand, swaying and using the wall for support as the world tilted dangerously, and blood thundered in her ears. On a nearby table, a heavy ceramic vase—a long-ago housewarming gift—stood as a beacon. Without hesitation, she snatched it up; its solid weight provided reassurance amid the chaos.

The masked attacker recovered quickly, lurching toward her with murderous intent. Instinct took over as she swung the vase in a broad arc, striking the side of the attacker's head. The force reverberated up her arms, jarring her shoulders as the vase shattered into a cascade of blue and white fragments.

The attacker staggered sideways, colliding with the wall as a framed photograph tumbled to the floor, its glass cracking on impact. For a brief, shining moment, it seemed as if the attack might have been stopped.

It was not.

Shaking their head, blood seeped from beneath the mask where shards of ceramic had lacerated the skin. The dark eyes met hers once more, now filled with a furious resolve. Pushing off the wall with renewed determination, the attacker once again surged forward.

She turned to run, but her legs—weak and unresponsive—betrayed her. Before she could take more than a few faltering steps, the hands grabbed her hair and yanked her backward. Pain exploded across her scalp as her cry, raw and animalistic, filled the air.

They grappled against the wall, caught in a grotesque mimicry of an embrace as family photos—from graduations to cherished moments at the beach, snapshots of a life—fell around them and shattered on the floor.

With desperation as her fuel, she drove her elbow back repeatedly into the attacker's ribs. Each blow seemed to count for less, or perhaps her strength was waning. A strong arm snaked around her neck from behind, the forearm pressing into her windpipe with the practiced precision of a professional hold.

In a moment of blurred determination, her hand reached behind, fingers seeking the face through the mask. She clawed desperately, finding softness and provoking a pained howl as the grip loosened enough for her to twist free.

Stumbling forward just two steps before the attacker recovered, she found it insufficient. The attacker slammed into her from behind, the force carrying both into a decorative mirror hanging in the hallway. The mirror shattered on impact, glass cascading in a deadly shower. A shard sliced a wound across her cheek, while another embedded in her palm as she attempted to cushion their fall.

They tumbled to the floor together, the attacker's weight robbing her of breath as she was flipped onto her back with terrifying ease. Exhausted, she realized that every ounce of her energy had been spent, yet the hands found her throat once again, their grip relentless.

Gazing up at the masked face, she mustered a final act of defiance. "Why?" she gasped—a single word that cost her precious oxygen.

She did not get an answer. The pressure mounted, her airway closing completely. Her hands reached weakly to pull at the wrists, but strength had abandoned her. They fluttered helplessly like wounded birds against the arms.

As the hallway dimmed around her and the pain in her throat gave way to a strange, floating numbness, the distant murmur of the ocean seemed to beckon one last time. Her right hand dropped, coming to rest beside a sharp shard of mirror glass, long as a knife, cold and deadly.

Everything grew darker and quieter. The face above blurred as her lungs screamed for air that would not come. In a final act of defiance, her fingers closed around the shard, cutting into her own flesh. There was no time for pain—only the desperate need to fight back one last time.

Slowly, almost imperceptibly, her hand rose. The shard caught a beam of late-afternoon sunlight, glinting with the promise of resistance.

Then, darkness swallowed everything.

# Part I

Cocoa Beach, FL

Tuesday evening

# Chapter 1

THE LAUGHTER around our coffee table reminded me why I fought so hard to keep moments like these alive. Monopoly money was scattered between bowls of popcorn and half-empty soda cans, my family's faces lit by the soft glow of our living room lamps. These were the hours that made the darkness of my work bearable—these stolen evenings when I wasn't Agent Thomas but just Mom, just Eva Rae.

"Mom, Christine's stealing from the bank again!" Alex complained, pointing an accusatory finger at his older sister.

Christine rolled her eyes. "I'm the banker. I'm supposed to handle the money."

"Yeah, handle it, not pocket it," Angel chimed in, her smile revealing the gap where she'd lost a tooth last week.

Matt caught my eye across the board, his lips quirking in that half-smile that still made my stomach flip after all this time. He winked, and I felt the warm rush of gratitude for this patchwork family we'd stitched together.

"Christine," I said, keeping my voice deliberately light, "we have enough criminals in this world without you starting a career in bank fraud."

"Says the FBI agent," she shot back, but her fingers slid a five-hundred-dollar bill back into the game box.

I leaned back against the couch cushions, taking in the scene before me. Christine sat cross-legged on the floor, her dark hair pulled into a messy bun that somehow looked intentional on her. Alex had sprawled halfway across the coffee table, his elbow dangerously close to toppling his soda. Angel perched on Matt's lap, occasionally whispering strategic advice in his ear that made him nod solemnly. These small gestures—the way Christine's eyes found mine when she made a clever move, Matt's hand absently rubbing Angel's back, the competitive nudges between the kids—they were the invisible threads that bound us.

Matt had arranged a plate of sliced apples and cheese on the side table. The living room smelled of the cinnamon candle Angel had picked out at the farmers' market last weekend. Outside, rain tapped gently against the windows, cocooning us further in our private world. I'd left my phone in the kitchen—a deliberate choice to be present, not to let the job intrude.

"Your turn, Mom," Alex nudged my knee. "You're falling behind."

"I'm playing the long game," I said, picking up the dice. "You never see the FBI coming until it's too late."

Their groans made me laugh. These were the moments I stored away, mental photographs for the days when work pulled me into humanity's darkest corners.

The dice clattered across the board. Seven. I moved my piece—the thimble, always the thimble—and landed on Boardwalk.

"That's mine!" Angel squealed. "With a hotel! Pay up, Mom!"

"Highway robbery," I muttered, counting out colorful bills.

Matt's laughter joined Angel's. "She's ruthless. Gets that from you."

"I'm choosing to take that as a compliment," I replied, handing over my Monopoly fortune to my youngest.

The thump was so sudden, so out of place, that for a second no one reacted. Then came the unmistakable sound of something falling over—from the garage. It was followed by a cry. My smile froze, muscles tensing like a switch had been flipped. I set down my depleted stack of money and listened.

"What was that?" Christine asked, her voice dropping to a whisper.

"Probably just the wind knocking something over," Matt offered, but his eyes met mine, reading the change in my posture. There was no wind inside the garage; we all knew that much. And wind doesn't make a crying sound like that.

Angel clutched Matt's arm. "Is someone out there?"

"I'll go check," I said, already rising. "It might be a raccoon or an opossum."

Matt started to stand, shifting Angel to the side. "I can go."

"No." The word came out sharper than I intended. I softened my tone. "I'll go. It's fine."

But it wasn't fine. My heart had quickened, not with fear but with the familiar rush of adrenaline. The agent in me never truly slept, just dozed with one eye open. Since Matt lost his leg in the line of duty, I had been overly protective of him, terrified something bad would happen to him again.

"Stay here," I told them, moving toward our bedroom.

Inside, I unlocked the drawer of my nightstand and removed my service weapon. The cool metal against my palm shifted something in my brain—the mother receded, and the agent emerged. I checked the chamber with practiced movements, the routine as familiar as brushing my teeth.

When I returned to the living room, Matt's eyes locked onto the gun.

"Is that necessary?" he asked quietly, angling his body to block the younger kids' view.

"Probably not," I admitted. "But I'd rather be cautious. There's been a series of break-ins lately in Cocoa Beach, and I can't be too careful."

Christine watched me with narrowed eyes. She'd seen this transformation before, understood the weight behind it.

"We'll pause the game," Matt said, his voice deliberately casual for the kids' benefit. "Angel, how about you and Alex pick out a movie for after?"

I gave him a grateful nod, then moved toward the door that connected to the garage. The laughter from moments ago felt distant now, replaced by the focused clarity that came with assessing potential threats.

My fingers closed around the doorknob. Behind me, my family waited in a tableau of interrupted joy. Whatever waited on the other side of this door would have to answer for that crime first.


I pushed the door open with my shoulder, leading with my weapon. The garage was a cave of half-shadows. Every sound amplified in the enclosed space—the tick of cooling engines, the hum of the beer refrigerator in the corner, my own controlled breathing. I moved like I was treading through water, each step deliberate, my senses stretched to their limits.

The concrete floor felt solid beneath my bare feet—I'd left my slippers behind in the rush. A forgotten beach towel draped over a bike handlebar created a human-sized silhouette that made my finger twitch against the trigger guard. The air smelled of motor oil and the faint mustiness of cardboard boxes stacked against the far wall.

Something had fallen—there. A rack of garden tools lay toppled by the workbench, rakes and shovels sprawled across the floor like pickup sticks. But tools don't fall on their own.

I sidled along the wall, keeping my back protected. Matt's car offered too many hiding spots—beneath it, behind it, even inside it.

"FBI," I called out, my voice firm and steady. "I'm armed. Show yourself. Now."

The silence stretched, punctuated only by the soft buzzing of the fluorescent light I'd flipped on. I waited, counting heartbeats. One. Two. Three.

A scuffing sound came from behind Matt's car. I adjusted my stance, weapon trained on the source of the noise.

"Last warning. Come out with your hands where I can see them."

A sneaker emerged first. Then a leg in rumpled jeans. Finally, a thin figure rose slowly from behind the vehicle, hands raised shakily.

"Elijah?" I lowered my weapon instantly. The boy looked like he'd been through hell. His dark hair stuck up in greasy clumps. His hoodie was wrinkled and stained, hanging off one shoulder. His face was ghost-pale except for the red rims around his eyes—eyes that darted nervously between me and the door behind me.

"Don't shoot," he whispered, a feeble attempt at humor that fell flat in the charged air.

The garage door behind me banged open. Matt burst in, eyes wild with concern.

"Eva? What's—" He stopped short. "Elijah? What are you doing here?"

The change in Elijah was immediate and striking. The boy's body went rigid, shoulders hunching inward. He took a half-step back, bumping against the car. His eyes, which had held a certain frightened openness when looking at me, now narrowed and shifted to the floor. The fingers of his raised hands curled inward.

"I tipped over the tools, and they landed on my foot. I'm sorry. I just needed somewhere to go," he mumbled, addressing the concrete.

Matt moved forward. "Son—"

Elijah flinched—a small motion, but unmistakable. In that tiny movement, I read volumes: fear, distrust, perhaps even anger. I'd seen similar reactions in trauma victims, though comparing Matt to an abuser felt wrong. This was something else—something broken between them that I wasn't entirely privy to.

I holstered my weapon, tucking it into the waistband of my jeans at the small of my back. The transition from Agent Thomas to maternal figure happened with practiced ease.

"Are you hurt?" I asked, keeping my voice neutral, neither the sharp command of an agent nor the softness that might embarrass a teenage boy.

Elijah shook his head, still not looking at Matt. "I'm fine." The standard teenage response, belied by everything about his appearance.

"You're not fine," Matt said, frustration edging his tone. "Does Grandma know you're here? Or are you hiding from her?"

Elijah had been living with Matt's mother ever since Matt lost his leg in the line of duty. Matt had told me it was Elijah's own choice, that he wanted to live with his grandmother.

Elijah's jaw tightened. Another step back. "Grandma is… gone."

"She's what?" Matt said a little too loudly, and Elijah winced.

I moved slightly, positioning myself between them without making it obvious. "Matt," I said quietly, a warning in my tone. To Elijah, I said, "How long have you been in our garage?"

"A few hours," he admitted. "I didn't want to… interrupt your family thing."

The words carried weight. Your family thing. Not our family thing. The distinction wasn't lost on Matt, whose face flickered with hurt.

"You're not an interruption," Matt said, softening his approach. "You're my son."

Elijah's eyes finally lifted to me, not Matt—a silent plea.

"Let's go inside," I suggested, taking control of the situation. "It's hot out here, and whatever's going on, we can figure it out where it's comfortable."

"I don't want to be a problem," Elijah muttered.

"You're not," I assured him. "But those garden tools didn't knock themselves over."

A ghost of a smile touched his lips. "Sorry about that. I was trying to move around in the dark."

"Why were you in the dark?" Matt asked, unable to keep the accusation from his voice. "Why didn't you just come to the door?"

The fragile connection snapped. Elijah's face shut down again.

"Matt," I said gently, "why don't you go tell the kids everything's okay? I'll bring Elijah in."

Matt hesitated, clearly torn between asserting his paternal role and recognizing that his approach wasn't working. Finally, he nodded and backed toward the door.

"I'll make some hot chocolate," he offered, a peace offering that Elijah didn't acknowledge.

After Matt left, Elijah's shoulders dropped an inch. I didn't miss the significance of that subtle relaxation.

"You don't have to tell me everything right this second," I told him, "but I do need to know if anyone's in danger. Are you running from something?"

He hesitated, then shook his head. "Not exactly. It's… complicated."

I nodded, not pushing. "Most things worth talking about are. Come on."

I gestured toward the door, careful not to touch him or crowd his space. As he moved past me, I caught the scent of fear-sweat and something else—something that had me puzzled. He smelled like bleach.

<hr>

# Chapter 2

<hr>

THE LIVING ROOM had transformed in our absence. The scattered Monopoly pieces remained, but the warm bubble of family fun had burst. Christine stood by the window, arms crossed, watching us enter with undisguised curiosity. Angel and Alex huddled together on the couch beside Matt, who'd taken the edge seat, poised for action. I guided Elijah to the armchair, noting how he deliberately chose the seat farthest from his father. The space between them might as well have been filled with concrete.

"Elijah!" Alex exclaimed with the unfiltered enthusiasm of youth. "Are you staying for game night?"

Elijah's hands twisted in his lap. "No, I—"

"This isn't exactly a social visit," I cut in gently, sparing him the explanation. My eyes met Christine's, and I saw the wheels turning behind her analytical gaze. At seventeen, she missed nothing.

"Is that blood on your sleeve?" she asked Elijah directly.

The room went still. I glanced down and noticed what my daughter had spotted immediately—a small, rust-colored stain on Elijah's cuff. He tucked his arm quickly against his body.

"It's just dirt," he mumbled, but the damage was done.

"Christine," I said, using my this-is-not-negotiable voice, "take Angel and Alex upstairs."

"But Mom—"

"Now."

She rolled her eyes but complied, herding her siblings toward the staircase.

"This is so unfair," Alex protested. "We never get to hear the good stuff."

"I'll tell you later," Christine promised in a whisper she clearly meant me to hear.

"No, you won't," I countered, giving her a look that stopped further argument.

Once their footsteps faded upstairs, I pulled the ottoman closer to Elijah and sat facing him. Not too close—giving him space—but close enough to establish a connection. Matt remained on the couch, leaning forward with his elbows on his knees, face tight with concern.

"Elijah," I began, "when did you last see your grandmother?"

His eyes fixed on a point just past my shoulder. "Three days ago. Tuesday morning. She made pancakes."

"And you haven't heard from her since?"

He shook his head. "Her car's still in the garage. Her purse is on the kitchen counter. But she's gone."

"Did you call her friends? Check the hospital?" Matt interjected.

Elijah's jaw tightened. "I'm not stupid. I called everyone. Nobody's seen her."

"We don't think you're stupid," I assured him, shooting Matt a warning glance, telling him to take it down a notch. "We're just gathering information."

"Why didn't you call the police?" Matt asked, his voice softening with effort. "Or us?"

Elijah's fingers gripped the armrests. "Because of what I found."

The room seemed to cool by several degrees. My skin prickled with the change in atmosphere.

"What did you find, Elijah?" I kept my voice steady and professional.

His eyes finally met mine, red-rimmed and haunted. "There was blood in her bedroom. It was a complete mess, with broken photo frames and vases, glass everywhere, and even a broken mirror. I got scared, so I hid, hoping she'd come home, but she never did."

Matt's face drained of color. "Blood? How much blood?"

"A lot," Elijah whispered. "On the carpet. I tried to clean it up, but I couldn't get it all." His voice cracked. "There was too much."

My mind immediately cataloged possibilities, none of them good. In my experience, significant blood loss coupled with a missing person rarely had a happy ending. But I kept my expression neutral.

"Why did you try to clean it up?" I asked carefully.

"I don't know." His hands trembled. "I panicked. I thought… I thought if I cleaned it up, maybe it meant nothing happened." A tear escaped, which he wiped away roughly. "That's stupid, right?"

"No," I said softly. "It's human."

Matt stood suddenly, pacing to the window and back. "We need to call this in. Now."

I nodded but stayed focused on Elijah. "Why didn't you come inside earlier? Why hide in the garage?"

He glanced at the board game and the scattered snacks. "You were having family time. I sat in the garage for hours, trying to figure out what to say. How to explain." His shoulders hunched. "I didn't want to ruin everything."

"You couldn't ruin anything," Matt said, his voice rough with emotion. He moved toward his son, hand outstretched.

Elijah leaned away from the touch. Matt's hand hung in the air for a moment before dropping heavily to his side.

The rejection was palpable. I watched Matt struggle with it, saw the hurt flash across his face before he masked it. "I need to go see the house."

I placed a hand on his arm. "Not tonight. It's late. She's been gone for days. One more night won't matter. It will all be there tomorrow. Let's go together. And we'll need to file a missing person's report."

Elijah nodded, exhaustion evident in every line of his body.

"But first we need to get you to bed," I added. "It's late, and you look like you haven't slept in days."

"I haven't," he admitted. "Every time I close my eyes, I see the blood."

Matt cleared his throat. "Your old room is still set up. You should stay here."

The offer hung awkwardly between them. They hadn't seen much of one another for the past few years. In the meantime, the boy seemed to have grown up… maybe a little too quickly.

"We'll figure this out together," I promised, stepping into the void. "First thing tomorrow, we'll go to your grandmother's house, and I'll assess the scene."

"Professional assessment?" Elijah asked, a flicker of hope in his voice.

"Yes," I nodded. "FBI assessment."

For the first time since he'd emerged from behind the car, Elijah's posture softened slightly. He trusted my credentials, if nothing else.

"You should get some rest," Matt tried again, his voice gentler. "I can find you some clean clothes. You've grown so much, you might fit into some of mine."

Elijah nodded without looking at his father. "Thanks," he said, the word short and clipped.

I stood, offering my hand to help him up. He took it briefly, his fingers cold against mine.

"I'll show you upstairs," I said. As we walked toward the staircase, I caught Matt's gaze over Elijah's shoulder. The worry there wasn't just for his mother—it was for the chasm between him and his son, a gap I wasn't sure how to bridge.

But first things first. Tomorrow, I'd see the blood for myself. Tonight, we'd give this boy sanctuary. My FBI brain was already constructing timelines and possible scenarios, but I pushed those thoughts aside. Right now, Elijah needed safety more than he needed questions.

The game pieces sat abandoned on the table, colorful money scattered like fallen leaves. The evening had started with family bonds and ended with bloodstains. The contrast wasn't lost on me. This was how cases often began—with small disruptions that revealed deeper, darker currents running beneath seemingly calm waters.

---

# Chapter 3

---

THEN:

The Thompson family car hummed along the country road, a bubble of warmth and pride cutting through the cool spring night. Michael kept glancing in the rearview mirror at Ellie, his six-year-old daughter, who sat in her booster seat, clutching her ballet costume's tutu like it might float away if she let go. Sarah reached back to smooth a stray curl from Ellie's forehead, her fingers lingering for just a moment longer than necessary.

"Our little star," Michael said, his voice carrying that special softness he reserved just for Ellie. "I think that was your best performance yet."

"Really?" Ellie's voice was pitched high with excitement. She hugged the sparkly pink tutu tighter, her small fingers tracing the sequins that caught the passing streetlights in tiny bursts of color.

Sarah turned in her seat, her smile visible even in the dim car interior. "Really. When you did that perfect pirouette, Dad nearly fell out of his chair."

"I did not!" Michael protested, but his laugh betrayed him. "Though I might have gasped a little."

Ellie giggled, kicking her feet against the bottom of her seat. The rhinestones on her ballet slippers twinkled with each movement. Just an hour ago, she had been center stage at Miss Patty's Dance Academy's Spring Recital, a spotlight turning her into something magical. She could still feel the flutter in her stomach when the music started, could still hear the applause washing over her when she held her final pose.

"Mrs. Jenkins said I was the best flower fairy they've ever had," Ellie announced, sitting up straighter. "She said I had natural talent."

"Mrs. Jenkins is absolutely right," Sarah agreed. She reached for Michael's hand on the console between them and squeezed it. Their shared look spoke volumes—pride, love, and that particular wonder of seeing your child shine.

The car rounded a bend in the road, headlights sweeping across trees that lined either side. The route home from Maplewood's community center was familiar but winding, cutting through stretches of woodland before reaching their neighborhood.

"What do you say we stop for ice cream to celebrate?" Sarah suggested. "I think Benson's might still be open."

Ellie bounced in her seat. "Can I get chocolate with sprinkles? And whipped cream? And a cherry?"

"I don't know," Michael teased, pretending to consider it seriously. "That's an awful lot of toppings for such a tiny dancer."

"I'm not tiny! I'm the biggest in my class!"

"That's true," Sarah laughed. "Miss Patty had to order her costume specially because our girl is growing like a weed."

The car slowed as they approached another curve. Through the windshield, the night pressed close, the road visible only in the sweep of their headlights. Michael turned the wheel with practiced ease, the tires humming against asphalt.

"Maybe I'll be a real ballerina someday," Ellie mused, twirling a ribbon from her costume around her finger. "With pointe shoes and everything."

Michael nodded, glancing at her in the mirror again. "You can be anything you want to be, Ellie-belly. Your mother and I will…."

The brightness came without warning—twin beams of light spearing through the darkness ahead, wobbling and veering across the center line. The approaching car swung wildly into their lane, its high beams blinding.

"What the…?" Michael tensed, his knuckles going white on the steering wheel.

Sarah's hand flew to the dashboard. "Michael!"

"Hold on!" he shouted, jerking the wheel hard to the right.

Time stretched like taffy. Ellie felt the car lurch beneath her and heard the squeal of tires against the pavement. The world outside the windows blurred. Her stomach lifted the way it did on playground swings, but wrong, all wrong.

The other car screamed past them, missing by inches. Ellie caught a flash of red paint, a driver's shadowed face. Then came the horrible moment of suspension as their own car left the road entirely, front wheels spinning over empty air at the edge of an embankment.

Sarah's scream tangled with Ellie's. Michael fought with the wheel, but gravity had already claimed them. The world tilted, then rolled. The seatbelt cut into Ellie's chest. Her tutu fluttered upward, sequins catching the chaos of movement like tiny, disoriented stars.

Metal groaned. Glass shattered. The crunching sounds came from everywhere at once, percussive and final. Ellie's head snapped sideways, then forward. One of her ballet slippers flew off her foot. The family Polaroid photo they'd taken before the recital—propped on the seat beside her—tumbled across the car's ceiling as it became the floor.

They were rolling and tumbling, an awful carnival ride that wouldn't stop. Ellie screamed until her voice cracked, her small body held in place by the straps of her booster seat while everything else in the world turned upside down and broke apart.

When the motion finally ceased, the silence felt like another kind of violence. The car settled at a twisted angle, one headlight still miraculously shining, casting eerie shadows through the trees.

Something hissed and ticked beneath the crumpled hood. The sweet scent of Ellie's strawberry shampoo mixed with sharper smells: gasoline, hot metal, the copper tang of blood.

In her booster seat, Ellie hung suspended, the world around her shattered beyond recognition.

The world had turned sideways. Ellie blinked, trying to make sense of what she was seeing. The car rested at an impossible angle, nose crumpled against the earth, one side partially caved in. Her booster seat held her firmly in place, the straps digging into her shoulders. Outside, trees stood like silent witnesses, their leaves stirring in a breeze she couldn't feel.

Something warm trickled down her forehead. She touched it with trembling fingers. Sticky. Red in the strange half-light. Not much, just a small cut where her head had struck something during the tumble down the embankment.

"Mommy?" Her voice sounded wrong—too small, too quivery. It didn't sound like the voice of a dance recital star at all.

The front of the car was worse than the back. Much worse. The dashboard had folded inward like a paper fan. The windshield was a spiderweb of cracks, some sections missing entirely. Through the gaps, Ellie could see dirt and twisted metal and the night sky beyond, stars indifferent to the broken things below them.

"Daddy?" she tried again, louder this time.

Her mother didn't move. Sarah Thompson sat unnaturally still in the passenger seat, her head at an angle that made Ellie's stomach hurt to look at. The pretty blue dress she'd worn to the recital was darkened with something wet. Her eyes were open but didn't blink, didn't move, didn't see.

A soft groan came from the driver's seat. Michael Thompson shifted slightly, his movements slow and pained. The steering wheel pressed against his chest, pinning him. When he coughed, a red mist appeared on his lips.

"Ellie." His voice was a rasp, barely recognizable. "Ellie-belly. Are you hurt?"

"I'm okay," she whispered, though she wasn't sure if that was true. Nothing hurt exactly, but everything felt wrong. "Daddy, Mommy won't answer me."

Michael tried to turn toward his wife but winced sharply. "It's okay," he said, though his voice cracked on the words. "Help is coming. Someone will have seen. They'll come."

The smell inside the car made Ellie's nose wrinkle: gasoline, sharp and chemical, and the sweet-salty tang of blood. The lingering scent of her mother's perfume seemed absurdly normal. From somewhere beneath the crumpled hood came a steady tick-tick-tick, like an angry clock.

"I'm scared," Ellie admitted, her lower lip trembling. She was a big girl—Mrs. Jenkins had said so—but now she felt very small indeed.

"I know, sweetheart." Michael shifted again, grimacing with effort. He managed to free his right arm and reached awkwardly between the seats, trying to touch her. "I'm here."

Their fingers brushed, and Ellie felt a spark of relief so intense it nearly hurt. His hand was wet with blood, but it was warm and it was Daddy's, and that was all that mattered.

"Your mother…," he began, then stopped, his breath catching. "Your mother loves you so much, Ellie. So, so much."

Something in his voice made the tears come then, spilling hot down Ellie's cheeks. "I want to go home," she sobbed. "I want to go home with you and Mommy."

Beyond the broken windows, a sound emerged, distant at first, then growing—a wailing that cut through the night… sirens. Michael's eyes flickered with relief.

"See? They're coming." His words slurred slightly. "They'll help us."

But his fingers had grown cooler in Ellie's grasp. His breathing turned shallow, each inhale a struggle that made his whole body shudder. Somewhere in the woods below, branches cracked as if someone was approaching.

"Daddy?" Ellie's voice rose with panic. "Daddy?"

Michael's eyes found hers in the dimness. He tried to smile, but it looked all wrong, twisted with pain. "My beautiful girl," he whispered. "My little dancer."

His chest hitched oddly. When he spoke again, the words were faint, as if coming from much farther away than the front seat. "Be brave, Ellie-belly."

His fingers went slack in hers.

"No!" Ellie yanked at her seatbelt, trying to reach him. "Daddy! Wake up!"

Outside, lights flashed through the trees—red, blue, white. The sirens were louder now, almost upon them. Voices called in the darkness. Flashlight beams swept down the embankment, illuminating the twisted path the car had carved through underbrush and saplings.

"Down here! We've got a vehicle!" someone shouted.

Boots slid on loose earth. Uniformed figures appeared like ghosts through the broken windows, their faces grim masks in the emergency lights. A woman in a paramedic's uniform crouched by Ellie's window, her gloved hand testing the jammed door.

"Hey there, sweetheart," she said, her voice gentle but urgent. "We're going to get you out. Can you tell me your name?"

Ellie couldn't answer. Her eyes remained fixed on her father's motionless form, on the hand that had held hers moments ago but now hung limp and cooling.

More people arrived—firefighters with strange equipment, more paramedics with bags and stretchers. They swarmed around the car like ants, speaking in strange phrases Ellie couldn't understand. Someone used a tool that made a horrible screaming noise as it cut through the car's frame.

"Pulse?" asked a paramedic who had managed to reach Sarah.

"Nothing," came the reply.

"This one's still got a faint cardiac rhythm," said another, leaning over Michael. "But he's fading fast."

The door beside Ellie finally gave way with a screech of metal. The female paramedic reached in, her hands gentle as she assessed Ellie for injuries.

"You're doing great," she soothed, though Ellie hadn't done anything at all. "We're going to get you out now, okay?"

Ellie watched, numb and distant, as the emergency workers fought a battle she already somehow knew they would lose. Her father's chest no longer rose and fell. Her mother remained terribly, finally still. The lights flashed across their faces, painting them in alternating red and blue, making them look almost alive again in brief, cruel moments.

By the time they cut through her seatbelt, both her parents had stopped moving entirely.

The paramedic's hands were warm through her latex gloves as she carefully unfastened the straps of Ellie's booster seat. "Almost there, honey," she murmured, her voice steady despite the chaos surrounding them. "You're doing so well."

Ellie didn't feel like she was doing anything at all. She sat perfectly still, her eyes never leaving the front seats where other emergency workers hunched over her parents.

"Can you wiggle your toes for me?" the paramedic asked, her flashlight beam sweeping over Ellie's legs. The rhinestones on her remaining ballet slipper caught the light, sending tiny rainbows across the crumpled ceiling. Ellie wiggled her toes. "Good girl. How about your fingers?"

Ellie complied mechanically, her body responding while her mind floated somewhere above the scene, watching it all happen to someone else. The tutu she'd been so proud of was crushed and torn now, one of the sequined flowers hanging by a thread.

Outside the car, a firefighter called something to his team. The grinding sound of metal cutting tools paused. "Ready for extraction. Cervical collar in place?"

"Affirmative," the paramedic beside Ellie responded. She fitted a stiff plastic collar around Ellie's neck, explaining softly, "This is just to keep you safe while we move you, sweetie. Nothing to worry about."

But Ellie wasn't worried. She felt nothing at all as they slid a board behind her and secured straps across her body. The world had narrowed to a tunnel where only certain details penetrated: the blood drying tacky on her father's hand; the unnatural angle of her mother's neck; the way the paramedics' voices changed when they spoke about her parents—hushed, clipped, their hope bleeding out with each passing second.

"On my count," someone said. "One, two, three."

They lifted her from the wreckage with careful precision, six hands supporting the backboard. As they carried her up the embankment, Ellie caught glimpses of the scene around her. The night was no longer dark. Emergency vehicles lined the road above, their lights turning the forest into a pulsing, otherworldly landscape. Radio chatter crackled between responders. Someone had spread a silver blanket on the ground. Another paramedic waited beside a stretcher, medical bags open and ready.

"Any family we should contact?" one of the firefighters asked, his voice low.

The paramedic carrying Ellie's backboard shook her head slightly. "Not now."

At the top of the embankment, they set her stretcher down on stable ground. The paramedic leaned over her, checking pupils, pulse, and asking questions that Ellie answered in monosyllables. Yes, she could feel that. No, nothing hurt too badly. Yes, she remembered what happened.

Down below, there were more shouts. More urgency. The medical team working on her parents grew larger, then smaller. Equipment was passed up the hill, then down again. Someone called for more blood. Someone else reported stats in clipped, professional tones that couldn't hide the futility underneath.

A police officer approached, his uniform neat except for the mud caking his boots and pant cuffs. His face was kind in the harsh emergency lights, lines etched around eyes that had seen too many nights like this one. He knelt beside Ellie's stretcher, removing his hat. His hair underneath was flattened with sweat, despite the cool night air.

"Hello there," he said softly. "My name's Officer Parker. Can you tell me your name?"

"Ellie Thompson," she whispered. "I'm six."

He nodded, his smile gentle but strained. "Ellie, the doctors are working very hard to help your mom and dad." He paused, choosing his words with painful care. "But they were hurt badly in the accident."

Ellie stared at him, waiting. Adults always thought children couldn't understand things, but she did. She understood the way his eyes couldn't quite meet hers. She understood the hushed voices and the slowing pace of activity below. She understood the paramedic who now stood beside her, a hand resting lightly on her shoulder.

"Your parents," the officer continued, his voice cracking slightly, "they've gone to heaven, Ellie. Do you understand what that means?"

She understood. It meant they weren't coming back. It meant she was alone. It meant everything was broken in a way that couldn't be fixed.

She didn't cry. The tears from earlier had dried on her cheeks, leaving salty trails that tightened her skin. Instead, she turned her head to look down at the wreckage of their family car. Something caught her eye—a rectangular piece of paper that had landed on a patch of grass near the vehicle's shattered rear window.

"My picture," she said suddenly, the first words she'd spoken unprompted since the crash.

The officer followed her gaze. "What's that, sweetheart?"

"Our picture. From tonight." Her voice grew stronger with urgency. "I need it."

It was the family photo taken just hours earlier at the dance studio. Her father had asked another parent to snap it—Ellie in her tutu and flower headdress, flanked by her smiling parents. Their last photo together.

Before anyone could stop her, Ellie wriggled free of the loose straps and slid off the stretcher. Her bare feet found purchase on the damp earth, and she was moving, half-sliding down the embankment toward the car. The officer called after her, but she was quick and determined, driven by a need she couldn't articulate.

She reached the photo, where it lay in the dirt, miraculously intact. In the flash of emergency lights, she could see their faces—

her own gap-toothed smile, her father's proud grin, her mother's elegant profile. Frozen in time, perfect and whole and together. She pressed it to her chest, the paper already going soft with dew.

The officer had followed her down. He didn't scold her for running off. Instead, he knelt beside her again, his face level with hers. "That's a beautiful picture, Ellie."

She nodded, her fingers clutching the edges so tightly they bent. "It's mine now," she said, a fierce protectiveness in her voice.

"Yes, it is." He held out his hand. "Will you come back up with me? The doctors still need to make sure you're okay."

Ellie put her small hand in his much larger one, the photo pressed against her heart with her other arm. As they climbed back up the embankment, she looked over her shoulder one last time at the crumpled car that had carried her family home from so many dance lessons, so many grocery trips, so many ordinary days they'd taken for granted.

The final emergency workers were emerging from the wreckage, their shoulders slumped in defeat. Someone had placed a sheet over her mother's form. Another covered her father. The firefighters began packing away their equipment, the urgent energy of rescue giving way to the somber routine of recovery.

The officer's hand was warm around hers as he led her to the waiting ambulance. The family photo crinkled against her chest with each step, a fragile talisman against the long, uncertain journey ahead. Behind them, the lights continued to flash, painting the night in emergency colors that would forever mean the end of everything Ellie had known.

# Chapter 4

I PULLED the car into Crystal's driveway at 7:13 a.m., killing the engine as the tires crunched over the last bit of shell-flecked concrete. Matt didn't move. His eyes fixed on his mother's house—a single-story ranch with cream stucco and blue shutters that looked exactly like a dozen others on the street. Nothing out of place. Nothing to suggest anything had happened. I touched his arm. He flinched.

"She's probably fine," I said, not believing it.

Matt nodded, a mechanical gesture.

The Florida sun hadn't yet burned through the morning haze, and dew glittered on the perfectly trimmed hedges that lined Crystal's walkway.

Matt pulled his key from his pocket. It trembled between his fingers.

"Mom?" His voice broke the silence as we stepped inside. The air conditioning hit us, set to precisely 72 degrees, as Crystal always kept it. "Mom, it's Matt and Eva Rae."

The echo of his words in the silent house twisted something in my stomach. I moved past him, my FBI training kicking in before I could stop it. As I entered the front room, the signs of a struggle were unmistakable: a toppled lamp lay shattered on the floor, and the coffee table was askew, its contents strewn across the carpet. "This isn't right," Matt whispered behind me, his voice filled with unease.

I moved to the kitchen: clean counters, empty sink, and dishes stacked in the drying rack. I opened the refrigerator—milk, eggs, vegetables, all fresh. She hadn't planned to be gone long. A pack of cereal was on the counter along with a used bowl with dried-up milk on the bottom, which I assumed was what Elijah had been using and living off for the past few days.

"When's the last time you talked to her?" I asked, scanning the room for a calendar, a note, anything.

"Friday morning."

At the master bedroom door, Matt hesitated. I placed my hand on the small of his back and felt the tension in his muscles. We stepped in together.

The lamp lay on its side, shade dented where it had hit the nightstand. The duvet hung half off the bed. A water glass had spilled, leaving a dark stain on the pale carpet. Glass was scattered on the floor. A vase had broken, as well as photo frames and a mirror, just like Elijah had told us.

The blood drained from Matt's face until his skin matched the eggshell walls.

"Don't touch anything," I said, my voice dropping into the calm, detached tone I used at crime scenes.

I circled the room, cataloging details. Scuff marks scored the wall near the closet—a struggle, someone thrown against it. The nightstand drawer hung open. A bottle of pills had rolled under the edge of the bed.

And then I smelled it. Sharp. Astringent. Bleach.

I approached the closet, pulling my phone from my pocket. The chemical smell grew stronger. I switched on my flashlight and directed the beam at the carpet inside. In the harsh light, I could see it—the rusty-brown stains of blood that someone had tried to clean.

Elijah. The edges showed the characteristic feathering pattern of blood spatter.

"Matt," I said carefully, "has your mother mentioned anyone bothering her? Any strange calls or visitors?"

He didn't answer. I turned to find him kneeling by the bed, holding something small in his palm. A pair of wire-rimmed reading glasses, one lens cracked. His hands shook.

"She needs these," he whispered. "She can't read a menu, a book, anything without them."

I took photos of everything—the lamp, the broken glass, the scuff marks, the blood spatter, the glasses—while maintaining my distance from the evidence. My mind switched fully into agent mode, analyzing, categorizing. Multiple scenarios played through my thoughts, none of them good.

"We need to call this in," I said, watching Matt's face carefully. "This is a potential crime scene."

Matt stood up, still clutching his mother's glasses. "You think something happened to her." Not a question.

"I think we need to be thorough. Your mother is missing. There are signs of a struggle. There's blood." I kept my voice even, clinical. "I need a forensics team in here. I need access to her phone records and her bank statements."

His shoulders slumped, and for a moment, I saw not my boyfriend but a frightened child. The thought of Crystal—prickly, private, precise Crystal—lying hurt somewhere sent a wave of nausea through me. I pushed it down. I had known her since I was in pre-school, and she was the one who had always been there for me when my parents couldn't because they were mourning the loss of my sister, who had been kidnapped. I was always welcome in her house, it didn't matter how often. This was like a second home to me. Crystal was my second home.

"We'll find her," I said, the only promise I could make.

Matt nodded, his eyes never leaving the glasses in his hand. "Elijah," he said suddenly. "I need to call Elijah."

I watched his face, noted the flicker of something—guilt? Fear?

—When he mentioned his son. I filed it away, another data point in the growing puzzle.

"Who would hurt her, Eva? Who would want to hurt my mother?"

I had no answer for him. Only the certainty that Crystal Miller's carefully ordered life had been violently disrupted.

Chapter 5

"SHE KEEPS her calendar in her desk," Matt said, breaking a few minutes of silence. He moved to a small cherrywood secretary in the corner of the room, sliding open the center drawer.

I followed, careful to step around the areas I'd photographed. "Anything I should know about your mother's routine?"

"Everything was routine with Mom." A ghost of a smile crossed his face. "Sunday brunch with her friends, the usual bottomless mimosas. Tuesday book club. Thursday grocery shopping. Always the same stores, in the same order."

He pulled out a leather-bound planner and opened it on the desk's surface. I leaned in, studying Crystal's precise handwriting. Each appointment was noted in blue ink, and each completed task was marked with a small checkmark.

"Here," Matt pointed to the day before. "She was supposed to meet someone at the library. Just says 'L – 2 p.m.'"

"Library staff? Friend? Author event?" I suggested.

Matt shook his head. "She would've mentioned an event. And she abbreviates her friends' names with two letters, not one." His finger traced down to Friday. "Look, she had a doctor's appointment she never told me about."

Dr. Klein, 11 a.m. was written in the same meticulous script, but circled twice in red.

"She hates doctors," Matt muttered.

I took a photo of the calendar pages. "Any other appointments that seem unusual?"

Matt flipped back through the previous weeks. Nothing stood out.

His cell phone vibrated. He pulled it from his pocket, checked the screen, then returned it without answering—the third time in thirty minutes.

"Elijah?" I asked.

Matt nodded. "I texted him that we're at the house. He wants to come here."

"But you don't want him to."

"Not until we know… not until we know what we're dealing with." Matt turned away, resuming his search through the desk drawers.

I moved to the bathroom, noting the orderly row of products on the counter. Everything was aligned, labels facing forward. I opened the medicine cabinet and found prescription bottles arranged by size. One stood out—newer than the others, dated just two weeks ago.

"Matt," I called. "Did you know your mother was taking Lorazepam?"

He appeared in the doorway, frowning. "What's that?"

"Anti-anxiety medication. Pretty strong dose." I read the label. "Prescribed by Dr. Klein."

"She never mentioned anxiety." Matt took the bottle from me, studying it. "She never mentioned any of this."

His phone vibrated again. This time, he stepped out to answer it, his voice a low murmur from the hallway. I continued examining the bathroom, finding nothing else noteworthy until I checked the trash can. It contained wadded tissues with smudges of makeup and a torn piece of paper with a phone number, no name. I bagged it as evidence.

When Matt returned, his face had hardened.

"Elijah's insisting on coming over," he said, running a hand through his hair—a nervous gesture I'd rarely seen from him. "I told him to stay put."

"You're worried about him," I observed.

"He and Mom were close. In their own way." Matt leaned against the doorframe. "They're a lot alike—stubborn, private. She's been like a mom to him for a long time."

"But?" I prompted.

"But nothing." He straightened. "What else should we be looking for?"

I studied him. The tension in his shoulders. The way his eyes wouldn't quite meet mine. There was something he wasn't telling me about his and Elijah's relationship, but pushing now would only make him shut down completely.

"Her car isn't missing," I said instead. "No sign of forced entry. Either she left willingly on foot, or..."

"Or she was taken by someone in their car," Matt finished.

We moved back to the bedroom. Matt picked up a small silver frame from the nightstand—a photo of Elijah at about twelve, gap-toothed and grinning on a fishing pier.

"She'd never just leave," Matt said quietly. "Not without telling Elijah or me. Not without her glasses. And look at this mess."

His fingers traced the frame's edge. The gesture was tender, worried. But something else flickered in his eyes when he looked at his son's photo—something that made me wonder about the dynamics in this family.

"I need to call this in now," I said, pulling out my phone. "Step outside with me."

In the driveway, I dialed my contact at the Sheriff's Office while Matt stood a few feet away, staring at his mother's closed garage door. The morning had fully bloomed now, neighbors beginning to emerge for their daily routines. A jogger passed, nodding curiously.

"This is Agent Thomas," I said when the call connected. "I need a forensics team at 114 La Rivera Road. Possible abduction, signs of struggle, evidence of blood. The victim is Crystal Miller, seventy-three." I gave the rest of the details efficiently, ending with, "And run the name Dr. Klein. Prescribed the victim anxiety medication recently."

When I hung up, Matt was watching me, his expression unreadable.

"Is there something you're not telling me?" I asked directly.

"No," he answered too quickly.

The space between us vibrated with unspoken words. I made a mental note of every hesitation, every omission. Professional instinct told me that family secrets often held the key to cases like this. I realized I never knew why Elijah chose to live with his grandmother when he still had a room with us at our house. Matt never told me why—only that it was easiest for us all. Back then, Matt had said it was hard for him to deal with Elijah, that it was too much when he had just lost his leg and had to learn how to do daily things again, like walking on a prosthetic. I had just thought he was depressed and didn't want to deal with a teenager while going through what he did. But now I was beginning to sense that maybe it was something else.

His phone buzzed again in his pocket. He ignored it this time, but I saw his knuckles whiten as he clenched his fist. "The team will be here in twenty minutes," I said. "I need everything, Matt. Everything you know about your mother's life. No matter how small it seems." He nodded, but his eyes drifted back to the house, to whatever invisible thread connected him to his missing mother and his troubled son—a thread I couldn't yet see but would need to unravel if I was going to find Crystal Miller.

I decided to approach the neighbor, an elderly woman with twinkling eyes and a warm smile that creased her rosy cheeks. She was renting the house through Airbnb, she told me, while visiting her grandchildren. Despite the seriousness of the situation, her presence was comforting, like a gentle breeze on a hot summer day.

"Oh, dear, she's missing? I'm afraid I haven't heard much," she confessed. "I spend most of my time on the beach with the little ones, you know."

She paused, tapping her chin thoughtfully with a frail finger.

"But I did notice a car pull up about three days ago, a white Ford Fiesta. I hadn't seen it before. Maybe that is of importance?"

"Did you happen to see the license plate?" I asked. "Maybe what state it was from?"

She shook her head, concerned. "No, I'm afraid not. I'm sorry."

"Did you notice anything about the car? Any bumper stickers or significant dents that might help identify it?"

"I didn't. I'm sorry I can't be of more help. I really do hope you find her." Her eyes twinkled with a mix of curiosity and concern as I thanked her for the information, wondering if this small detail could be the key to uncovering the mystery of Crystal's disappearance.

---

# Chapter 6

---



The Bakers' house squatted at the end of the street like an animal too tired to stand up straight. Paint curled away from the siding in brittle ribbons, and the porch sagged in the middle as if something heavy had sat there too long. Ellie clutched her small duffel bag closer to her chest as the social worker's car pulled into the cracked driveway, her fingernails digging into the worn fabric. Foster home number four—but who was counting?

"This is it," chirped Ms. Winters, the social worker, her cheerfulness as artificial as the silk flowers pinned to her lapel. "The Bakers are very experienced foster parents."

Experienced, Ellie had learned, rarely meant kind.

The front door swung open before they reached the porch steps. Mrs. Baker emerged, a thin woman stretched like taffy, with elbows and knuckles that looked sharp enough to cut paper. Her smile was a mathematical equation—precise, measured, temporary.

"You must be Ellie," Mrs. Baker said, her voice hitting all the right notes of welcome without carrying any actual warmth. Her eyes performed a quick inventory of Ellie's appearance, lingering briefly on the scuffed sneakers and the too-short jeans. "We've been expecting you."

Ms. Winters gave Ellie's shoulder a squeeze that lasted exactly three seconds—long enough to appear caring but short enough to move things along. "I'll check in next week," she promised, already backing toward her car. The betrayal was as familiar as an old bruise.

"Come along, dear," Mrs. Baker said, the endearment hanging awkwardly in the air. "Let's get you settled."

Inside, the house smelled of pine cleaner and something else—something stale and resigned. The living room furniture all faced the television like faithful worshippers, the cushions dented in specific spots that clearly belonged to specific people. Not visitors. Not temporary additions.

"We have four children living here now, including you," Mrs. Baker explained as she led Ellie up the stairs that creaked under their weight. "Our son Clay is sixteen—he has his own room. Then there's Jenny and Tara, both twelve. You'll be sharing with them."

The hallway was lined with framed school portraits and vacation snapshots. Ellie counted six faces that appeared repeatedly: Mr. and Mrs. Baker, their son, and what looked like three grown children who had moved away. Not a single image contained any of the foster children Mrs. Baker had just mentioned.

The bedroom door stuck slightly, and Mrs. Baker nudged it with a practiced hip. "Here we are."

Three narrow beds were jammed into a space meant for one, maybe two. Two of the beds had rumpled comforters in faded florals. The third was covered with a thin, gray blanket that reminded Ellie of the kind they put on dogs at the animal shelter. A single dresser stood against the wall, its wood veneer peeling at the corners.

"That one's yours," Mrs. Baker pointed to the bed closest to the door, the one with the shelter blanket. "The girls have divided the dresser. Bottom drawer is yours." She opened the curtains, which hung limply, too narrow for the window. Outside, a streetlight buzzed, promising to keep Ellie company all night with its sickly yellow glow.

"Bathroom's down the hall. You'll share with Jenny and Tara."

Ellie nodded, not trusting her voice.

Mrs. Baker's initial performance of welcome was already evaporating, her words coming faster, checking off items from a mental list. "Now, the rules. Breakfast at seven, lunch you get at school, dinner at six. Miss a meal, you go hungry. Chores are posted on the refrigerator. Do them without being told."

Ellie had heard variations of this speech before. She let the words wash over her, focusing instead on the woman's hands, which twisted around each other like nervous animals.

"Lights out at nine on school nights, ten on weekends. No food in the bedrooms. No phone calls after eight. No friends over without prior approval." Mrs. Baker paused, seeming to remember something. "Oh, and Clay's room is off-limits. He values his privacy."

Translation: the biological son's comfort mattered more than the foster kids'.

"Any questions?" Mrs. Baker asked, not waiting for a response. "Good. Get unpacked and come down for dinner in thirty minutes. Mr. Baker likes punctuality."

The door closed behind her with a soft click. Ellie sat on the edge of the bed, feeling the springs protest beneath her. She placed her duffel bag beside her, not ready to unpack, not prepared to admit this was happening again.

On the wall opposite her bed hung a school portrait of Clay, grinning with the confidence of someone who knew exactly where he belonged. Next to it was a family vacation photo—the Bakers on a beach somewhere, their arms around each other, frozen in genuine happiness.

She unzipped her bag but didn't take anything out of it. Instead, she cataloged the room's exits: one door, one window that probably stuck but might open with enough force. She located the creaky floorboards by the closet, testing them with her toe, noting which ones to avoid at night.

Outside, the maple trees of the neighborhood swayed in the

afternoon light. Ellie watched their shadows dance across the faded wallpaper and wondered how long she would stay this time. Long enough to unpack all her clothes? Long enough to learn everyone's full names? Long enough to care?

Probably not. It was easier that way.

The bedroom door banged open just as Ellie had worked up the courage to begin unpacking. Two girls tumbled in, their voices dropping into sudden silence when they spotted her. The taller one—hair cut in a jagged line just below her ears—narrowed her eyes like a cat assessing whether something was worth pouncing on. The other, shorter but stockier, leaned against the doorframe with a smirk that suggested she'd already found Ellie lacking.

"So, you're the new kid," said the taller one, flicking her gaze over Ellie like she was reading a boring billboard. "I'm Tara. That's Jenny."

Jenny didn't wave or smile, just tilted her head and said, "You're smaller than the last one." It was unclear whether this was a good or bad thing.

Ellie nodded, not sure what response would smooth things over. "I'm Ellie."

"We know," Tara said, moving to the middle bed and flopping down. "Mrs. Baker already told us all about you. Said you don't talk much."

"Which is fine," Jenny added, crossing to the dresser. "The last girl cried every night for two weeks. Drove me crazy."

Tara pointed to the dresser. "Bottom drawer is yours. Don't touch our stuff. Ever."

Jenny pulled open a drawer stuffed with wrinkled clothes. "The left side of the bathroom sink is yours—just the edge, though, not the whole side. And you can put your toothbrush in the blue cup. The hairdryer is ours—you can use it if you ask first."

Ellie nodded again, mentally cataloging the invisible boundaries being drawn around her. It was always like this in the beginning—learning the unwritten rules, figuring out where the land mines were buried.

"And don't get any ideas about using my stuff," Tara added,

gesturing to a collection of nail polishes lined up on the windowsill. "Last girl 'borrowed' my blue polish and returned it all goopy."

"I won't," Ellie said, her voice smaller than she intended.

Jenny snorted, exchanging a look with Tara that said volumes about how many times they'd heard similar promises. Ellie recognized it as the look of girls who had seen too many temporary roommates come and go.

Ellie turned back to her duffel bag, unzipping it slowly. She pulled out two T-shirts, three pairs of underwear, and some socks with thinning heels. She was aware of the other girls watching, measuring her possessions against some invisible standard. As she reached the bottom of the bag, her fingers found the photo that had been nestled between her folded clothes.

She withdrew it carefully, intending to place it on the small table beside her bed—the one truly personal touch in this impersonal space. She had gotten the frame from the paramedic who had come to visit her in the hospital, the nice woman who had taken care of her that night three years ago. It was a gift, she said. So she could keep the photo safe. It was her favorite thing in the world. The picture showed her parents at the recital on the night of the accident, her younger self sandwiched between them, all three faces caught mid-laugh at something long forgotten. Ellie wasn't even sure she remembered how her mother's laugh sounded anymore. But looking at the photo, she believed she could sometimes still hear it.

"What's that?" Tara's voice had shifted, suddenly interested.

Before Ellie could respond, Tara was beside her, plucking the frame from her hands with nimble fingers. "Ooh, is this your family?" She held it up to the light, studying it with exaggerated interest.

"Can I have that back, please?" Ellie asked, her heart speeding up.

Tara turned the photo toward Jenny. "Aww, look at the happy family," she said, her voice mockingly sweet. She held it just high enough that Ellie would have to reach for it. "Mom and Dad look so nice. Where are they now? Too busy to take care of their daughter?"

Ellie's cheeks burned. "They died. Car accident. Please give it back."

Something flickered across Tara's face—perhaps a moment of genuine regret—but it was quickly replaced by a harder expression. Jenny moved closer, examining the photo over Tara's shoulder.

"Don't get too attached to this place," Jenny said, her voice matter-of-fact. "Nobody stays here long anyway. Either your relatives show up because they're out of jail, or you get moved again."

"She's right," Tara nodded. "The record is four months. That was Miguel. Then his uncle suddenly remembered he existed."

Ellie stood up, her patience snapping. "I don't care. Give me back my photo."

Tara raised an eyebrow, holding the frame even higher. "Or what? You'll tell Mrs. Baker? She doesn't care as long as we don't break anything or make too much noise."

Something cold and familiar settled in Ellie's chest—the knowledge that there was no adult who would step in, no authority who would make things right. It was a feeling she'd had many times before.

She lunged forward, reaching for the photo. Tara sidestepped, but Ellie was quicker than she expected. Her fingers caught the edge, and for a moment, they were engaged in a tug-of-war, Tara's surprise giving way to determination.

"Let go!" Ellie demanded, pulling harder.

"You're going to—"

The frame slipped from both their grasps, tumbling through the air in a lazy arc before hitting the edge of the bedside table. The crack of plastic was small but definitive. The frame bounced once on the worn carpet, the protective cover popping loose, and the photo sliding partially out.

For a heartbeat, no one moved. Then Tara shrugged, the deliberateness of the gesture making it clear she was hiding guilt beneath indifference. "Oops. Accidents happen."

Jenny laughed, a short burst that held no humor. "At least the picture didn't tear. That would be really sad." Her tone made it clear she wouldn't have found it sad at all.

Ellie dropped to her knees, gathering the broken pieces. Her hands trembled as she examined the damage. The frame had cracked along one corner, and the plastic cover was scratched, but the photo itself was undamaged. Still, something about seeing it broken sent a wave of hot tears to her eyes, which she fought back fiercely.

"Ugh, please don't cry," Tara said, retreating to her bed. "The babies who cry don't last long here."

Jenny nodded in agreement. "Mr. Baker hates criers. Says they give him a headache."

Ellie swallowed hard, blinking rapidly. She wouldn't give them the satisfaction. Carefully, she reassembled the frame as best she could, pressing the broken pieces together. It would never look right again, but it would hold the photo, and that was what mattered.

The other girls had already lost interest, turning to discuss plans for the weekend as if Ellie weren't even there. She gently placed the damaged frame on the bedside table, positioning it so the crack was less visible from where she would lie in bed.

It was just a frame, she told herself. The picture—the memory—was still intact. She'd need to be more careful about what she revealed in this house, about what she allowed to become vulnerable.

The lesson had cost her a broken frame. Next time, it might be something worse.


The kitchen smelled of overcooked vegetables and something Ellie couldn't identify—a bland, mushy scent that suggested food made out of obligation rather than love. Six mismatched chairs crowded around a table meant for four, their uneven legs making small screech-and-thump noises whenever someone shifted their weight. Mrs. Baker moved between the stove and the table with rigid efficiency, her elbows tight against her sides as if navigating a much smaller space than actually existed.

Ellie perched on the edge of her chair, a wobbly thing with a cushion that had long ago surrendered its stuffing. Across from her, Jenny and Tara sat with the practiced boredom of veterans, their eyes occasionally darting to the kitchen doorway. Waiting.

Heavy footsteps announced Mr. Baker before he appeared. A stocky man with shoulders perpetually hunched forward, as if he were walking into a stiff wind. His eyebrows formed a continuous line of displeasure across his forehead, and when he spoke, his voice seemed to start in his chest and gather gravel on its way up.

"Clay still at basketball?" he asked no one in particular as he dropped into the chair at the head of the table. The chair—sturdier than the others—accepted his weight without complaint.

"Practice runs late on Thursdays," Mrs. Baker answered, setting a casserole dish in the center of the table. The dish contained a beige mixture that might have been chicken and rice, or perhaps tuna and pasta. It was the color of surrender.

Mr. Baker nodded, then noticed Ellie. His gaze swept over her with neither interest nor welcome. "You're the new one."

It wasn't a question, but Ellie nodded anyway. "Yes, sir."

He grunted, a sound that completed the interaction as far as he was concerned.

Mrs. Baker began serving, her movements as precise as a machine. The spoon dipped into the casserole, depositing food onto plates in a counterclockwise motion. Mr. Baker's plate received a generous helping, mounded in the center like a small beige mountain. Jenny and Tara got moderate portions. When the spoon reached Ellie's plate, it seemed to hover for a moment before delivering a noticeably smaller scoop, spread thin across the ceramic surface.

An empty chair—Clay's—waited beside his father, its plate already served with a portion matching Mr. Baker's. A small dish of what looked like chocolate pudding sat beside it—the only dessert on the table.

"Vegetables," Mrs. Baker announced, placing a bowl of limp green beans beside the casserole. Again, the serving process repeated, with portions distributed according to some unspoken hierarchy that left Ellie with exactly four green beans.

Mr. Baker stabbed his fork into his food without waiting for the others, a signal that dinner had officially begun. The only sounds for several minutes were the scrape of forks against plates and the occasional request to pass the salt. Ellie ate slowly, trying to make her small portion last.

"Coach says Clay might make varsity next year," Mr. Baker finally said, his voice suddenly animated. "Said he's got the best three-point shot he's seen in a decade."

Mrs. Baker nodded with practiced enthusiasm. "That's wonderful. I told him his extra practice would pay off."

"Kid's got natural talent," Mr. Baker continued, his chest expanding. "Gets it from my side of the family. My brother almost went pro, you know."

Ellie had nearly finished her small portion when her stomach gave an embarrassing growl. Without thinking, she glanced at the casserole dish, where a substantial amount still remained.

"Could I have a little more, please?" she asked, her voice barely above a whisper.

The table went silent. Jenny and Tara exchanged looks of mingled horror and fascination, like witnesses to an impending car crash. Mrs. Baker's hand froze midway to her water glass.

Mr. Baker's face darkened, his eyebrows drawing even closer together. "You think food grows on trees?" he asked, his voice deceptively quiet. "Learn to be grateful for what you're given."

Heat crawled up Ellie's neck. "I am grateful. I just—"

"You just what?" he cut her off. "You just thought you'd come into our home and start making demands on day one?" He gestured toward her empty plate. "That's a perfectly adequate portion for a girl your size. We can't have you developing bad habits on our watch."

Mrs. Baker cleared her throat. "Ellen, why don't you help me clear the table?" It wasn't a suggestion.

"My name isn't Ellen…" she started, but then paused. It was no use. They didn't care what her name was.

As Ellie gathered plates, she noticed Mrs. Baker scraping the leftover casserole into a plastic container labeled "Clay" in permanent marker.

Jenny and Tara disappeared upstairs immediately after dinner. Ellie helped wash dishes in silence, her empty stomach clenching periodically. When they finished, Mrs. Baker nodded toward the stairs without a word. Dismissal.

The bedroom was dark when Ellie entered, the other girls already in their beds, their breathing not quite slow enough to be asleep. Ellie changed into her pajamas in the bathroom—faded flannel pants and a T-shirt with a cartoon character she'd outgrown years ago but couldn't bear to part with.

Her bed creaked loudly as she climbed in, the thin mattress offering little barrier between her body and the protruding springs beneath. The streetlight outside cast yellow bars across the ceiling through the gap in the curtains. Down the hall, she could hear the muffled sound of a television, occasional laughter from the living room where the Bakers waited for their son.

Ellie lay still, listening to the unfamiliar noises of the house—a pipe knocking somewhere in the walls, the refrigerator humming downstairs, the occasional car passing on the street outside. Different sounds from her last foster home. Different from the home before that. Different from her parents' house, where she'd fallen asleep to the gentle whir of the ceiling fan and her father's off-key humming from the next room.

The memory of her father's voice tightened her throat. She swallowed hard, determined not to cry. But as the minutes stretched into an hour, as the sounds of the television downstairs went silent and footsteps moved from room to room turning off lights, as the darkness seemed to press closer, something inside her cracked.

The first sob was silent, nothing more than a hitch in her breath. The second shook her shoulders. By the third, tears were tracking sideways across her face, soaking into the pillow. She tried to muffle the sound with her blanket, but grief has a way of demanding to be heard.

"Mom," she whispered into the darkness. "Dad." The words hung in the air, unanswered.

A floorboard creaked in the hallway. Ellie froze, holding her breath. Light spilled into the room as the door opened, illuminating Mr. Baker's hulking silhouette. For one wild moment, Ellie thought he might ask if she was okay, might offer some awkward word of comfort.

Instead, his voice cut through the darkness like a cold blade. "Toughen up," he snapped. "There's no room for crybabies in this house. You'll wake everyone up."

The door closed with a decisive click, plunging the room back into darkness. From the other beds came the sound of Jenny or Tara—Ellie couldn't tell which—shifting under covers, a small sigh that might have been sympathy but was more likely annoyance.

Ellie curled into a tight ball, making herself as small as possible. Her hand reached for the broken photo frame on the bedside table, fingers closing around it carefully to avoid the sharp edges. She pulled it to her chest, cradling it like something living.

The house settled around her, indifferent to her presence. Tomorrow, she would need to be stronger. Tomorrow, she would remember to be invisible, to ask for nothing, to expect less. Tomorrow, she would be whatever the Bakers wanted, if only to survive until something better came along.

But tonight, alone in the dark with only the broken frame to anchor her, Ellie allowed herself to feel the full weight of her solitude. It pressed against her chest, heavy as stone, cold as winter. She'd never felt more alone, never felt more like a visitor in someone else's life, a footnote in someone else's story.

Sleep, when it finally came, offered no escape—only a temporary pause in a loneliness so complete it had become its own kind of company.

## Chapter 7

I CHOPPED the green pepper with quick, precise movements, my knife hitting the cutting board in a rhythm that matched my heartbeat. Behind me, the murmur of teenage voices drifted from the living room, too low for casual conversation. My ears perked up.

Matt stirred the pasta sauce beside me. We had spent the entire day at his mother's house watching the forensics team do their work, but nothing had come of it so far. No trace of what happened to his mother, and it was tearing him up, I could tell. The strain showed in the tight corners of his mouth, the mechanical way he moved through dinner preparations.

"Something smells good," I said, keeping my voice light.

"Secret family recipe." He shrugged. It felt sad. "Garlic powder."

I laughed on cue, then tilted my head slightly toward the living room. Elijah's voice had dropped even lower, forcing Christine to lean forward on the sofa. My daughter's face was focused, serious—a mirror of my own interviewing expression.

"I'm telling you," Elijah said, his words barely reaching the kitchen, "something was wrong with Grandma. Real wrong."

I handed Matt the chopped peppers, then moved to the refrigerator, positioning myself at an angle that gave me a better view of the kids while appearing to search for ingredients. The maneuver was second nature—the same careful repositioning I'd use when watching a suspect in an interrogation room.

"She kept checking the locks," Elijah continued, fingers picking at a loose thread on his hoodie sleeve. "Like, three, four times a night. And the curtains—she'd peek through them, then slam them shut if she saw headlights."

Christine's voice was softer, but I caught it anyway. "Did she say who she thought was out there?"

"No names. Just 'they' and 'them.'" Elijah's face twisted. "Mumbling something like 'they'd found her again'."

"Do you think maybe she went nuts?" Christine asked. "Like old people sometimes do?"

The refrigerator door grew cold against my palm. I'd been standing there too long, staring at nothing. I grabbed the butter with purpose and returned to the counter.

"Pass me the salt," I said to Matt, while my brain cataloged Elijah's rigid posture, the slight tremor in his hands, the authentic fear that edged his voice. Not the manufactured drama of a teenager seeking attention. Something had genuinely frightened him.

The wooden spoon in Matt's hand made slow, deliberate circles in the sauce.

"I'm thinking," I said carefully, measuring my words, "that perhaps your mother might be experiencing some cognitive issues." I kept my tone gentle, professional—the same voice I used when suggesting difficult possibilities to victims' families. "Early-onset dementia can sometimes present with paranoid delusions."

Matt's hand froze mid-stir. The silence stretched between us, broken only by the soft bubble of the sauce and the distant murmur of the teenagers.

"My mother," he said finally, each word precise and sharp, "is perfectly lucid. She's only seventy-two, for God's sake."

"She's seventy-three," I corrected him. He gave me a look.

I recognized the defensive posture, the slight squaring of shoulders I'd seen in a thousand interviews—people protecting their loved ones from unpleasant truths.

"I'm not diagnosing her, Matt." I kept my voice even. "But paranoia and hiding are consistent with several conditions. It might explain her disappearance better than…"

"Better than what?" His stirring paused. "Better than someone actually being after her?"

I measured my response, careful not to push too hard. "I'm just saying we should consider all possibilities."

"You're thinking like an FBI agent." The words weren't a compliment. "This isn't one of your cases, Eva. This is my mother."

Heat crept up my neck, not from anger but from the uncomfortable recognition that he was right. I'd slipped into investigator mode, analyzing his family like suspects rather than supporting them as partners.

"I know that." I touched his arm, felt the tension in his muscles. "But my training might help find her."

"Then use it to find her, not to explain her away."

From the living room, Elijah's voice rose slightly. "She kept saying they'd never stop looking. That's why she had to be so careful."

Matt's eyes met mine, challenging. We both knew that paranoid delusions typically lacked the consistency and specific focus that Elijah described. But acknowledging that meant accepting a more troubling alternative: that Crystal Miller might have real reasons to be afraid.

I turned back to my vegetables, knife moving with mechanical precision. Factual analysis was my refuge, my strength. The weight of the blade in my hand was certain.

"We'll find her," I said, but even to my ears, the promise sounded hollow.

# Chapter 8

THE PASTA STEAMED on our plates, untouched. I'd arranged the food with unnecessary precision—the sauce centered perfectly on the noodles, and the garlic bread sliced at exact angles. My hands needed something to do while my mind raced ahead, connecting dots that refused to form a coherent picture. Across the table, Elijah's spine was ramrod straight, his eyes tracking every movement of my hands like I might be concealing evidence instead of serving dinner.

"Water?" I lifted the pitcher.

No one responded. The dining room felt airless, compressed.

Matt cleared his throat, fork tapping against his plate with nervous energy. "So, Christine, how's that science project coming along?"

My daughter opened her mouth to answer, but Elijah cut in, his voice sharp as broken glass.

"Dementia?" The word hung between us. "You think Grandma has dementia?"

I'd underestimated the boy's hearing, or perhaps overestimated the soundproofing between kitchen and living room. Either way, my theory had traveled, and the reception was hostile.

"I simply mentioned it as one possibility," I said, slipping into my professional voice without meaning to. "Many conditions can cause—"

"She's not crazy." Elijah's knuckles whitened around his fork, the metal pressing deep into his palm. The tendons in his wrist stood out like cords. "She knew exactly what was happening. She was scared, feared for her life."

Matt set down his utensils, his movements deliberately gentle. "No one's saying she's crazy, Elijah. Eva's just trying to understand what might be going on."

"She's an FBI agent. Why isn't she out there looking instead of sitting here eating spaghetti?" The accusation hit its mark. I'd wondered the same thing myself.

"Because officially, your grandmother hasn't been missing long enough for FBI involvement," I explained. "Local police are—"

"Doing nothing." Elijah's eyes blazed. "Because they think she's just some confused old lady who wandered off."

His shoulders hunched forward, protective and defiant. I'd seen the same posture in a hundred interview rooms—the stance of someone defending their truth against disbelief.

Matt reached across the corner of the table, placing his hand on Elijah's shoulder. "We'll find her, son. I promise."

The reaction was immediate and volcanic. Elijah's body jerked as if the touch had burned through his hoodie. His chair screeched against the hardwood floor as he shoved backward, the sound slicing through the room.

"Don't call me that." Each word was a bullet. "You don't get to make promises about her."

I caught every microexpression on Matt's face—the initial confusion, eyes widening slightly; the flash of hurt that followed, pulling at the corners of his mouth; then the careful, practiced neutrality that slid over his features like a mask. In less than two seconds, he'd hidden his pain behind a wall of calm I recognized all too well.

Matt's hand retreated to his lap. "I'm sorry," he said simply.

Elijah remained standing, his breath coming in short bursts. No one moved. From my peripheral vision, I saw Christine's fingers drumming silently against her thigh—her anxiety tell since childhood.

"The pasta looks great, Mom," Christine said, her voice too bright, too forced. "Did you use that basil from the garden?"

The transparent attempt at normalcy hung awkwardly in the air. Elijah slowly sank back into his chair, his body still vibrating with tension.

"Yes," I answered mechanically. "Fresh basil."

Silence settled over us again. Matt twirled pasta around his fork without lifting it to his mouth. Elijah stared at his plate as if it contained coded messages. Christine tried twice more to spark conversation—comments about school, a question about weekend plans—but each attempt fizzled into uncomfortable quiet. Alex and Angel kept quiet and focused on their food.

I observed them all through my professional lens, cataloging details I couldn't help but notice. The way Matt's eyes kept darting to Elijah with a mixture of concern and caution. The protective angle of Elijah's shoulders curved forward as if expecting a blow.

Something was fractured in the foundation of this blended family—a crack that had existed before Crystal's disappearance but now threatened to split wide open. The "son" that had triggered Elijah's outburst. The promise that Matt had no right to make.

I added these observations to my mental case file, alongside Crystal's paranoia and Elijah's conviction that someone was after his grandmother. Professional detachment was my refuge, my defense against the uncomfortable reality that I was both investigator and participant in this unfolding drama.

My fork pierced a piece of pepper with unnecessary force. The sauce had congealed on my plate, cooling into an unappetizing mass. No one had eaten more than a few bites.

"I think," Matt said finally, breaking the silence, "we should all remember we're on the same side here."

Elijah's eyes flicked up, meeting mine with unexpected direct-ness. "Are we?"

The question wasn't just for me. It hung in the air between all of us—a challenge, an accusation, and underneath it all, a plea for someone to take his fears seriously.

I measured my response carefully. "I believe you, Elijah. About your grandmother's fear." I held his gaze. "Tell me more about what she said. About who might be looking for her."

The tension in his shoulders eased fractionally. Matt's eyes caught mine across the table—a silent question, a moment of connection amid the strain.

Beneath the formal dining room light, we were not quite a family and not quite strangers. We were something more complicated—six people connected by obligation, affection, and now by the void left by a missing woman whose secrets were only beginning to surface.

## Chapter 9

THEN:

Ellie Thompson lay rigid under the threadbare blanket, counting the cracks in the ceiling she couldn't see. Darkness pressed against her eyes, but she'd memorized the seventeen jagged lines that spread like bony fingers across the plaster. The house creaked and sighed around her, settling into the night with reluctant groans that matched the protests of the springs beneath her thin mattress.

She shifted slightly, and the bed frame squeaked in betrayal. Ellie froze, her heart stammering against her ribs as she listened for heavy footsteps in the hallway. Nothing came except the distant gurgle of ancient pipes and the soft wheeze of wind through the poorly sealed window.

The threadbare blanket did little to shield her from the chill. Goosebumps pebbled her skin despite the two pairs of socks and the oversized sweatshirt she wore to bed because it was so cold in the house. "Heating costs money, and money doesn't grow on trees," Mr. Baker reminded her weekly, as if she might have forgotten since the last telling.

Three years. Three years since the accident that took her parents. Three years of bouncing between homes like a pinball, gaining momentum with each rejection. The Wilsons had been kind but overwhelmed. The Garcias already had four children and barely noticed when Ellie didn't speak for three days straight. The Moores had returned her after two weeks because she "wasn't a good fit" for their family. And now the Bakers, who had made it clear from day one that she was a source of income, not a child to be loved.

The memory surfaced like a bruise being pressed—Mr. Baker's face, flushed and contorted, looming over her just three days ago. She'd come home from school with an empty stomach that growled loud enough for her teacher to hear. The cafeteria had served fish sticks, and after finding a still-frozen center in her first one, she'd lost her appetite. By the time she reached the Baker house at 3:30, her hunger had become a hollow ache.

"Mr. Baker?" she'd asked, finding him in the kitchen. "Is it okay if I have a snack? I didn't really eat lunch today."

His eyes had narrowed, bloodshot and suspicious. "Didn't they feed you at school? We pay for that lunch, you know."

"They had fish sticks, but mine wasn't cooked all the way—"

"So, you're being picky now?" His hand had shot out faster than she could react, connecting with her cheek in a stinging slap that knocked her sideways. "You think we're made of money? You think food just appears by magic?"

The memory of that slap tingled across her skin now as she lay in bed. Her stomach had remained empty until the meager dinner of canned soup and crackers that evening.

It wasn't just the Bakers. Foster care had labeled her somehow, marked her as different in ways that other children sensed like predators scenting weakness. At her current school, a group of fifth-graders had cornered her on the playground.

"Hey, trash kid," the ringleader had called, a girl with perfect blonde braids and a pink backpack that probably cost more than all of Ellie's belongings combined. "Is it true your parents didn't want you?"

"My parents died," Ellie had responded, her voice flat and practiced.

"That's what they all say," another girl had chimed in. "Orphan girl's making up stories."

The words shouldn't have hurt—she'd heard worse—but they'd burrowed under her skin anyway, sharp little hooks that tugged at her insides when she least expected it.

The acrid smell of alcohol wafted under her door, signaling that Mr. Baker was having another "difficult night." The odor was as familiar to Ellie as the scent of school cafeterias and social workers' offices—institutional and depressing. She could track Mr. Baker's moods by the strength of the smell; tonight, it was potent enough to make her nose wrinkle—a bad sign.

Her body felt like a single taut muscle, stretched to breaking. Every noise, every shift in the house's atmosphere registered in her heightened awareness. Social services had visited last week, but as usual, the Bakers had transformed into model foster parents for the forty-five-minute home inspection. Mrs. Baker had even baked cookies—cookies that disappeared into a locked tin as soon as the social worker's car pulled away.

Ellie's hands curled into fists beneath the blanket. Her fingernails dug crescents into her palms, the slight pain grounding her, keeping her thoughts from spinning too far into the darkness that sometimes threatened to swallow her whole. She was nine years old but felt ancient, her childhood compressed into a before—before the accident—and an after filled with temporary beds and conditional welcomes.

In the quiet darkness, a resolve crystallized within her like frost forming on glass. She had tried being good. She had tried being invisible. She had tried to be helpful and agreeable, everything the endless parade of adults in her life had asked her to be. None of it had earned her safety or a sense of belonging.

Perhaps it was time to try something else entirely.

．　．　．

The digital clock on her nightstand blinked 1:37 a.m. when Ellie finally made her move. The house had fallen into the deep, settled silence that came after midnight, punctuated only by the occasional rumble of Mr. Baker's snores from downstairs. She slid her legs over the edge of the bed with the careful precision of a bomb technician, wincing as her weight shifted and the old springs gave a mournful squeak.

Ellie held her breath, counting to thirty in her head. When no sounds of stirring came from down the hall, she placed her bare feet on the cold wooden floor and crept to the corner where she'd hidden her backpack behind a loose baseboard, careful not to wake up Tara, who was still sound asleep. Jenny had been sent away a couple of weeks ago after some incident with Clay. Ellie didn't know what it was, and frankly, she didn't care.

She placed the backpack on her bed and began her practiced routine in the sparse light from the street lamp outside. First came two T-shirts, one pink and one yellow, both faded from countless washes. She folded them with military precision, smoothing each wrinkle with careful fingers. Next, a pair of jeans and two pairs of underwear, followed by three mismatched socks. The fourth sock had disappeared during the move to the Bakers' house, like so many things in Ellie's life—there one moment, gone the next.

Her toothbrush went into the front pocket, its bristles splayed and frayed from months of use. Mrs. Baker had promised a new one two months ago, but had "forgotten" every time she went to the store. Beside it, Ellie tucked a travel-sized toothpaste tube she'd found in the school's lost and found, still half-full. She hesitated, then added the stub of a pencil and a small spiral notebook with most of its pages still blank.

Then came the most important item. From beneath her mattress, Ellie retrieved a folded square of tissue paper. Her hands trembled slightly as she unwrapped it to reveal the cracked frame holding the photograph—the last one taken of her family together.

The memory of that night washed over her. Her mother had worn her special occasion earrings, the dangly ones with tiny stars that caught the light when she moved. "For my little star," she had said, tapping Ellie's nose.

Ellie blinked back the hot pressure behind her eyes. She didn't have time for that now. With reverent care, she slipped the photo between two shirts where it would be cushioned and protected. The tissue paper went in as well—she couldn't bear to leave any part of it behind.

She changed out of her pajamas, layering herself against the cool spring night. First came a long-sleeved thermal shirt, threadbare at the elbows but still warm. Over that went her school polo—the only clean one left—and then her one sweater, a gray pullover with a stretched-out neck. She stepped into her jeans, the knees worn thin, and pulled on both pairs of socks before lacing up her sneakers tightly. The right one had a small hole forming near the big toe, but it would have to do.

Ellie padded to the window and peered through a gap in the crooked blinds. The night was clear, stars sprinkled across the black canvas of the sky—no rain in sight, which was a small mercy. The oak tree outside her window cast lacy shadows on the lawn, and the streetlight at the corner cast an orange glow that could either be helpful or dangerous, depending on who might be watching.

Her movements had the fluid quality of a performance rehearsed many times in the mind before being executed in reality. For weeks, she had planned this escape, mentally cataloging the house's noises, learning which floorboards creaked and which didn't, noting Mr. Baker's drinking patterns and the heaviness of his sleep afterward. She had squirreled away a granola bar from Monday's lunch and two apple juice boxes from Wednesday, storing them in her backpack's side pocket for the journey ahead.

Ellie zipped the backpack closed with methodical care, easing the zipper over each tooth to prevent the telltale sound of a quick pull. She slung it over both shoulders, adjusting the straps so it sat snug against her back—another lesson learned from experience. A loose bag that swung or bumped made noise, and noise meant getting caught.

At the door, she paused, her ear pressed against the wood,

listening for any sound that might signal danger. Her hand hovered over the doorknob, small fingers curled like the legs of a nervous spider. This was the point of no return. Once she stepped outside this room, she was committed to her plan. If she were caught now, the consequences would be severe—Mr. Baker's hand was heavy even when he was sober.

Ellie took a deep breath, twisted the knob with exquisite slowness, and pulled the door open just wide enough for her slender frame to slip through. The hallway beyond stretched dark and forbidding, but somewhere at the end of it lay freedom.

The living room soon lay ahead, the final and most dangerous obstacle. Through the archway, she could see the flickering blue light of the television casting spectral shadows across the walls. The sound was turned nearly all the way down, just a murmur of voices and music from some late-night rerun. Ellie took a steadying breath and peered around the corner.

Mr. Baker sprawled across the sagging couch like a felled tree, one leg dangling off the edge, the other propped on the coffee table amid a graveyard of empty bottles. His mouth hung open, emitting snores that rattled and caught in his throat before resuming their rhythm. He wore the same clothes as earlier—khaki pants now wrinkled beyond salvation and a button-down shirt with a dark stain spreading across the pocket. His right arm dangled toward the floor, fingers loosely curled around an invisible bottle.

The stench hit Ellie like a physical force—alcohol sharp and sour, mixed with sweat and the musty smell of the aging upholstery. She breathed through her mouth, thankful for once that she hadn't eaten much. The path to the back door required her to skirt past the couch where Mr. Baker lay, leaving barely two feet of clearance between her and his dangling arm.

Inch by excruciating inch, Ellie edged forward. The television cast her shadow across the wall, elongated and distorted. She froze when it seemed to move independently of her, then realized it was just responding to the changing images on the screen. Three steps more. Two. She was nearly past him when Mr. Baker shifted.

A strangled grunt escaped his throat. His leg slid off the coffee table with a thud, sending an empty bottle spinning. Ellie turned to stone, not even daring to blink as Mr. Baker's head rolled to the side. His eyes remained closed, but his lips moved, mumbling something unintelligible that sounded like "payment" and "due Friday." Then his breathing settled back into its rhythmic rattling, and his body went slack once more.

The back door stood before her like a portal to another world. The deadbolt posed the final challenge—a stiff, temperamental lock that sometimes took Mrs. Baker several tries to open. Ellie wrapped her small hand around it and turned with steady pressure, wincing at the metallic click that sounded obscenely loud in the quiet house. The bolt slid back, and she eased the door open just enough to slip through, careful not to let it swing wide and catch the breeze.

The night air rushed to meet her like a living thing, cool and sweet and impossibly fresh. It filled her lungs with a crispness that made her dizzy after the stale, alcohol-laden atmosphere of the house. Ellie stepped onto the back porch, easing the door closed behind her with a soft click that felt like punctuation—the period at the end of a chapter she never wanted to read again.

Stars scattered across the sky above her, more than she'd ever been able to see through her bedroom window. The moon hung low and half-full, providing just enough light to make her way across the unkempt backyard with its patchy grass and forgotten garden tools. Each step took her farther from the house, and with each step, the invisible weight on her shoulders seemed to lighten fractionally.

By the time she reached the gap in the fence that separated the Bakers' yard from the alley behind it, Ellie was almost running. The night embraced her, wrapping her in shadows that felt not threatening but protective. For the first time in months, perhaps years, she felt something unfurling in her chest—something that might, with proper care, grow into hope.

# Part II

# Chapter 10

CRYSTAL'S CASE file spread across my desk like the aftermath of a paper hurricane. Five days missing, and we were still no closer to finding her. The photos from her bedroom showed the same story I'd memorized: blood spatter on the wall, a toppled lamp, signs of a desperate struggle. My phone buzzed against the wooden desk. When I answered, the voice on the other end was clipped, urgent.

"Agent Thomas, we've got a homicide in Cocoa Beach. A woman in her seventies was attacked in her home." The dispatcher's voice carried no emotion—just facts.

"Address?" I grabbed my jacket, already moving.

Twenty minutes later, I pulled up to a single-story ranch house with cream-colored stucco walls and a well-maintained yard. Palm trees stood like sentinels, their fronds barely moving in the heavy air. Yellow crime scene tape created a perimeter that neighbors peered past from their driveways, whispering behind cupped hands. The neighborhood was upscale but not flashy. Quiet. The kind of place where nothing bad was supposed to happen.

I ducked under the tape, flashed my badge at the uniformed officer, and stepped inside. The air conditioning hit me like a wall of ice compared to the Florida heat outside. The living room was undisturbed—family photos, a stack of paperback mysteries on the coffee table, a half-finished crossword puzzle. Everyday life, interrupted.

But the bedroom told a different story.

"Jesus," I whispered, stopping in the doorway.

The forensic team worked methodically, taking samples and photographs. They moved like ghosts around the room, careful not to disturb what was already disturbed. Blood flecked the beige walls in a familiar pattern. The bedside table was on its side, and the lamp was shattered. The sheets were half-dragged onto the floor.

And it all looked exactly like Crystal's room.

"Victim is Eleanor Blackwood, 74, retired librarian," said a voice beside me: Detective Wilson, clipboard in hand. "The neighbor noticed her newspapers piling up. The victim's been dead for some time, at least ten days, the ME said. Blunt force trauma to the head, multiple."

I nodded, stepping carefully into the room. "Same signs of struggle as the Miller case."

Wilson raised an eyebrow. "You think they're connected?"

"Let me see the rest first."

I moved deeper into the room, crouching to examine scuff marks on the hardwood where something—or someone—had been dragged. The forensic photographer captured my movements with mechanical clicks.

"Check the closet," I said.

The walk-in closet door stood ajar. Inside, clothes hung in neat rows, color-coordinated and pressed. But the carpet beneath told a different story. Dark stains. Blood. This was where the first blow fell. Someone was hiding in the closet and surprised Mrs. Blackwood.

My stomach clenched. Not coincidence. Not anymore.

I pulled out my phone, taking my own photos. I compared them side by side with the ones from Crystal's house. The similarity made my skin crawl.

"Drag marks from the closet to the door," I noted, pointing to the slight but unmistakable lines in the carpet pile. "Killer tried to clean up, but didn't have enough time to be thorough."

Wilson scratched his chin. "The body has been dragged across the carpet. It was found, wrapped in a shower curtain. We think they tried to move her, but gave up."

"Too heavy?" I asked, looking down at Mrs. Blackwood.

He nodded. "It's possible. She wasn't very big, though, so maybe they were disturbed."

I stood, knees cracking. "What do we know about the victim?"

"Mrs. Blackwood. Retired librarian, moved here about twelve years ago. Husband died of cancer eight years ago. Kept to herself mostly. Did some volunteer work at the literacy center. No known enemies, no valuables missing that we can determine."

The echoes of Crystal's life made my chest tight. Crystal Miller, 73. Retired engineer from Kennedy Space Center. Lived alone in Cocoa Beach—no known enemies.

"Build? Height? Weight?" I asked, already knowing the answer.

"About five-five, slight. Maybe 130 pounds."

Crystal's exact measurements.

I swiped through more photos on my phone, comparing angles, entry points. The similarities weren't just striking—they were deliberate. The same person had done both crimes. I felt it in my gut.

"We're looking at the same perp," I said, my voice dropping. "Same victim type, same methodology, same cleanup attempt."

"And Eleanor's actually dead," Wilson said bluntly. "Which means—"

"Which means we need to find Crystal. Fast." I cut him off, not wanting to hear the rest of his sentence. My fingers tightened around my phone until the case creaked.

Wilson's radio crackled. He stepped away to answer it.

I returned to the closet, studying the bloody handprint. Smaller than an average man's hand. The victim's? Or someone else's? I snapped more photos, comparing them with Crystal's case file images. There was something else here, something I was missing.

Wilson returned. "What do you make of this, Agent Thomas?"

"I think we've got a predator who targets older women living alone." I straightened, pocketing my phone. "But why? I need all the evidence processed ASAP," I said. "Compare everything to the

Miller case. DNA, fibers, fingerprints—everything. And I need a list of any other missing women matching this profile in the area."

As I walked out, the sun hit my face, but I felt cold. The puzzle was coming together, forming a picture I didn't want to see. But at least now we were looking in the right direction.

And if Crystal was still out there, we had a new chance to find her.

## Chapter 11

I DROVE TOO FAST HOME, the crime scene photos burning a hole in my mind. The connections were falling into place like the tumblers of a lock I didn't want to open. If I was right, Crystal Miller hadn't just disappeared. She'd been taken by someone who'd already killed once—maybe more. My tires screeched as I pulled into my driveway.

"Matt?" I called out, moving through the living room.

"In the kitchen."

I found him standing at the counter, pouring coffee into a mug with steady hands. He wore the same faded T-shirt from yesterday, his eyes ringed with the shadows of sleepless nights. Chief Annie had told him to take the day off today since his mother was missing, and he needed rest. It was really me who had called her and told her to do it, since I knew he had been up pacing all night, and finally fallen asleep when morning broke. But he didn't need to know that. It was two in the afternoon, but it was obvious that he had just gotten out of bed. When he looked up and saw my face, his hand froze mid-pour. Coffee spilled over the rim, pooling black on the white countertop.

"What happened?" His voice was flat, prepared for the worst.

"I need to show you something." I set my bag on the counter and pulled out my phone, containing the photos I had taken earlier this morning. "There's been another incident. A murder."

Matt set the coffee pot down with deliberate care. "My mother?"

"No. A woman named Eleanor Blackwood." I paused, gauging his response. "But there are… similarities."

I showed him the crime scene photos and let him swipe through them on my phone. Matt stared at them, his breath coming faster.

"These were taken this morning," I explained, pointing to the first photo. "A woman in her seventies was attacked in her home in Cocoa Beach. Retired librarian, lived alone. Been dead for at least a week, probably as long as ten days."

Matt's gaze darted between the photos and my face. "A lot like Mom."

"Yes." I pointed at one of the photos. "There was a struggle in the bedroom. Overturned furniture, broken photo frames, vases, and blood spatter on the walls. Most of the blood was by the walk-in closet, suggesting that's where she met her killer when opening the closet door."

"Just like at Mom's house."

I nodded. "Same age range, similar build, both no husbands, both retired professionals. And the same MO—struggle in the bedroom, blood by the closet."

Matt's hands shook as he gave me back my phone. "You think whoever did this also hurt my mother?"

"I do." I kept my voice steady and professional. "I think we're dealing with a predator who targets older women living alone. Someone who knows their routines and knows when they're vulnerable."

"If she's still alive…" Matt's voice broke. He couldn't finish the thought.

"There's a chance she is." I moved a photo showing the victim's body. "Eleanor Blackwood was found wrapped in a shower curtain. It looks like the killer was planning to transport her somewhere, but was interrupted."

"But no one interrupted whoever took Mom."

"Exactly. But I noticed that the shower curtain was missing from your mother's bathroom. I didn't think anything of it when we were there, but now I do."

Matt's face contorted. His fist slammed down on the counter, sending his coffee mug flying. It shattered against the tiles, spraying dark liquid across the white floor. The sound hung in the air between us.

"Goddammit!" His voice was raw. "Five days! She's been gone five days, and we're just now—"

I grabbed his hand—it was hot, vibrating with anger and fear. "We're going to find her, Matt. This is the break we've been waiting for."

His fingers curled around mine, squeezing so hard it hurt. We stood like that for a moment, connected by pressure and pain and something else—a determination that bordered on desperation.

"How?" His voice was barely a whisper. "How do we find her now?"

I let go of his hand. "We have new evidence to compare. Hair, fibers, fingerprints—and now we have a pattern. We know what to look for."

"And if she's..." He couldn't say it.

"She's a fighter, Matt. You know that better than anyone."

He nodded, bending down to pick up the larger pieces of the broken mug. His movements were mechanical, an attempt to restore order to something he could control.

"So, what are our next steps?" he asked, straightening up. His eyes were red-rimmed but dry. "What do we do now?"

"The lab is rushing the analysis on everything we found. We're comparing it to what we collected from your mother's house. If it's the same person, there will be connections."

Matt threw the ceramic shards into the trash. "And then?"

"Then we find out who had access to both women. Who knew their routines and their vulnerabilities. We're checking phone records, friends, former co-workers, volunteer organizations, service providers—anyone who might have come into contact with both of them."

"That's not enough." Matt's voice hardened. "We need to do more. I can help. I can talk to Mom's friends, former colleagues—"

"You've done that already."

"I'll do it again. There must be something we missed."

I watched him, this man holding himself together through sheer force of will. His determined expression reminded me of Crystal—the same stubborn set to the jaw, the same intensity in the eyes. More than once while growing up, I had seen her get angry when I talked about my parents and how dismissive and cold they acted toward me. She would get that burning look in her eyes while telling me that "some people simply shouldn't be allowed to have children." She would also, often in the same breath, tell me that we shouldn't judge, and that we didn't know what they were going through… missing their daughter. That was Crystal for you. Always feeling empathy for everyone.

"Okay," I agreed. "But stick to people, not places. Don't go near any potential crime scenes. This person is dangerous, Matt. They're meticulous, careful. They plan."

He nodded, already reaching for his phone. "I'll start making calls."

My phone rang, the shrill tone cutting through the tension. I answered immediately, turning slightly away from Matt but feeling his eyes boring into my back.

"Thomas," I said.

The lab technician's voice was clipped, excited. "We got a preliminary DNA match between the samples from both scenes. It's not in the system, but it's definitely the same person. And there's something else—"

I held my breath.

"The blood in Crystal Miller's closet? It's not all hers. Some of it belongs to the killer."

I turned back to Matt, who was watching me with desperate hope in his eyes.

"Crystal fought for her life," I told him. "And now we have a trail to follow."

---

## Chapter 12

---



The darkness was absolute in the narrow alcove behind K-Mart's dumpster when Ellie Thompson opened her eyes. No alarm clock needed—her body had learned to wake before the garbage trucks arrived, before the store employees showed up, before anyone could discover her makeshift home. The cardboard beneath her had gone soft with use, but it was better than bare concrete, and the blanket wrapped around her slender frame still held some warmth against the pre-dawn chill.

Ellie sat up, her curly brown hair a tangled mess atop her head. Her small hands, chapped from the spring morning air, automatically began folding the blanket with practiced precision. There was a certain dignity in keeping things orderly, even here. The sliver of sky visible between buildings was just beginning to lighten from black to deep blue.

"Another day," she whispered to herself, a ritual that somehow made the silence less oppressive.

Her backpack—a faded green thing with a broken zipper she'd fixed with safety pins—contained everything she owned. She tucked the blanket inside, making sure her most precious possession remained protected between the folds: the photograph. Ellie touched the corner of the photo briefly, then secured it back in its place.

She changed her socks—one of the few luxuries she allowed herself was clean socks whenever possible—and slipped on her sneakers, which were holding together despite being half a size too small. The laces had broken weeks ago, but a piece of string worked almost as well.

The backpack went into a hollow space behind a loose brick in the building's foundation—a hiding spot she'd discovered after her third night in the alley. No one had found it yet.

Ellie emerged from her alcove like a small ghost, eyes scanning for movement. The street was empty, streetlights still casting pools of yellow light on wet pavement from last night's rain. She walked with purpose, head down but alert, counting the blocks in her mind. Tuesday meant the Riverside Community Center—she never visited the same place two days in a row. Patterns made people notice you, and being noticed was dangerous.

Five blocks east, two blocks north. Her stomach growled, but breakfast would have to wait. Maybe there would be something at school—sometimes kids threw away perfectly good food. The thought sustained her as she walked, her steps quick but not running. Running attracted attention.

The community center's lights were already on when she arrived. Perfect timing—6:02 a.m., just two minutes after opening. Early enough that the place was nearly empty, late enough that she wouldn't be the first person the staff saw.

"Morning," she mumbled to the attendant, a college-aged guy with heavy eyelids who glanced up briefly from his phone.

"Hey," he replied without really looking at her, just as she'd counted on. Ellie had observed him for three Tuesdays before choosing this location—his shift started at 6:00 a.m., and he never really woke up until after 7:00.

The women's locker room was empty, and Ellie moved quickly to the showers. The water was lukewarm, but it felt wonderful against her skin. She allowed herself exactly three minutes—long enough to get clean, short enough to avoid suspicion. Her tiny sliver of soap was getting smaller; she'd need to find more soon.

Under the spray, her mind calculated the day ahead. Classes until 3:15. Lunch would be tricky—it always was. After school, she'd need to check the church—sometimes they put out boxes of free bread on Tuesdays.

Ellie shut off the water and dried herself with a paper towel, each movement efficient and deliberate. Her fingers felt numb from the cold water, but her chest held a familiar warmth—determination, the feeling that had kept her going these past three months. Survival required planning, and she was good at planning.

A woman entered the locker room, and Ellie casually moved to the sinks, keeping her head down. She brushed her teeth with a finger and the tiniest amount of toothpaste squeezed from a sample packet she'd found.

When the woman set her gym bag down and went into a stall, Ellie quickly borrowed a swipe of deodorant from the bag's side pocket. She'd never take anything valuable—just borrowed necessities. Her foster mother's voice echoed in her head: "Stealing is wrong." But this wasn't stealing, not really. Just surviving.

At the mirror, she combed her fingers through her curly brown hair, taming it as best she could. The reflection showed a small, thin girl with alert green eyes who looked older than nine. A spray of freckles across her nose gave her a deceptively carefree appearance. She practiced a neutral expression—not too happy, not too sad—the kind that didn't invite questions.

"You look normal," she whispered to herself, adjusting the worn friendship bracelet on her wrist—the last birthday gift from her best friend before she'd been moved to her third foster home.

By 6:30, Ellie was back on the street, clean and presentable enough for school. Thursday was the YMCA across town. Friday was the community college gym where the morning attendant thought she belonged to the family that came in for early swim lessons. She never used the same bathroom more than once a week, and she always, always acted like she belonged.

The sky had lightened to a pale blue now, and Ellie walked toward Oakwood Elementary, her shoulders straightening with each step. To anyone watching, she was just another kid heading to school, maybe from a home where parents left early for work. Nobody would guess that the neat little girl with the green backpack had spent the night behind a dumpster, counting stars through a gap in the buildings overhead.

Ellie approached Oakwood Elementary with the careful timing she'd perfected over weeks. Being too early meant standing alone and being noticeable; being too late meant encountering teachers who were monitoring tardy students. The sweet spot was 8:17 a.m., when the largest cluster of students poured through the front doors, creating a current she could slip into unnoticed. She kept her eyes trained on the ground, shoulders slightly hunched—not enough to look troubled, just enough to deflect attention to more interesting targets around her.

At 8:30, the morning bell echoed through hallways lined with construction paper art and motivational posters. Ellie navigated through the crush of bodies, backpacks, and morning chatter with the precision of someone who'd mapped every inch of the territory. She avoided the center of the hallway where teachers stood watching, instead hugging the wall where taller students blocked the adults' sightlines.

Classroom C-12, Ms. Brennan's fourth-grade homeroom. Ellie slid into her desk in the third row, second seat from the wall—not the front row where teachers focused their attention, not the back row where troublemakers sat, not by the windows where daydreamers were easily spotted. She'd chosen this seat carefully on her first day, and Ms. Brennan had never changed the arrangement.

In the beginning when she had just run away, she had worried that the Baker's would look for her at school, but they never did. They probably didn't care enough that she was gone. It was only if it was discovered that she wasn't there by her social worker that they would stop getting their money. Then they'd probably start looking for her.

"Good morning, everyone," Ms. Brennan called out, her voice cheerful but tired around the edges. "Let's get our math worksheets out from yesterday."

Ellie's hand went to her folder, extracting the neatly completed worksheet. Math was safe—it required no personal stories, no family details, just numbers that either worked or didn't. She'd completed it last night by the light of the convenience store window, sitting on the curb behind the building where the clerk couldn't see her.

"Who would like to share their answer for number six?" Ms. Brennan asked.

Ellie counted silently. One, two, three… On four, she raised her hand, not first, which teachers remembered, not last, when desperation set in. Third or fourth hand was the sweet spot for invisibility.

"Ellie?"

"Twenty-four," she answered, voice clear but not too loud.

"That's correct. Good job."

No follow-up questions, no extra praise—just the right amount of interaction to be unremarkable. Ellie's stomach clenched around nothing, the hunger a dull ache she'd grown accustomed to managing. She'd learned that hunger came in waves; if you didn't feed it, it eventually retreated to a manageable hum.

English class followed math. Mrs. Garcia was discussing a book about a family's cross-country road trip. "Who has gone on a family vacation?" she asked brightly.

Ellie kept her expression neutral as hands shot up around her. She bent slightly, pretending to search for something in her backpack until the moment passed. She'd become an expert at these small evasions—tying a shoe, finding a pencil, checking a page number—any activity that prevented eye contact during dangerous questions.

Between classes, she stopped at the water fountain, letting the cool liquid fill her stomach, creating the illusion of fullness. The trick was to drink slowly, three steady swallows, then move on before anyone noticed how desperately thirsty she always was.

Science class was in Mr. Abernathy's room, with its smell of pencil shavings and the faint tang of chemicals. Tables instead of desks. Groups instead of individuals. Ellie slipped into her assigned seat, nodding politely to the three other students at her table. Jamie, Marcus, and Sophie—known quantities, predictable in their disinterest in her.

"Today, we're conducting our seed germination experiment," Mr. Abernathy announced, pushing his glasses up his nose. "Each group will check your seedlings, measure them, and record the data."

Sophie pulled their group's tray of lima bean seedlings from the shelf. "Ours are growing really well!" she exclaimed, pointing to the pale green shoots.

"My dad says it's because the classroom is warmer than the other rooms," Marcus offered.

Ellie reached for the ruler, focusing on the task rather than the conversation. Measurement, recording, and observation—these were safe activities.

"What about you, Ellie?" Jamie asked suddenly. "Did your beans at home sprout yet?"

The take-home seedling kits. Ellie had carried hers dutifully out of class last week, then disposed of it in a trash can three blocks from school—no place to grow plants behind a dumpster.

"Not yet," she replied with just the right amount of disappointment. "I think my window doesn't get enough light."

"That's too bad," Sophie said, already losing interest. "My mom put ours in the kitchen and they're huge now."

Crisis averted. Ellie continued measuring, her face a careful mask of concentration. Mr. Abernathy passed by their table, nodding approvingly at her neat handwriting on the chart. He moved on without comment—exactly as she'd hoped.

The next period was history, with Ms. Delgado, who was young, enthusiastic, and dangerous. She asked personal questions, made connections with students, and noticed details. Ellie had developed a specific strategy just for her class: contribute one fact-based comment early in the period, then develop a slight cough that made calling on her uncomfortable for the teacher.

"The Oregon Trail was difficult for families because of the harsh conditions," Ellie offered five minutes into the lesson, her timing perfect.

"Excellent point, Ellie," Ms. Delgado smiled. Three minutes later, Ellie covered her mouth with her elbow and produced a convincing dry cough. Ms. Delgado's eyes slid past her for the rest of the period.

In the hallway between history and lunch, Ellie ducked into the bathroom. The mirror showed a small girl with watchful eyes, her curly hair pulled back with a rubber band she'd found on the playground. Her green T-shirt was clean enough, her expression carefully neutral—neither happy nor sad, existing in the unremarkable middle ground where questions didn't land.

She splashed water on her face, both to refresh herself and to create a plausible reason for her slightly damp appearance should anyone notice. Damp meant just washed, which meant clean, which meant normal. Normal was the goal, always.

The five-minute warning bell rang, signaling the approach of the most challenging part of her day: lunch period. Ellie practiced her "just fine" expression in the mirror one last time, straightened her shoulders to the precise angle between confidence and meekness, and rejoined the flow of students in the hallway.

As they lined up outside the cafeteria, chatter increased around her—lunch trades being negotiated, weekend plans discussed, complaints about parents who packed the wrong snacks. Ellie kept her hands busy arranging and rearranging the items in her pockets, creating the impression of someone organizing lunch money.

"...And then my mom said we could get pizza after," a boy behind her was saying.

"Lucky! My dad never lets us get take-out on weeknights," his friend replied.

Ellie focused on the line moving forward, on her breathing, on the precise placement of her feet on the linoleum tiles. One foot in front of the other. One moment at a time. One more day of passing as normal in a world where normal meant having parents, having a home, having enough to eat.

The cafeteria doors swung open, releasing a wave of noise and the tangled smells of institutional food. Ellie Thompson, nine years old and invisible by design, stepped into the chaos with her chin held carefully level, hunger a familiar companion, and her survival plan for lunch period already unfolding in her mind.

## Chapter 13

I HUNCHED OVER MY DESK, the fluorescent lights of the station humming above me like persistent insects. The screen glowed blue-white in the dimness, casting shadows across the scattered papers—Matt's birth certificate, Crystal's property deeds, employment records. Crystal Miller's life was laid out in bureaucratic bread-crumbs. But the trail went cold forty-seven years back, vanishing like footprints on wet sand. My stomach tightened.

The clock on the wall read 2:17 p.m. I'd been at it for hours, following threads that frayed at their ends. Coffee grew cold in my mug, forgotten.

"Anything worth finding takes time," I muttered to myself, a mantra from my first supervisor at Quantico.

I pulled up another database and typed "Crystal Anne Miller" again. Different search parameters this time. People leave traces. Always.

The monitor flickered as results populated the screen. Same dead end—Crystal Miller appeared in Cocoa Beach records in 1978. Purchased a modest home four blocks from the beach. Got a job at Kennedy Space Center. Credit history was established. But there was nothing on her prior to that.

I printed the documents and added them to my growing pile. Matt had given me her birth certificate that he found among her papers in her office. My fingers traced the edges of it. The paper felt wrong—too new. The hospital listed didn't match regional naming conventions for the era.

Her college transcripts showed a woman who existed only in graduation records. No student activities. No campus housing. Just a name on a list.

My throat felt dry. Matt's mother. My boyfriend's mother. Grandmother to Elijah, who spent weekends in our home. The woman who baked lemon bars for our family gatherings and kept her gardening gloves neatly folded in her back pocket.

I reached for my phone, thumb hovering over Matt's contact. My chest tightened with the weight of what I'd found. This would hurt him.

I pressed call.

"Hey, Eva Rae," his voice was warm but troubled through the speaker

"I need you to come to the station." My voice sounded strange, too professional. The way I spoke to witnesses, not to the man who slept beside me. "Now, if you can."

"What's wrong?"

"Better to discuss in person."

Silence hung between us for three heartbeats.

"I'll be there in fifteen."

The call ended. I arranged the documents in order, using sticky notes to mark the most damning inconsistencies. My fingertips pressed against my temples, fighting back a headache born of eye strain and ethical knots.

When Matt appeared in my doorway, his face was etched with worry.

"Eva Rae? What's happened? Did they find my mother?"

I shook my head and gestured to the chair across from me. "Please, sit."

He lowered himself into the seat, eyes never leaving mine.

"This is about your mother," I said, pushing the first document

across the desk. "I've been going through her past, and I found…
inconsistencies."

His brow furrowed. "What kind of inconsistencies?"

"The kind that suggest Crystal Miller didn't exist before 1978."

Matt's laugh was short and uncomfortable. "That's ridiculous.
My mom's lived here for decades. I was born forty-five years ago."

I handed him the property deed. "This is her first appearance in
any public record I can access."

"That's impossible. She—"

"Her birth certificate was issued retroactively in 1979. The
hospital listed on it closed in 1975, making verification conveniently
impossible." I slid another document forward. "Her supposed alma
mater has no record of her attendance; there's no record of her
graduating from the university she has put on her records. Only a
certificate, which she put with her job application, that could have
been fabricated. Employment history begins with her engineering
position here, at the space center."

Matt's fingers trembled slightly as he leafed through the papers.
He ran a hand through his hair once, twice. A nervous habit I'd seen
a hundred times over breakfast, during movie nights, when helping
the kids with challenging homework.

"There must be a mistake." His voice lacked conviction. "This is
all a very long time ago. Records aren't always correct. She came
from North Carolina, a small town called Hendersonville. That's
where she grew up."

"I checked up on that as well, and there are no records of a
Crystal Miller there. No school records, nothing. Did you ever meet
your grandparents?" I asked.

"No, they died before I was born. My mom got a job at the
space center, that's why she moved here," he said. "She got pregnant
right after, when she met my father. They never married. He died
from lung cancer when I was twelve."

I leaned forward, elbows on the desk. "Matt, I'm not going to
sugar coat it. I have a feeling that your mother isn't who she claims
to be."

His eyes met mine, defensive anger flashing briefly before uncertainty washed it away. He looked again at the documents, squinting as if they might rearrange themselves into something more palatable.

"Why would she—?" he started, then stopped.

"I don't know," I admitted. "But whatever she's hiding, she went to considerable expense and trouble to conceal it."

Matt's shoulders slumped. "She always was private about her past. Said it was too painful." He paused and looked at me. "What if I don't know my mother at all?"

I had no answer. In my line of work, I'd seen identities shed like snakeskins, lives reinvented for reasons ranging from the mundane to the monstrous. I squeezed his wrist gently, the only comfort I could offer against the uncertainty ahead.

## Chapter 14



The cafeteria hummed with the chaos of a hundred conversations, the clatter of plastic trays, and the squeak of tennis shoes on linoleum. Ellie slid onto the bench at the far end of table six, her back to the wall, her eyes level with the emergency exit sign. Perfect position—partially obscured by the large trash can, clear sightlines to both entrances, and just enough distance from the lunch monitors to avoid their sweeping gazes. She'd occupied this exact spot every day for two weeks, and not once had anyone attempted to join her or ask her to move.

With methodical precision, Ellie unwrapped her treasure—half a peanut butter sandwich she'd found abandoned on a picnic table at the park yesterday afternoon. The bread had gone slightly stiff around the edges, but the filling was still good. She'd wrapped it carefully in a napkin she'd taken from the dispenser at the gas station, keeping it safe in her pocket overnight.

The first bite she took was small, deliberate. Chew slowly. Make it last. Twenty-two careful chews per bite—she'd read somewhere that proper digestion required thorough chewing, and she couldn't afford to waste a single calorie. Between bites, she sipped water from the half-filled bottle she'd refilled at the drinking fountain, the liquid helping to expand the sensation of fullness in her stomach.

Three tables away, a burst of laughter drew her attention. A boy with tousled blond hair was gesturing animatedly, his blue eyes bright with excitement, his lunch—a whole sandwich, apple, yogurt cup, and cookies—spread untouched before him. Will Johnson. Same grade, different class. Always talked too loudly. Always had clean clothes and food that came in store-bought packages with brand names.

"My mom's making a chocolate cake with three layers!" Will exclaimed, his hands spread wide to indicate something enormous. "And we're doing pin the tail on the donkey!"

The children around him responded with appropriate awe, their voices rising in a chorus of "awesome," "no way," and "that's so cool." Will beamed under the attention, his untied shoelaces flopping as he bounced slightly in his seat.

"Dad said I could invite fifteen kids this year," he continued proudly. "And Mom's making goodie bags."

Ellie took another tiny bite of her sandwich, her eyes fixed on her own hands while her ears strained to catch every detail. Three-layer cake meant leftovers. Sounded like an outdoor party. Fifteen kids meant chaos—perfect cover for someone who didn't quite belong. Her mind calculated possibilities with the precision of a much older person, weighing risks against potential rewards.

"We're having hot dogs and hamburgers too," Will was saying, "and Mom's special mac and cheese that she puts the crunchy stuff on top of."

Mac and cheese. Ellie's stomach tightened painfully at the thought. Hot food, warm from the grill or oven, mac and cheese with the crispy breadcrumb topping that meant someone had taken extra time, had cared enough to add that final touch of comfort. She couldn't remember the last time she'd had mac and cheese. Last year, maybe? At the Petersons', before Mrs. Peterson had caught her taking food from the pantry to save for later. She'd only stayed there for two weeks.

She broke off a crumb of her sandwich, rolling it between her fingers before placing it on her tongue. Make it last. Always make it last.

"Should we bring presents?" asked a girl with a tight ponytail and sparkling earrings.

"Yeah, but my mom said no one has to," Will replied, though his expression suggested gifts would be very welcome. "My birthday list is mostly books and Legos."

A home with space for toys. A mother who baked. A father who helped plan parties. Ellie studied Will with scientific detachment, cataloging the details that marked him as a child who had never worried about where he would sleep or whether he would have enough to eat. His skin had the rosy glow of regular meals and warm baths. His hair, though messy, had been recently cut in a style that probably cost actual money. His backpack was new this year, with all its zippers intact.

Ellie's fingers absently traced the worn friendship bracelet on her wrist as she calculated how much food might be available at such a party. Fifteen kids, plus parents and possibly some siblings. That meant at least twenty people. Adults always overestimated food quantities. There would be leftovers, possibly substantial ones. The question was whether she could take any without being noticed.

"We're starting at two o'clock," Will was saying, "and you can stay until six if your parents say it's okay."

Four hours in a warm house. Four hours with access to a bathroom that no one would question her using. Four hours of pretending to be just another kid with a home to return to afterward.

The last bite of her sandwich disappeared too quickly. Ellie kept the napkin spread on the table, picking up imaginary crumbs to maintain the illusion of still eating. Her water bottle was nearly empty now, but she rationed the last few sips, knowing the hollow feeling in her stomach would only intensify throughout the afternoon.

Around her, the cafeteria continued its symphony of normal childhood—trading desserts, complaining about siblings, and planning weekend activities. Will's voice rose above the general din as he described the party games his mother had planned. Something about prizes. Something about teams.

Ellie wrapped her empty napkin into a tight ball and tucked it into her pocket—no evidence left behind, nothing to mark her passing. The clock on the wall showed that there were twelve more minutes left in the lunch period. She extracted a dog-eared library book from her backpack. She opened it to a random page, creating a barrier between herself and potential conversation while allowing her to continue observing Will's table.

A party meant adults who would ask questions. Adults who might notice that her clothes, while clean, didn't quite fit. Adults who might wonder why no parent dropped her off or picked her up. The risk was considerable.

But a party also meant food, warmth, and a few hours of pretending that she belonged somewhere. Her stomach growled its vote on the matter, and Ellie pressed her arm against it to muffle the sound.

Will was writing something now, tearing pages from a notebook and passing them to his friends. Invitations, probably. Ellie watched, keeping her expression carefully neutral, a practiced mask of mild disinterest. No one would invite her. No one ever did. She was too quiet, too careful, too invisible by design.

The bell signaling the end of lunch would ring soon. Ellie slipped her book back into her backpack and took a final sip of water. Around her, students began gathering their trash, voices rising in a crescendo of last-minute conversations. Will's friends clustered around him, examining what were indeed homemade invitations decorated with drawings of cake and presents.

Ellie stood, slinging her backpack over one shoulder in a practiced motion that didn't reveal the emptiness inside, her face composed in the expression she'd perfected in countless bathroom mirrors—not happy, not sad, just passing through, nothing to see here.

Four hours in a warm house. Four hours of food and normalcy. Her practical mind was already calculating the walking route to Will's neighborhood, the time it would take, and the story she would need to construct about where her parents were and why they couldn't stay. But those calculations were academic, she reminded herself. The invitation would never come. Girls who sat alone at lunch tables weren't on birthday party guest lists.

The cafeteria emptied in waves, like a tide pulling back from shore. First went the eager students, then the dawdlers finishing conversations, and finally the stragglers savoring last bites or avoiding what came next. Ellie remained seated, timing her exit for the perfect moment of minimum visibility. She watched the clock, waiting for the sweet spot when most supervisors had followed the main crowd but before the final sweep for lingerers began. Three more minutes. Two. She gathered her water bottle and zipped her backpack with unhurried movements. One minute. She stood, calculating her path to the east doors where fewer teachers stood watch. That's when she saw Will Johnson breaking away from his friends and walking directly toward her table.

Ellie froze, her fingers tightening around her backpack strap. This wasn't part of the routine. Direct interactions were dangerous and unpredictable. Her eyes darted toward the exit, measuring whether she could leave before he reached her, but it was too late. Will was already there, standing across the table with a rectangle of bright blue paper in his hand.

"Hey, Ellie," he said, with the easy confidence of someone who'd never had to calculate the risks of human interaction. His blond hair stuck up slightly on one side, as though he'd been running his hand through it. "I'm having a birthday party this Saturday. Do you want to come?"

He held out the invitation—homemade, drawn with markers in different colors, slightly crooked letters spelling out "You're Invited!" across the top. A cake with candles dominated the center of the page, surrounded by balloons.

Ellie's mind raced, cataloging details and assessing threats. Will Johnson. Good at kickball, terrible at keeping his voice down during quiet reading time. Always had Band-Aids on his knees. Never said mean things about other kids. No apparent reason for him to single her out—no class project requiring partners, no teacher's instruction to include the quiet girl. The invitation appeared genuine, not a setup for some cruel joke.

Still, she hesitated. Her carefully constructed invisibility was at stake. Being noticed was dangerous. Being remembered was worse.

"I'm not sure if I can make it," she responded, her voice deliberately casual, neither too eager nor too dismissive. Noncommittal was safest. Leave an exit route.

Will rocked forward on his toes, undeterred. "It'll be fun! We're having games and cake and everything." His enthusiasm was almost tangible, his smile widening. "My mom makes the best chocolate cake. Do you like chocolate cake?"

Their fingers brushed as he pushed the invitation closer to her, and she flinched slightly before catching herself. Human contact was rare in her carefully maintained bubble of isolation. His hand was warm, the paper smooth between them.

"I don't know," Ellie said, her voice softening despite her best efforts to remain neutral. "My, um, situation is kind of complicated." The half-truth was her standard deflection.

Will shrugged, undaunted. "That's okay. My mom says people can come for whatever part they can make it to. It starts at two." His blue eyes were earnest, with none of the calculation or hidden intent Ellie had learned to spot in adults who asked too many questions. "There'll be goodie bags too."

Ellie glanced down at the invitation, her eyes automatically registering the address. Maple Ridge subdivision. The nice part of town, with the big houses and well-kept lawns. Not too far—maybe a forty-minute walk from the library where she often spent Saturday afternoons. Her mind mapped the route, noting bus stops to seek shelter in should the weather turn bad.

The promise of food made her empty stomach contract painfully—hot dogs, hamburgers, three-layer chocolate cake. But more than that, the prospect of a few hours in a normal house, with heating and comfortable furniture and adults who made special mac and cheese with "the crunchy stuff" on top—it pulled at something deep inside her, something she usually kept carefully wrapped and hidden away.

"I don't have a present," she said, testing for conditions, for the catch that must surely exist.

"That's okay," Will replied easily. "My mom said presents are optional."

Ellie's fingers tightened around the invitation, creasing one corner. The paper felt substantial and important in her hand, a passport to four hours of normalcy. Her gaze flickered to the address again, confirming it was within walking distance. She mentally calculated risks versus rewards, as she did with every decision.

Risks: Adults asking questions. Other kids noticing inconsistencies in her story. Potential involvement of authorities if someone became suspicious.

Rewards: Food. Warmth. Four hours of pretending she was just another kid with a home to return to. Four hours of not being hungry and alone.

"Okay," she said finally, a small, genuine smile breaking through her careful mask. "Thanks for inviting me."

Will grinned, looking pleased and slightly surprised, as though he hadn't been sure of her answer. "Great! It'll be awesome!" He bounced slightly on his toes, his untied shoelaces slapping against the floor. "I gotta go, but I'll see you Saturday, okay?"

Ellie nodded, carefully tucking the invitation into the front pocket of her jeans. "Saturday," she confirmed.

Will waved as he jogged back to his waiting friends, immediately launching into an animated conversation that Ellie couldn't hear but could easily imagine: "She said yes! Now we have twelve people coming!"

As she pulled out the invitation to look at it again, her mind was already working, planning the story she would need. If anyone asked about her parents, they were busy working. If asked where she lived, she'd mention a street near enough to be plausible but far enough that no one would offer a ride home. She'd need to arrive looking clean and presentable, which meant timing a visit to the community center shower just right. The library had a bathroom where she could change into her best outfit—the blue T-shirt without any holes and the jeans that almost fit.

The near-empty cafeteria suddenly seemed too exposed. The last lunch monitor was looking her way, probably wondering why she hadn't moved on. Ellie slipped the invitation back into her pocket and slung her backpack over her shoulder, her movements deliberately casual as she headed for the exit.

# Part III

# Chapter 15

CRYSTAL MILLER AWOKE TO COMPLETE, absolute darkness that pressed against her eyeballs as if it were a tangible weight. Her head pounded where something—or someone—had struck her, and when she tried to move her hands toward the tender spot, they remained stubbornly still. A surge of panic overcame her, electric and immediate, only to be supplanted by the methodical voice of her mind, urging her to catalog, assess, and survive.

She was bound. Zip ties—cold, rigid plastic—bit into her wrists behind her back, and the same restraints encircled her ankles. A cloth had been forced into her mouth, held in place by what felt like duct tape pressed across her lower face. She could neither call out nor scream, and the realization made her heart beat fiercely against her ribs.

"Breathe through your nose, Crystal," her internal command whispered, slow and deep.

Crystal tested the restraints; the zip ties offered no slack, a testament to the captor's skill. Each tug sent searing pain across her skin, so she ceased struggling, understanding that panic would lead nowhere—only clear, frozen facts could help her now.

The air was thick with dust and disuse—a musty atmosphere

mingled with a weak chemical scent, possibly from cleaning supplies. Beneath her, the cheap vinyl tile floor felt cold and slightly tacky against her bare legs; she was still wearing her dress, though her shoes were gone. Behind her, a hard, unyielding object pressed into her spine: metal shelving with a jutting corner that dug painfully into her back. Shifting away elicited a wince from her protesting shoulders.

How long had she been imprisoned here? Days at the very least, as fragments of memory flickered into her mind: a driveway, returning home with groceries, a noise in the closet, followed by nothing but darkness.

Straining her ears in the oppressive silence, she discerned the low mechanical hum of an air conditioner and the distant ticking of a clock—until heavy, unhurried footsteps began to echo from another room. Her captor was still present.

Tilting her head back, she sought to understand the space around her. Her shoulder blades pressed against a wall; as she pivoted, her fingertips felt drywall, then wood—a door frame—and finally, a narrow shelving unit too petite to be a pantry. A closet, she realized with mounting dread. She was bound within a four-by-six-foot prison, with shelves on one side, a wall on the other, and a door before her, she sensed a hanging garment brushing her hair from a rod above.

Then the footsteps ceased. A distant chair scraped against a floor, followed by the clink of glass and the muted sound of a television coming to life. Swallowing against the dryness in her throat and the lingering taste of cotton and fear from the gag, Crystal steadied her trembling fingers on the cold plastic. She needed to think.

The footsteps drew nearer, and she froze, not daring to breathe. They paused at the door, and a shadow blocked the thin line of light at its base—a silent figure listening. Her pulse thundered so loudly she was sure it could be heard. Then the shadow receded, and the footsteps moved away. Slowly, she exhaled, controlled and measured, while hot tears gathered behind her eyes—tears she refused to release now, knowing that only calm and clarity would suffice.

As she shifted again, the sharp edge of the metal shelving jabbed into her back. Desperate, Crystal angled her bound wrists toward it, seeking the jagged corner with her fingertips. There it was —a rough cut in the metal, far from ideal, yet her only hope. With each movement, her headache intensified, but leaning against the wall, she gathered both strength and purpose.

Crystal listened intently to the pattern of her captor's movements—a routine of five minutes in the kitchen, eight in what sounded like the living room, with the television droning quietly in the background. Predictability was her ally now.

Her trembling fingers brushed against the metal edge once more, positioning the zip tie against it. With the silence around her and the discipline forged from years of quiet determination, she began to saw.

In the cramped darkness of the closet, the metal edge she used was disappointingly dull, barely sharp enough to make an impact. Her wrists twisted painfully behind her as she worked the zip tie against the metal, forcing her shoulders into an unnatural, contorted position. Back and forth she worked, the plastic catching on the metal then slipping free without cutting. Each time, she adjusted, seeking a sharper point—and slowly, time stretched on, marked only by the persistent scrape of plastic and the mounting pain in her arms.

When footsteps approached, Crystal froze, holding her breath as the same shadow reappeared at the bottom of the door, lingering with unnerving intent. Her muscles screamed in protest from the awkward strain, yet she dared not move. After what felt like an eternity, the shadow receded once more, and she exhaled slowly, her heart hammering so fiercely she felt its beats in her temples.

Steadying herself, she resumed sawing. This time, the edge caught the plastic with a bit more determination; she felt a slight give—a small, promising victory. Pushing through the burning pain in her shoulders and wrists, she worked faster, even as a single drop of blood began to roll down her palm. The metal had nicked her, but she dared not stop—every notch carved into the zip tie was progress, however meager.

Minutes bled into what seemed like hours, her sense of time warped by the solitude in the darkness. The television outside fell silent; indistinct footsteps moved toward what she guessed was a bathroom—water ran, a toilet flushed, the squeak of furniture echoed. Still, she continued sawing, her clumsy movements betraying her fatigue. Blood slicked her hands, making each motion a delicate balancing act as she bit down on the gag to stifle any noise when her raw wrists scraped harder against the zip tie.

Strand by strand, the plastic weakened. With a twist of her wrists and increasing pressure, Crystal felt the zip tie stretch, then, with a frenzied sawing motion fueled by fear, snap. The break was sudden, and she nearly cried out in surprise. Her arms dropped to her sides as her shoulders protested the abrupt release, while pins and needles burst through her hands as blood returned in a rush. Amid the exquisite, terrible pain lay hope—freedom had come.

In the murky darkness, she brought her trembling hands forward to inspect them. Rubbing raw, crusted skin, her pale, spider-like fingers twitched as the tingling sensation slowly returned. Gently, she reached up and peeled away the tape from her mouth, biting her tongue to keep any sound at bay. The cloth gag, now saturated with saliva, was next to come off. After a brief moment of liberation, she listened for any external reaction—only the distant, low hum of the air conditioner met her ears.

She rolled onto her side and fumbled for the zip ties binding her ankles. Those restraints were even tighter, their plastic biting into her skin through thin socks. Despite her swollen fingers, she tried to manipulate the locking mechanism with her fingernails to no avail. She needed something thin and rigid.

Her searching hand brushed along the shelving unit, coming into contact with various bottles, boxes, and cleaning supplies, until her fingers found a thin piece of wire protruding from beneath the shelf. She worked it back and forth until it snapped free—a stray piece of metal from the shelving's construction. Perfect.

Crystal slipped the wire into the ankle zip tie's locking mechanism. Her trembling fingers applied careful pressure as she felt for the internal catch. The plastic resisted briefly before yielding.

Crystal attempted to stand, but her legs buckled beneath her. Relenting, she lowered herself back to the cold floor, massaging her calves until some strength gradually returned. As her fingers grazed the shelf once more, they felt something cylindrical and smooth—a small flashlight, the kind kept for power outages. She flicked it on and cupped her hand around the beam, concentrating the light to reveal the contoured interior of the closet: white metal shelving laden with household supplies, a hanging rod above holding a few old coats, and a plain hollow-core interior door fitted with a basic privacy lock.

She shone the light onto the lock mechanism. There was no deadbolt, just a simple latch. The same wire that freed her ankles might work on this lock, too. Crawling toward the door, each movement negotiated with her body's protests, she advanced carefully. The steady rumble of snoring coming from outside both comforted and terrified her. Could attempting to open the door wake them? Was the snooze merely an act?

Pressing her ear against the door, she listened: the snoring emanated from a room farther away, not right at the door. There was a chance. With determined precision, her hands worked the wire into the lock. Feeling for the internal mechanism amid trembling fingers, she slowly turned the catch until, with a satisfying click, it gave way.

The door opened with a soft click that exploded in Crystal's ears like a gunshot. Immobilized for a heartbeat, she clutched the wire in her bleeding fingers. The snoring in the other room stuttered momentarily before resuming its steady drone. Edging the door open another inch, then another, she created a narrow opening just wide enough to slip into the unknown.

Crawling on hands and knees, she emerged from the closet into a dim hallway. The beam of her flashlight illuminated cheap beige carpet stained with what looked like coffee—or perhaps something worse. To her right, a doorway led to a kitchen; to her left, the source of the snoring resounded from a living room.

There, in a recliner, her kidnapper slept, the face swallowed by shadow. Silently, she turned off the flashlight and tucked it into her pocket, preferring to move under the cover of darkness.

The front door lay beyond the living room, and her escape required crawling past the slumbering captor. Lowering herself flat against the carpet, careful to distribute her weight so as not to creak the floorboards, she inched forward, her raw wrists painfully scraping against the carpet as her elbows carried most of the strain.

Keeping close to the wall and dissolved into the shadows, her racing heartbeat thumped so loudly she imagined it echoing throughout the room. A coffee table blocked her path, forcing a detour that brought her perilously close to the recliner. The close proximity allowed her to smell stale beer and cigarettes, and she saw the rise and fall of a chest—dangerously near.

Stealing past in deliberate, measured motions, she held her breath to avoid a single sound. An accidental bump against a solid object—a floor lamp whose base shifted on the carpet—threatened to expose her. Reacting swiftly, she lunged forward with bloody, trembling hands to steady the lamp, easing it back into place even as pain shot through her wrists.

Then, as suddenly as it had started, the snoring stopped. Crystal froze, flattening herself against the floor so completely that she barely breathed. A grunt and a shift from the recliner followed, and soon the snoring resumed its deep, rhythmic pattern.

Undeterred, she started moving again. She passed the lamp and the recliner, drawing ever closer to the front door—a dark rectangle with a silver deadbolt. On her knees, her legs still wobbly but determined, Crystal reached the door and examined its locks: an easily turned deadbolt, a chain, and a simple sliding bar lock partway down the door.

The deadbolt turned with an easy click that sent a jolt of fear through her; glancing back, she reassured herself as the snoring continued undisturbed. The chain posed more difficulty, her swollen fingers struggling to free it until it finally yielded, and a short effort liberated the bar lock with its simple horizontal slide.

Turning the knob, she eased the door open just wide enough to slip through. As the night air swept over her face—the first fresh breath in days—Crystal longed to run, yet forced herself to move slowly and methodically. She squeezed through the gap and pulled the door closed behind her with painstaking care until it latched with a soft click.

Only then did she allow herself to look around.

She found herself on a small concrete stoop before a nondescript ranch house, surrounded by identical houses with darkened windows and driveways that held little more than the occasional parked car. There were no distinctive landmarks or street signs—only the generic Florida suburban landscape, with palm trees and hibiscus bushes dotting manicured lawns, all rendered in muted tones under the weak yellow glow of widely spaced street lamps.

Yet she knew exactly where she was.

And she knew where to go.

# Chapter 16

THE BANGING STARTED JUST after eleven, three hard knocks that cut through our quiet evening like gunshots. Matt and I exchanged glances across the living room, his book lowering as my head snapped up from case files. Nobody visits this late, not in our neighborhood, not without calling first.

"Stay here," I said, already moving toward the door.

Our Cocoa Beach home, usually a sanctuary from my work, suddenly felt exposed. The knocking came again, more desperate this time. Through the front windows, I caught glimpses of our dark yard, palm shadows swaying against the driveway.

I flipped on the porch light and peered through the peephole. A woman's hunched figure stood there, face downturned, shoulders heaving. Something wasn't right.

"Who is it?" Matt called from behind me.

My fingers closed around the baseball bat we kept in the umbrella stand. Old habits. "I don't know."

I unlocked the door and pulled it open, keeping my body positioned to move quickly if needed. The woman's head jerked up.

Her face hit me like a physical blow.

Crystal Miller stood on my doorstep, but not the Crystal I knew

—the buttoned-up, perfectly coiffed mother-in-law who measured her words like ingredients. This woman was a wreck. Her silver hair hung in dirty clumps, dark with what looked unmistakably like dried blood. Her usually immaculate clothes were torn and filthy, streaked with dirt and darker stains. But it was her eyes that chilled me—wide, darting frantically past me, scanning the darkness behind her like she expected someone to materialize from the shadows.

"Crystal?" I breathed.

She opened her mouth, but no sound came. Her lips trembled, cracked and dry. Those watchful eyes locked onto mine for one lucid second before rolling back. Her knees buckled.

I dropped the bat and lunged forward, catching her as she collapsed. Her body felt impossibly light against mine, bird-boned and fragile. Up close, the smell of sweat and fear rolled off her in waves.

"Matt!" I shouted, struggling to keep her upright. "It's your mother!"

Footsteps pounded across hardwood. Matt appeared beside me, his face transforming in rapid succession—concern shifting to shock, then blooming into raw relief.

"Mom?" His voice cracked. "Oh, my God, Mom!"

He reached for her, arms outstretched.

"She's been hurt," Matt whispered, cradling his mother against his chest. His eyes met mine over her head, wild with questions I couldn't answer.

I stepped back, professional instincts kicking in. Cataloging. Observing. The bruises circling her wrists were dark and defined—restraint marks. The gash above her eyebrow had crusted over but looked deep enough for stitches. Her fingernails were broken, dirt packed underneath—defensive wounds.

"Get her inside," I said, already scanning the street beyond our yard. Empty. Quiet. But something in me didn't trust the stillness. "Now, Matt."

He nodded, guiding Crystal through the doorway. Her feet dragged. I locked the door behind us, throwing the deadbolt with a satisfying *thunk*.

"What happened to her?" Matt's voice shook. "Who would do this to my mom?"

The living room felt different now, charged with a sense of urgency. The case files I'd been reviewing—old kidnappings, cold trails—lay scattered on the coffee table. Ironic. For days, we'd been living with our own missing person case, and now Crystal had returned, bringing more questions than answers.

Looking at her now—the wounds, the terror in her eyes—I knew right away. Someone had taken her. Someone had hurt her. And she'd escaped.

"I'll call for an ambulance," I said, moving toward the phone.

"No hospitals." Crystal's voice cracked through the room, surprisingly strong. Her hand clamped around my wrist with shocking force. "Please. No hospitals."

Matt hovered beside her, his expression stricken. The laugh lines around his eyes had deepened into channels of worry. His hands opened and closed at his sides—wanting to comfort, afraid to touch.

"Mom, you're hurt—" he started.

"No hospitals," she repeated, each word distinct and hard. Her eyes found mine again, clearer now. "Promise me. They'll find me there. I didn't know where else to go. I can't go… I can't go home… I know you both have guns. You can… help me, protect me."

A cold feeling settled in my stomach, heavy and certain. Something was very wrong here—something beyond the obvious trauma. The hair on the back of my neck stood up. Whatever had happened to Crystal Miller, she believed it wasn't over.

I nodded slowly. "Okay. No hospitals. But you need help."

She released my wrist and sank back against Matt, the burst of energy gone. I felt the weight of responsibility settle over me like a second skin, familiar and unwelcome. My chest tightened with that uncomfortable heat I recognized instantly—not guilt, but determination.

Someone had hurt my family. And I would find out who.

# Chapter 17

I MOVED WITH PRACTICED EFFICIENCY, years of crisis management kicking in. The living room transformed into command central. I pointed Matt toward the couch where Crystal now sat hunched, her shoulders drawn tight against some invisible threat.

"Get her water. Room temperature, not cold." My voice came out clipped, the way it did when I couldn't afford emotions getting in the way. Matt hesitated, torn between hovering and helping. "Matt. Now."

He nodded once, backing toward the kitchen. His eyes never left his mother.

Crystal rocked slightly, her gaze fixed on something none of us could see. Up close, the damage was worse than I'd first thought—bruises in various stages of healing patterned her exposed skin like spilled ink. Whatever had happened to her hadn't been quick.

The floorboards creaked in the hallway. I turned to find Elijah frozen in the doorway, his lanky frame silhouetted against the hall light. The thirteen-year-old had Matt's height but none of his ease. He stood with his shoulders hunched forward, his dark hair falling across his eyes.

Those eyes widened as they landed on his grandmother.

"Gran?" The word came out small, childlike.

Something shifted in Crystal's expression—the first real change I'd seen. Her vacant stare focused, sharpened. She straightened slightly, her trembling hands stilling in her lap.

"Elijah," she breathed.

I watched the complex emotions play across the boy's face—relief crashing into anger, confusion into something like pain. He glanced briefly at his father in the kitchen, a look I couldn't decipher passing between them, before stepping into the room.

"You're okay," he whispered, the words sounding more like a question than a statement.

Crystal's hand reached out—the first voluntary movement she'd made since collapsing. Elijah crossed to her, ignoring my instructive glance to move slowly. He dropped to his knees beside the couch, and Crystal's fingers closed around his with surprising strength. A silent communication passed between them; the grandmother and grandson were locked in a bubble I couldn't penetrate.

Matt returned with water, hovering at the edges of this tableau, an outsider to their connection. I caught the hurt that flashed across his face before he masked it.

"I'm going to get some supplies," I said, standing. "Matt, your friend Mike. He's a doctor. Maybe call him? Perhaps he can take a look at her, make sure she's okay?"

He nodded, pulling out his phone. "He's close by, too. Lives just down the beach."

I moved quickly, gathering what I needed—the first aid kit from the bathroom, clean towels, and a blanket from the hall closet. My mind categorized Crystal's visible injuries: contusions, abrasions, and possible fractures. Dehydration… definitely. Malnutrition… likely. The rest I couldn't assess without a proper examination.

When I returned, Elijah had settled beside his grandmother on the couch. He hadn't released her hand. Matt stood by the window, phone pressed to his ear, speaking in low tones.

I knelt in front of Crystal, keeping my movements deliberate, telegraphed. "I'm going to clean some of these wounds, Crystal. Is that okay?"

She nodded once, her eyes never leaving Elijah's face. I started with the cut above her eyebrow—the most obvious injury. The antiseptic must have stung, but she didn't flinch. I worked methodically, cleaning each visible wound and cataloging them in my mind. Defensive marks on her hands, bruising consistent with restraints on her wrists and ankles.

"I need to check for other injuries," I said softly. "Under your shirt."

Her reaction was immediate and violent. She jerked away, arms wrapping protectively around her torso. Her eyes, finally breaking from Elijah, flashed with panic. "No!" The word exploded from her, raw and ragged. "No one touches me. No one."

Elijah's hand tightened on hers. "It's okay, Gran. She's just trying to help."

But Crystal shook her head, curling further into herself. "No touching. No looking. I'm fine."

I recognized the lie, saw the way she winced when she moved, the careful way she held her body. She was hurt. But I also recognized that pushing would do more harm than good.

Matt approached, his phone conversation finished. "Mike is on his way." His voice held barely contained frustration. "Mom, please. Just tell us what happened. Where have you been? Who did this to you?"

The questions hung in the air, heavy and unanswered. Crystal turned her face away, pressing closer to Elijah. The boy shot his father a warning look.

"She's exhausted, Dad," Elijah said, his voice hard. "Can't you see that?"

Matt's patience broke. "She's been missing for days! Do you understand that? Days of not knowing if she was alive or dead!" His voice rose with each word. "Someone did this to her, and you're acting like I'm the bad guy for wanting to know who!"

I moved between them, a physical barrier to the escalating tension. "Matt. This isn't helping."

But Elijah was already on his feet, his thin frame vibrating with anger. He stepped between his father and grandmother, his protective stance unmistakable. "Back off," he warned, voice low and tight.

Matt stared at his son, bewilderment mixing with his anger. "What the hell is wrong with you? Why are you mad at me instead of whoever hurt her?"

The air between father and son crackled with unspoken accusations. I'd sensed the tension between them before—Elijah's teenage rebellion mixing with lingering resentment toward his father—but this was different. Sharper. More personal.

"Both of you, stop." I used my professional voice, the one that brooked no argument. "Crystal needs rest, not a family showdown." I turned to Matt. "Your mother's been through something traumatic. Pushing her won't help."

Crystal had withdrawn completely, eyes closed, body curled against the couch cushions. She looked smaller somehow, diminished.

"Let's get her to the guest room," I said. "She can rest there until the doctor arrives."

Matt nodded curtly, his jaw still tight with frustration. Elijah remained planted between them, guardian and gatekeeper. The standoff continued until I touched Elijah's shoulder gently.

"Help me get her settled," I said. "She trusts you."

The tension in his shoulders eased slightly. He nodded, turning back to his grandmother. The tenderness with which he helped her stand contrasted sharply with the anger he'd directed at his father seconds before.

Matt watched them go, his expression a complex mixture of concern, hurt, and deepening suspicion. The cracks in this family ran deeper than I'd realized, and whatever had happened to Crystal had split them wider.

## Chapter 18



Ellie Thompson stood at the edge of the Johnsons' front lawn, one foot on the sidewalk as if ready to flee. The carefully wrapped gift in her hands—just a small box covered in newspaper she'd colored with borrowed markers—suddenly seemed pathetic compared to the two-story house with its perfect green lawn and cheerful red door. Balloons in primary colors bobbed from the mailbox, catching the afternoon sun and casting jittery shadows that matched the flutter in her stomach.

She tugged at the hem of her too-big T-shirt, wishing she'd had something nicer to wear. The other kids would probably be dressed in brand-new outfits with shiny shoes, not scuffed ones with a flapping sole held together by determination and a stolen paperclip. Ellie scanned the street out of habit—always know your exits—before forcing her feet forward across the invisible boundary between public and private property.

The stone path leading to the front door was lined with cheerful yellow flowers. Ellie counted seventeen steps from the sidewalk to the porch, memorizing the terrain like she did at every new place. The porch swing swayed slightly in the breeze, its cushions plump and inviting, nothing like the hard benches and concrete ledges where she sometimes rested. Through the large front window, she caught glimpses of movement—children darting past, streamers fluttering from the ceiling.

Her finger hovered over the doorbell. Maybe this was a mistake. Will was nice to her at school, sure, but that didn't mean she belonged here in this perfect picture-frame house with its breathing, intact family. Three seconds, she decided. She'd give herself three seconds to be brave.

One. Two. Thr—

The door swung open before she could press the bell, revealing a woman with auburn hair twisted into a bun, laugh lines around her eyes, and an apron dusted with flour. This had to be Will's mom.

"You must be Ellie!" The woman's smile created a sunburst of wrinkles at the corners of her eyes. "Will has told us so much about you. I'm Kathy, Will's mom. Please, come in!"

Ellie clutched her gift tighter, her knuckles white around the package. "Thank you for inviting me, Mrs. Johnson."

"Oh, honey, call me Kathy. Everyone does." Her hand hovered near Ellie's shoulder before dropping away, as if sensing the girl's aversion to unexpected touch. Instead, she stepped back, creating space for Ellie to enter on her own terms. "The party's in full swing. There are hot dogs and burgers in the kitchen, and Will's been watching the door for you."

Ellie stepped inside, and her senses immediately went into overdrive. The house smelled of chocolate cake, hot dogs, and something else—maybe furniture polish or laundry soap—that she associated with homes where people stayed. Music played from somewhere deeper in the house, punctuated by bursts of children's laughter. Birthday streamers hung from the ceiling in swooping arcs of blue and green, and a banner with "HAPPY 10TH BIRTHDAY WILL!" stretched across one wall, the letters obviously hand-painted with care.

She stood awkwardly in the entryway, one shoulder pressed

against the wall, taking in the framed family photos lining the hall-way. Will with missing front teeth. Will holding a trophy. Will sand-wiched between his parents at what looked like a beach. So many captured memories, all in one place, all preserved.

The living room beyond was filled with kids her age; some she recognized from school, while others were strangers. They circled around a blindfolded boy who was swinging his arms wildly while trying to find the donkey on the wall. None of them noticed her standing there, half-hidden by the coat rack, and Ellie was grateful for the moment to gather herself.

She watched the children—their easy laughter, their casual touches as they bumped shoulders or grabbed hands. Somewhere along the way, she'd forgotten how to do that, how to exist in the noise without constantly scanning for threats. Her fingers traced the friendship bracelet on her wrist, its threads worn thin from the same nervous gesture repeated countless times.

"ELLIE!" Will's voice cut through her thoughts. He abandoned the circle and bounded across the room, his blond hair flopping with each step, blue eyes wide with excitement. "You came! I was worried you wouldn't find us, or maybe you couldn't come, or—" He caught himself mid-ramble and grinned, a smile that creased his whole face. "I'm really glad you're here."

Ellie tried to match his smile and managed a small one that felt stiff on her face. "Happy birthday." She thrust the package forward. "It's not much."

Will took it like she'd handed him a treasure. "Thanks! Come on, we're about to finish putting the tail on the donkey, and then we'll have cake, and then presents, and I've got a new board game for after—" He grabbed her hand, then immediately released it when she flinched. "Sorry," he said, his voice dropping. "I forget sometimes."

The simple acknowledgment of her boundaries—so rare in her experience with other kids—loosened something in her chest. "It's okay," she said, and meant it. "Lead the way."

Will beamed and walked backward toward the living room, gesturing for her to follow. "Mom made the best chocolate cake you've ever tasted. Like, ever. And there's ice cream. Do you like chocolate or vanilla better? We have both."

As she followed him into the brightness and noise, Ellie felt herself being pulled into the celebration—not quite belonging, not yet comfortable, but for the moment, included.

Candy was thrown into the air, and the kids dove to get it. But not Ellie. She tracked the movement of each person in the room—a habit she couldn't shake—noting how Henry Johnson laughed as he lifted a smaller child to reach a candy that had landed on a bookshelf, how Kathy gently reminded the kids to share, and how Will gathered extra pieces in his pockets with furtive glances in Ellie's direction.

"Didn't get any?" Will appeared at her side, slightly breathless from the candy scramble. Before she could answer, he emptied his pockets into her hands—a small mountain of wrapped sweets. "I got extras. The purple ones are the best."

"Thanks," Ellie said, surprised by his thoughtfulness. She tucked most of the candy into her pocket, saving it for later out of long habit. Resources were meant to be rationed.

The party flowed into a game of musical chairs, then a scavenger hunt through the backyard. Ellie participated with careful restraint, never entirely abandoning herself to the fun like the other children, but allowing small moments of enjoyment to slip through her guard. During freeze tag, she surprised herself by laughing when Will pulled a ridiculous face while "frozen."

Throughout it all, she observed the Johnson family like a naturalist studying exotic creatures. Henry moved through the party with easy confidence, his hand often finding his son's shoulder or ruffling his hair as he passed. Unlike some of the men Ellie had encountered in foster homes, his movements never seemed threatening. When he reached over to fix Will's crooked party hat, Ellie noticed how the boy leaned into his father's touch instead of away from it.

"Dad! You're embarrassing me," Will protested when Henry showed his friends a baby photo, but his smile betrayed his delight at the attention.

Across the room, Will's sister Carol—a teenage girl with her brown hair pulled back in a bun much like her mother's—organized the younger children into teams for the next game. Despite being years older than the party guests, she showed no signs of the typical teenage disdain Ellie had observed in other homes.

"Three steps back, Tommy," Carol guided a small boy with glasses. "Perfect! Now you're ready."

When Carol caught Ellie watching, she gave a slight, conspiratorial wink. "These little gremlins are a handful, huh?" she said as she passed. "Let me know if you need a break from the chaos. I've got a quiet spot on the porch swing."

Ellie nodded, filing away the offered refuge for later. The constant stimulation was beginning to wear on her nerves, like sandpaper on already raw skin.

A door closed somewhere with a bang, and Ellie flinched, her body tensing automatically. She quickly scanned the room, identifying the nearest exit (a sliding glass door to the backyard, approximately twelve steps away) and cataloging potential obstacles (coffee table, scattered toys, three running children). Only when she'd completed this assessment did her heartbeat begin to slow.

She caught Kathy watching her, a flicker of understanding in the woman's eyes that made Ellie drop her gaze to the carpet. She didn't want anyone's pity, especially not from this kind-faced woman who seemed to radiate maternal warmth as she moved through the party, making sure juice cups were filled and shy children were included.

"Does anyone need more hot dogs before we do cake?" Kathy asked, balancing a plate of buns. She paused beside Ellie. "Honey, have you had enough to eat? You've barely touched anything."

"I'm fine," Ellie said automatically, though the hot dogs smelled delicious. In her experience, it was better not to take too much, not to appear greedy.

Kathy set the plate down and pulled a clean paper plate from a stack. "Well, I'm going to fix you one anyway. Growing kids need food." She selected the largest hot dog, put it inside a bun, and added a squeeze of ketchup beside it. "No arguments," she said with a gentle smile that took any sting from the words.

The simple act of someone noticing she hadn't eaten, caring enough to feed her without expecting anything in return, made Ellie's throat tighten. She accepted the plate with a whispered thanks, turning away quickly so Kathy wouldn't see the emotion welling in her eyes.

"Cake time, everyone!" Henry called, flicking the lights to get everyone's attention. "Will, come take your place at the head of the table!"

Children scrambled for seats around the dining table, which had been decorated with a blue tablecloth and star-shaped confetti. Will's face lit up as Kathy emerged from the kitchen carrying a chocolate cake adorned with ten blazing candles. The gathered guests broke into an enthusiastic, if somewhat off-key, rendition of "Happy Birthday."

Ellie hung back, half-hidden in the doorway between the living room and dining area. She watched the family tableau—Henry with his arm around Will's shoulders, Kathy's face glowing with pride as she held the cake, and even Carol singing along with genuine enthusiasm. The candles cast a warm, flickering light across their faces, illuminating their easy affection for each other.

"Ellie!" Kathy called, spotting her in the doorway. "Come on, sweetie, you should be in the photo too."

Ellie froze, unsure if she'd heard correctly. Kathy gestured her forward with a warm smile that crinkled the corners of her eyes.

"Right here," she said, patting the spot next to Will. "Henry's going to take a picture before the candles melt completely."

Will grabbed her hand, tugging her into position beside him. "Come on! You have to help me make a wish."

Their fingers brushed, and Ellie felt a spark—not static, but something else that jolted her, nonetheless. For a moment, she was part of this circle of light and warmth. Henry raised the camera, and Ellie tried to remember how to smile naturally, how to look like she belonged.

"Make a wish, buddy," Henry said to Will.

Will closed his eyes tightly, his face scrunched in concentration, then took a deep breath and blew. The candles flickered, danced, and went out one by one, leaving thin trails of smoke curling upward. The room erupted in cheers and applause.

In that moment, as the smoke dissipated and Kathy began cutting the cake, Ellie found herself staring at the Johnson family—at the easy way they touched each other, the inside jokes that flowed between them, the invisible threads that bound them together. It was a perfect picture of everything she'd lost, everything she pretended not to want anymore.

And for the first time in a long while, Ellie let herself acknowledge the ache of longing that lived behind her ribs, constant as her heartbeat.

The party began to dissolve around the edges as the afternoon stretched into evening. Parents arrived in a steady trickle, collecting sugar-dazed children who clutched goodie bags and half-eaten slices of cake. Each goodbye tightened the knot in Ellie's stomach. While the other kids had homes to return to, she had… what, exactly?

"Did you have fun?" Kathy asked, appearing beside her with a trash bag for discarded paper plates and cups.

Ellie nodded, managing a slight smile that didn't reach her eyes. "Yes, ma'am. Thank you for having me."

"Any time, sweetheart." Kathy touched her shoulder lightly. "Will's been so excited to have you over. Is someone coming to pick you up, or do you need a ride home?"

Home. The word hung in the air between them, sharp as broken glass.

"My sister's coming," Ellie lied smoothly, the falsehood sliding off her tongue with practiced ease. "She's running late. That's so typical of her. Always late."

"Well, you're welcome to wait as long as you need." Kathy's smile was warm and unintrusive. "In fact, why don't you help us clean up while you wait? Many hands make light work."

Grateful for the reprieve, Ellie threw herself into the cleanup with unusual enthusiasm. She gathered stray cups and plates, straightened the cushions on the couch, and helped Will sort through his presents. All the while, her mind raced through her options, each one worse than the last.

In the kitchen, she heard Kathy and Henry talking as they loaded the dishwasher.

"After Will's in bed, we can watch that new mystery show on TV," Henry said, his voice low and comfortable. "It starts tonight. I picked up some of that ice cream you like."

"Perfect." Kathy's response was followed by the soft sound that Ellie recognized as a kiss. "It's been ages since we've had a proper date night."

Carol breezed through the kitchen. "I'm heading to Amber's now. Her mom says I can stay over since it's already getting late and she doesn't want me biking home in the dark."

"Be home by noon tomorrow," Henry reminded her. "We're having lunch with Grandma, remember?"

"I know, I know." Carol rolled her eyes good-naturedly.

Each casual exchange twisted the knife deeper. This was what a family sounded like—plans made and shared, boundaries set with love, the easy rhythm of lives intertwined. Everything Ellie had lost when her parents died, everything the foster system had failed to provide.

The thought of returning to the cold, dark alley behind the dumpster made her physically ill. Before she could reconsider, a plan began to form—desperate, wrong, but suddenly necessary.

While making sure no one was noticing, Ellie slipped quietly into the hallway. Will was distracted, showing his father a new book, while Kathy cleaned the dishes in the kitchen. No one noticed as Ellie crept up the stairs, her footsteps silent from long practice.

The upper hallway was dimly lit, with three closed doors and one ajar. Through the opening, she could see stars glowing on a dark blue ceiling—Will's room. She slipped inside, her heart hammering against her ribs.

The bedroom was everything a ten-year-old boy's room should be. Superhero posters decorated the walls, action figures stood in frozen battles on the shelves, and a child-sized desk was cluttered with Lego creations. The bed was unmade, its rocket ship comforter rumpled and inviting. It looked lived-in, permanent, secure—everything Ellie's transient existence was not.

She surveyed the space with the calculating eye of someone who'd hidden many times before. Under the bed? Too obvious. Behind the curtains? Too visible. Her gaze landed on the walk-in closet with its sliding doors—one partially open, revealing hanging clothes and stacked storage boxes.

From downstairs came the sound of Will's voice: "Mom, have you seen Ellie? Did she leave already?"

Time was running out. With trembling hands and a racing heart, Ellie crossed to the closet and slid the door open just wide enough to slip inside. The space smelled of clean laundry and the faint plastic scent of new toys. She nestled between hanging shirts and a row of storage boxes, pulling her knees to her chest to make herself as small as possible. Then she slid the door closed until only a crack remained, plunging her hiding spot into near darkness.

Her hands were cold, but she felt a heat in her chest—an uncomfortable burning that she recognized as shame. This was wrong. These people had been kind to her, had welcomed her into their home and their celebration. And she was repaying them by becoming an intruder, a trespasser in their private space.

But the alternative was worse. Just one night, she told herself. Just one night of safety and warmth, and she'd slip out in the morning before anyone woke up. They'd never have to know.

Footsteps on the stairs—heavier than Will's—made her press herself farther back between a winter coat and what felt like a base-ball bag. She held her breath as the bedroom light snapped on.

"—brush your teeth and into pajamas," Henry was saying as he and Will entered the room. "It's already past your bedtime, birthday boy."

"But Dad, I haven't played with all my new toys yet!"

"Tomorrow," Henry promised, his voice kind but firm. "You've had a big day."

Ellie watched through the narrow gap as Will collected his pajamas and a parent-child bedtime routine unfolded—so normal, so achingly ordinary. Will changing in the bathroom down the hall, returning to show his dad a loose tooth, Henry checking under the bed for monsters with exaggerated care.

Kathy appeared in the doorway. "Ready for goodnight kisses?"

Will climbed into bed, his face glowing in the soft light of his bedside lamp. "Today was the best birthday ever," he announced as his parents sat on either side of his bed.

"I'm glad, sweetheart." Kathy brushed his hair back from his forehead. "Was it nice having your friend Ellie here?"

"Yeah." Will yawned. "She's cool. Kind of quiet, but really smart. Did you know she can name all the planets and their moons?"

From her hiding spot, Ellie felt a strange warmth spreading through her chest that had nothing to do with shame.

"Sleep tight," Henry said, ruffling Will's hair one last time before standing. "Love you, buddy."

"Love you, too."

The light clicked off, plunging the room into darkness, broken only by a small night light shaped like a rocket ship. The door closed with a soft click, and the sound of retreating footsteps faded down the hall.

In the closet, Ellie remained perfectly still, barely daring to breathe. Outside, Will shifted in his bed, the springs creaking softly. Within minutes, his breathing deepened into the gentle rhythm of sleep.

Ellie curled tighter into herself, both terrified and determined. For tonight, at least, she was safe—a hidden guest in this home where love was as plentiful as the air they breathed. Tomorrow would bring its own problems, but for now, she allowed herself to absorb the security of these four walls, the steady sound of Will's breathing, and the lingering scent of birthday cake that clung to her clothes.

## Chapter 19

THE DOCTOR ARRIVED twenty minutes later—a gray-haired man with weathered skin and quick eyes that missed nothing. His casual Hawaiian shirt and cargo shorts couldn't hide the military precision in his movements. I recognized the type—retired military turned civilian, the kind who maintained operational security even when diagnosing the common cold. Perfect for our current situation.

"She's in the guest room," I said, leading him down the hallway. "She's reluctant to be examined."

Mike nodded. "Matt briefed me. No hospitals, no questions, no records."

"Exactly."

When we reached the guest room, Crystal was sitting rigidly on the edge of the bed. Elijah stood by the window, his silhouette sharp against the night sky. He straightened as we entered, protective energy radiating from his thin frame.

"Mrs. Miller, I'm Dr. Steiner, but you can call me Mike," the doctor said, his voice softening. "I'm a friend of Matt's. I'd like to take a look at your injuries, if that's all right."

Crystal's hands clutched the bedspread. "Just you?" Her eyes darted between the doctor and me.

"I'll step out," I offered.

"No." The word came fast, urgent. "You stay." Her gaze locked onto mine, surprisingly lucid. "Not him." She jerked her chin toward Elijah.

The boy's face fell. "Gran—"

"Please, Elijah." Her voice softened. "Just Eva Rae."

Something passed between them—an understanding I couldn't decipher. Elijah nodded slowly, slipping past us into the hallway. The door closed with a soft click.

Dr. Steiner opened his medical bag with practiced efficiency. "I'll need to examine you thoroughly, Mrs. Miller."

Crystal nodded once, her lips pressed into a bloodless line.

I positioned myself at the head of the bed, close enough to offer support but far enough to give the doctor room. He worked methodically, his face giving nothing away as he cataloged each injury. I did the same, my trained eyes tracking every mark.

Contusions on her wrists and ankles. Dehydration was evident in the skin's poor elasticity. The cut above her eyebrow needed butterfly bandages, not stitches. Defensive wounds on her forearms and hands. When she finally allowed her torso to be examined, I caught my breath at the bruising across her ribs—precise, targeted, administered by someone who knew exactly how much pressure to apply for maximum pain without breaking bones.

These weren't random injuries. They were calculated and meant to keep her alive long enough to feel the pain.

Crystal endured the examination in silence, her eyes fixed on the ceiling. Only when the doctor gently probed her ribs did she make a sound—a sharp intake of breath, quickly suppressed.

"Two bruised ribs," Dr. Steiner concluded. "No fractures that I can detect without X-rays." He continued his examination, his expression growing grimmer by the minute. When he finished, he repacked his bag with the same precision. "I'll leave you some pain medication and antibiotics for the cuts. Nothing appears life-threatening, but she needs rest and fluids."

Crystal pulled her shirt down, tugging it over the bruises as if hiding them would erase their existence. Her hands shook less now,

I noticed. The initial shock was wearing off, replaced by something harder to read.

We rejoined Matt and Elijah in the living room. They sat at opposite ends of the room, the space between them charged with unspoken tension. Matt jumped to his feet when we entered.

"How is she?" The question burst from him.

Mike set his bag on the coffee table. "Physically, she'll recover. Dehydration, malnutrition, numerous contusions, and abrasions. Two bruised ribs. No signs of sexual assault." He delivered the assessment with clinical detachment. "She needs rest, fluids, and minimal stress."

"What happened to her?" Matt pressed. "Who did this?"

"I don't know," Mike said. "And frankly, she's not in a state to be questioned right now. Whatever happened was traumatic, both physically and psychologically. Pushing her for details could do more harm than good."

Matt's frustration erupted. "She's been missing for days! Someone did this to her!" His voice rose, bouncing off the walls. "We need to call the police. We need to find whoever—"

"Back off!" Elijah was suddenly between them, his body vibrating with anger. The protective stance was back, but there was something else in his eyes when he looked at his father—something that bordered on accusation.

"What is wrong with you?" Matt demanded, staring at his son. "Why are you acting like I'm the enemy here?"

"Because you're not listening! She doesn't want the police. She doesn't want to talk. Why can't you respect that?"

I moved between them, hands up. "Enough. This isn't helping Crystal."

Mike gathered his bag. "I've done what I can. Call me if her condition changes." He lowered his voice, addressing me directly. "Keep an eye on her mental state. Trauma victims sometimes experience delayed shock."

I nodded, walking him to the door. When I returned, Matt and Elijah had separated again, the chasm between them wider than ever.

"Crystal needs to rest," I said firmly. "I'll help her get settled."

Matt nodded, shoulders slumping. The fight seemed to drain out of him, replaced by exhaustion. "I'll make up the guest room properly."

"I'll do it," Elijah said quickly. "I know where the sheets are in the linen closet."

I caught Matt's flinch at his son's words—another rejection, small but cutting.

I returned to the guest room alone. Crystal sat where we'd left her, staring at her bruised hands. She looked up when I entered, her eyes sharper now, more present.

"Let's get you comfortable," I said, helping Elijah get the bed ready. We then helped her under the covers. Her body felt brittle under my hands, like she might crack if I pressed too hard. Elijah kissed her forehead, then left.

Just as I turned to leave, her hand shot out, gripping my wrist with surprising strength. "Don't let them find me." The words were barely audible, breathed rather than spoken.

I leaned closer. "Who, Crystal? Who did this to you?"

She shook her head once, her lips pressing into a thin line. Then her eyes closed, the conversation over. Her grip loosened, hand falling limply to the coverlet.

I returned to the living room to find Matt and Elijah locked in silent combat, positioned at opposite ends of the room. Matt's face was etched with confusion and hurt. Elijah's shoulders were hunched, his hands shoved deep in his pockets, his entire body angled away from his father.

"What's going on between you two?" I asked quietly.

Matt spread his hands helplessly. "I have no idea. Elijah, why are you angry at me instead of whoever hurt your grandmother?"

The boy's jaw tightened. He said nothing, but his eyes spoke volumes—accusation, anger, and beneath it all, a flicker of something that looked almost like fear.

My mind raced, connecting dots that didn't quite align: Crystal appearing on our doorstep; her injuries—professional, calculated;

her terror of being found; Elijah's protective stance toward his grandmother and hostility toward his father; Matt's confusion.

I moved to the window, scanning the quiet street outside. Darkness pressed against the glass, the night holding its secrets close. Somewhere out there was the answer to what had happened to Crystal Miller. And judging by the terror in her eyes when she whispered her warning, that answer was still a threat.

*Don't let them find me.*

The question wasn't just who had taken Crystal, but why. I had a feeling the answer would shatter what remained of this family's fragile peace.

## Chapter 20

THEN:

Ellie Thompson woke at exactly 6:45 each morning, not because an alarm jolted her awake, but because fear was the most reliable time-keeper she'd ever known. She lay still in her nest of borrowed blankets and pilfered pillows, ears straining for the familiar sounds of the Johnson household stirring to life. The closet was dark and close, smelling of laundry detergent and the plastic of Will's action figures, but after three weeks of hiding here, it had become something dangerously close to home.

She'd learned to time her breaths with the rhythms of the house. The distant hiss of the shower meant Mr. Johnson was up. The clatter of plates downstairs meant Mrs. Johnson was setting break-fast. Will's grumbling complaints about school floated through the closet door like radio broadcasts from another world.

Ellie pulled her knees to her chest and waited. Waiting was what she did best now.

Her makeshift bed occupied the far corner of Will's closet, wedged behind a row of rarely-worn jackets and beneath a shelf of abandoned board games. She'd arranged the blankets in layers—thickest on the bottom to cushion against the hard floor, thinnest on top for the spring warmth. A small flashlight, stolen from a drawer in the kitchen, lay beside her pillow. Three books from Will's shelves were stacked neatly against the wall. Her backpack, containing everything she owned in the world, served as both storage and an emergency escape kit. She had gone to pick it up at her secret hiding spot one day when everyone was in school or at work, and the mom was grocery shopping.

The thump of footsteps on the stairs announced Mr. Johnson's descent to breakfast. Ellie mouthed the words along with him as he called out, "Morning, troops," the same greeting every day. She knew Mr. Johnson left for work at precisely 7:30 AM, his car backing down the driveway with a distinctive crunch of gravel that she could hear even from her hiding place.

Mrs. Johnson, Will, and Carol departed at 8:15 a.m., their routine so predictable that Ellie could almost set her watch by it. The slam of the front door. The jingle of keys. The car starting, then fading as they drove away. And then—blessed silence. Empty house. Freedom, of a sort. On days when Mrs. Johnson volunteered at the church, she'd have hours to herself in the house.

When the house fell quiet, Ellie counted to three hundred—five full minutes to ensure they hadn't forgotten anything and returned unexpectedly. Then she eased the closet door open, wincing at its slight creak. Will's bedroom looked different in daylight, his superhero posters and sports trophies taking on a cheerful glow that made her throat tighten with an emotion she refused to name.

The bathroom was her first stop. She'd timed herself—four minutes to use the toilet, wash her face and hands, and brush her teeth with the toothbrush she had stolen from the parents' cabinet in their bathroom.

Back in Will's room, she had filled her water bottle from the bathroom sink and checked her food supply. Two granola bars, an apple, and a packet of crackers—enough for emergencies if she couldn't make it to the kitchen at night. She rationed these carefully, never knowing when she might need to retreat to her hiding spot for extended periods.

The hours stretched before her, empty but dangerous. Ellie had developed a routine here, too. First, listening—pressing her ear to Will's bedroom door, mapping the house through its creaks and sighs, and then getting food downstairs, cereal or toast, always remembering to wash the dishes she used and place them back where she took them from. Then, reading books borrowed one at a time from Will's shelves, and always returned to their exact positions.

When reading tired her eyes, she drew, using paper liberated sheet by sheet from Will's school notebooks, pencils borrowed from his desk. She drew maps of the house, escape routes, and sometimes —when the loneliness pressed too hard against her chest—pictures of people with smiling faces and open arms.

"You're being stupid," she whispered to herself, carefully folding a drawing of a family—not the Johnsons, not exactly, but close enough that the resemblance made her hands tremble. Her voice sounded strange in the empty room, scratchy from disuse. She spoke aloud only rarely, afraid of the habit taking hold and betraying her at the wrong moment.

At 3:30 p.m., the distant slam of a car door sent her scrambling back to the closet. It was Will returning from school, and Mrs. Johnson's voice calling a greeting. Ellie's world narrowed again to the dimensions of her hiding place, ears straining for snippets of their conversation through the door.

She arranged herself carefully among the blankets, positioning her body to avoid cramping. Her muscles ached from the confinement, but it was a small price to pay for shelter. The alternative— going back to the streets, or the Bakers, or worse, another foster home like theirs—made her palms sweat and her heart race.

As daylight faded, Ellie lay in her nest, listening to the sounds of dinner preparation, of family life continuing on the other side of the wall. Her stomach twisted with hunger, but patience was another skill she'd perfected. Night would come. The house would sleep. And then, like a ghost, she would emerge to claim her share.

Her hands were cold in the closet's perpetual chill, but she felt a warmth in her chest—an uncomfortable heat that she recognized as both gratitude and shame. They didn't know they were keeping her safe. And she didn't know how long this fragile sanctuary would last.


The digital clock on the microwave read 1:37 a.m. when Ellie finally ventured from Will's closet. The house had settled into sleep two hours ago—Mr. Johnson's snores rumbling from the master bedroom, Will's even breathing from his bed across the room. She'd memorized their sleep patterns as carefully as their waking ones, knew the difference between Will's restless turning and his deeper slumber. Tonight, like every night, she counted to one hundred after his last movement before easing the closet door open and stepping into the darkened bedroom.

Will lie sprawled across his bed, one arm flung over his head, mouth slightly open. Ellie paused, watching the rise and fall of his chest beneath his spaceship pajamas. Something about his peaceful face made her chest ache. He had no idea she existed in his margins, borrowing space in his life without permission.

She picked her way across the floor in socked feet, avoiding the spot near his desk where the floorboards betrayed pressure with a telltale squeak. The hallway stretched before her, a canyon of shadows broken only by a thin slice of moonlight from the bathroom window. She moved like a shadow herself, keeping close to the wall where the floors were less likely to creak.

The fourth step from the top of the stairs always groaned, so Ellie stretched one leg over it, balancing precariously before continuing her descent. The banister felt cool beneath her palm, smooth from years of hands sliding along its surface. At the bottom, she paused again, listening for any disturbance in the house's breathing —nothing but the hum of the refrigerator and the ticking of the grandfather clock in the living room.

The kitchen was her destination, as it was every night. A low-risk target—food disappeared steadily throughout the week anyway, making her small thefts virtually undetectable if she was careful. And Ellie was very, very careful.

She approached the refrigerator first, opening the door slowly to minimize the sound of breaking suction and to prevent the interior light from flooding the kitchen too suddenly. The cool air washed over her face as she surveyed the contents, making strategic decisions. Never take the last of anything. Never take from a new container. Never leave evidence of cutting or handling.

She selected half an apple that Mrs. Johnson had sliced for Will's lunch the next day, carefully removing one piece and rearranging the rest to disguise the theft. A single string cheese from a package of twelve. Two baby carrots from a bag full of them. A carefully measured sip of orange juice directly from the carton—a luxury she allowed herself only occasionally.

The refrigerator's contents secured, she turned to the pantry. The Johnsons kept cookies in a ceramic jar shaped like a chicken. Ellie lifted the lid with practiced care, extracting a single chocolate chip cookie and replacing the lid without a sound. She added a handful of cereal from an already-opened box, a slice of bread from the middle of the loaf, and a single-serving package of peanut butter that would likely be attributed to Will's habit of snacking after school.

Her collection gathered, she returned to the refrigerator for the final item—a juice box hidden behind the milk cartons. As she reached into the back shelf, the overhead light suddenly blazed to life.

"Thought I heard something," Henry Johnson mumbled, his voice thick with sleep. He wore a navy bathrobe over striped pajamas, his hair standing up on one side. He rubbed his eyes, squinting against the light he'd just switched on.

Ellie didn't breathe. Didn't move. Didn't exist. She pressed herself against the wall beside the refrigerator, making herself as small as possible.

Henry shuffled to the cabinet above the sink, his movements clumsy with sleep. The sound of a glass being removed from the shelf seemed impossibly loud in Ellie's ears. The running tap roared like a waterfall. She watched through the crack between the refrigerator and its door as Henry filled his glass, his back to her position.

He turned, lifting the glass to his lips, water sloshing slightly over the rim. His eyes, heavy-lidded and unfocused, drifted toward the refrigerator. Ellie's lungs burned with her held breath.

Their eyes met—or almost met. Henry looked directly at the refrigerator door, his brow furrowing slightly. Ellie felt her stolen food turning to stone in her pockets. The moment stretched, rubberband taut and ready to snap.

"Huh," Henry said to himself, lowering the glass. "Someone must have left it open. Probably one of the kids."

He crossed the kitchen in three steps that seemed to take hours. His hand reached for the refrigerator door, inches from where Ellie stood frozen in terror. Their fingers almost brushed, and she felt a spark of pure panic—static electricity building in the dry night air, but it jolted her nonetheless.

Henry pushed the refrigerator door closed with a gentle thud. She stood pressed against the wall, listening to him set his glass in the sink, switch off the light, and shuffle back upstairs.

Only when his footsteps faded and the creak of the master bedroom door signaled his return to bed did Ellie permit herself to breathe again. Her legs trembled beneath her, threatening to collapse. The food in her pockets felt suddenly insignificant compared to the narrow escape.

She abandoned the juice box and made her silent way back upstairs, every nerve ending electric with lingering fear. By the time she slipped back into Will's closet and closed the door, her night's haul forgotten, all she could hear was the thundering of her own heart.

# Chapter 21

THE SOUND of shattering glass jolted me from sleep. Not the crash of a fallen picture frame, but the deliberate breach of a window. Beside me, Matt stirred but didn't wake. I slid open the bedside drawer in the darkness, fingers wrapping around the familiar weight of my Glock. My body moved before my mind fully surfaced from dreams—a response drilled into me through years at the Bureau.

I checked the digital clock: 2:17 a.m.

My bare feet found the floor, avoiding the creaky board by the foot of the bed. The house was silent now, which worried me more than continued noise. Deliberate silence. Calculated movements. This wasn't a drunk teenager who'd thrown a rock.

I eased into the hallway, gun held low. The darkness pressed against me, thick and humid from Florida's endless summer. A strip of moonlight cut across the carpet from the window at the end of the hall, illuminating framed photos of our blended family—smiling faces unaware of the danger below.

All doors remained closed. Matt's son Elijah and my three kids were all still safely asleep. I slipped toward the stairs, keeping my weight on the balls of my feet.

The lower floor waited, a landscape of shadows and hidden

corners. I paused at the base of the stairs, listening. The air conditioner hummed. A clock ticked in the kitchen. Then, a soft scuff of movement came from the other end of the house.

Where Crystal's room was.

I moved along the wall, staying in shadow. My heart pounded in my ears, but my hands remained steady. This was my family. My territory. The intruder had made a critical error.

A dark figure emerged from the hallway leading to Crystal's room. Tall. Slender. Wearing a ski mask and moving with purpose. I raised my weapon.

"FBI. Don't move." My voice cut through the darkness, controlled and authoritative.

The figure froze. One second. Two.

Then lunged.

The impact knocked me back, my gun hand smashing against the wall. Pain shot through my wrist. The Glock clattered to the floor, sliding across hardwood into darkness.

I twisted away from a wild punch, years of training taking over. The intruder was strong but untrained—all fury, no discipline. We crashed into the hallway table. A vase shattered. Photo frames rained down around us.

I caught an arm, leveraged my weight, and drove the attacker into the wall. The plaster cracked. A grunt—female, definitely female. She rammed her elbow back, catching me below the ribs. Air rushed from my lungs.

We grappled in the darkness, knocking against the walls, furniture toppling around us. I tasted blood where my lip had split. The metallic tang fueled me. I wasn't just an agent now—I was a mother protecting her home.

I caught her with a strike to the solar plexus. She doubled over. I moved to pin her, but she twisted away. A lock of silver hair stuck out below the ski mask.

She drove her knee up and caught me in the thigh. I stumbled. She bolted for the broken window, glass crunching under her feet.

"Stop!" I lunged after her, fingers grazing her jacket.

Too late. She slithered through the jagged opening, leaving behind a scrap of dark fabric caught on the glass.

I moved to follow, then stopped. Going outside, alone and unprotected, would be tactically unsound. The intruder was gone, melting into the night. My priority had to be securing the family.

"Eva Rae?" Matt's voice came from the stairs, thick with sleep and sudden fear. "What the hell—?"

"Call 911," I said, already scanning for my weapon. "Someone broke in."

The overhead light snapped on. Elijah stood at the switch, his teenage frame tense in the doorway, eyes wide as he surveyed the destruction.

"Is Grandma okay?" His voice cracked.

"Check on her," I ordered, retrieving my gun from beneath an overturned side table. "But be careful."

Matt was already on the phone, his free hand pressed against a bleeding cut on his foot where he'd stepped on glass. Our eyes met across the chaos of the living room—broken lamps, scattered photos, upended furniture.

The warm security of our home had been violated. And somehow, I knew this wasn't a random break-in. The woman had been heading directly for Crystal's room.

Elijah returned, his arm around his grandmother's shoulders. Crystal's face was pale, her hands trembling. When she saw the destruction, she stopped breathing for a second, her eyes fixing on the broken window.

"She found me," she whispered so quietly I almost missed it.

The night suddenly felt much colder.

## Chapter 22

THE LIVING ROOM transformed into an island of harsh light amid the darkness. Blood smeared the carpet in small, telling drops—not mine, not Matt's—the intruder's blood. I crouched beside a particularly clear spot, examining the pattern while my family huddled on and around the couch. The familiar weight of being both agent and mother pressed on me, pulling me in two directions. Evidence. Family. Procedure. Comfort. The blood told a story that Crystal already seemed to know.

Crystal sat with a blanket clutched around her shoulders, her fingers white-knuckled against the fabric. She trembled despite the night's heat. Elijah hovered beside her, a gangly sentinel refusing to move more than a foot from his grandmother. My children had been awakened by the commotion but remained upstairs after I'd assured them everything was under control.

Nothing was under control.

I took photos of the blood drops with my phone before calling Rick Mercer, my supervisor at the Bureau's Brevard County satellite office.

"Someone targeted Crystal specifically," I said quietly into the phone, stepping into the kitchen but keeping my family in view. "Female perpetrator, elderly but athletic build. Injured during the confrontation. Blood evidence on scene."

"Any connection to your active cases?" Rick's voice was sleep-rough but already analytical.

"None I can see." I watched Crystal's hunched form. "But there's something else going on here."

I ended the call with promises of a forensic team by morning. When I returned to the living room, Matt was kneeling in front of his mother, trying to get her to drink some water. Her hands shook so badly that he had to help her hold the glass.

"She found me," Crystal whispered again, louder this time. Her eyes darted to the broken window where a temporary patch of cardboard now covered the hole. "After all these years."

"Who found you, Crystal?" I asked.

Her gaze snapped to mine, suddenly sharp with fear or recognition, I couldn't tell which.

"I never thought…" she continued as if I hadn't spoken. "The name change… it was supposed to be enough."

My spine straightened. "What name change, Crystal?"

Matt looked between us, confusion etched on his face. "What are you talking about, Mom?"

She didn't answer him. Instead, she twisted the blanket between her fingers, a nervous gesture I'd never seen from this typically composed woman.

"Crystal," I pressed, gentling my voice, "if someone's threatening you, we need to know. That's the only way I can help."

"You can't help." Her voice turned flat. "No one can."

"Grandma, please." Elijah's adolescent voice cracked with worry. "Just tell us what's happening."

For a moment, Crystal seemed ready to speak. Her mouth opened, eyes focusing on her grandson's face. Then her expression shuttered closed like a door slamming shut.

"It's nothing. Just an old woman's confusion." She straightened her shoulders, attempting to reclaim her dignity. "Probably just a burglary gone wrong."

The deflection was so transparent it would have been comical in any other situation. I noted the widening of her pupils, the slight twitch at the corner of her mouth—textbook signs of deception I'd learned to spot during interview training.

"The intruder went straight for your room," I pointed out. "Ignored valuables in the living room."

Crystal's eyes darted toward the windows again. The blinds were closed, but she stared at them as if expecting to see a face pressed against the glass. Her fingers hadn't stopped trembling.

"I'm tired," she announced suddenly. "I just want to go back to bed."

"That's not happening tonight," I said. "We need to process this scene, and your room might contain evidence."

Heavy footsteps announced Matt's return from checking the perimeter of the house. I hadn't even noticed him leave during my conversation with Crystal. His face was grim as he reentered the living room.

"House is secure," he reported. He paused, looking at his mother with new eyes. "What did you mean about a name change, Mom?"

Crystal's gaze dropped to her lap. "Nothing, Matthew. I'm just shaken up."

Matt's eyes met mine over his mother's head. The doubt in them mirrored my own. He'd heard the words too, registered their significance.

"Nobody's going to hurt you," Elijah promised his grandmother fiercely. "I won't let them."

"The forensic team will be here by morning," I said, keeping my tone professionally calm. "I recommend we all stay together until then. "

Matt nodded, but his eyes hadn't left his mother's face. I recognized his expression—the disorienting feeling when someone you've known your whole life suddenly becomes a stranger.

"I'll make some coffee," I offered, more to break the tension than anything else. There was no way we were going to be sleeping anyway after all this. At least I wouldn't. I knew that much.

"She'll come back," Crystal whispered as I turned away. When I looked back, her eyes were fixed on the temporary patch covering the broken window, her face a mask of resigned terror.

# Chapter 23

DAWN CRAWLED THROUGH THE WINDOWS, painting everything in sickly yellow light. We'd been awake for hours, the adrenaline crash making everyone's movements slow and tempers sharp. I watched Matt pace the living room while Crystal sat rigidly on the couch, the same position she'd maintained since the break-in. Elijah hadn't left her side, his teenage frame somehow imposing despite his lankiness. I sipped cold coffee and catalogued their body language, the agent in me unable to switch off even as exhaustion dragged at my limbs.

"We need to move you to a hotel, Mom," Matt said, stopping his pacing to face Crystal directly. "Just until we figure out what's happening."

The words hung in the air. Reasonable. Logical. The same suggestion I'd been considering.

"No." Elijah's response came before Crystal could even open her mouth.

Matt ran a hand through his disheveled hair. "This isn't up for debate, Elijah. Someone broke in, specifically targeting your grandmother."

"So, your solution is to ship her away?" Elijah's voice rose sharply.

"It's for her protection," Matt said, his patience visibly wearing thin.

I watched the interaction silently, noting how Elijah's body angled forward, placing himself physically between Matt and Crystal. Not just protective but possessive. My gaze shifted to Crystal, who stared at her hands, offering neither support nor objection to her son's plan.

"You always want to ship people away when things get tough!" The accusation exploded from Elijah, his face flushing red. He stood up, forcing Matt to take a step back. "Every single time!"

Matt's expression hardened. "That's not fair. You know that's not true."

"When she fell and broke her ankle last year? Your first suggestion was a care facility." Elijah's hands clenched into fists at his sides. "When she needed help with the yard? You tried to convince her to sell the house and move to that retirement community."

Something old sparked between them—this wasn't just about today.

"I'm trying to keep her safe," Matt said, his voice deliberately calm in a way that only seemed to infuriate Elijah more.

"I'm not letting you make decisions for her anymore." Elijah's voice dropped, turning cold with anger rather than hot. More dangerous that way. "Or for me, by the way."

I noticed how Crystal's eyes flickered between them, her expression unreadable. She didn't defend Matt, her own son. Didn't contradict Elijah, her grandson. The silence felt deliberate.

Matt stepped forward, reaching toward his mother. "Mom, please. Be reasonable…"

Elijah moved with surprising speed, physically inserting himself between them.

"Don't touch her." The warning came out in a near-growl.

The tension in the room crystallized into something dangerous. Matt froze, shock registering on his face at his son's aggression. His jaw tightened, eyes narrowing.

I tracked their positioning, the distance between them, and the angle of their bodies—an automatic threat assessment ingrained from years of fieldwork. Matt's shoulders tensed, preparing to assert his authority. Elijah's stance widened, rooting himself to the spot.

"This isn't about some hotel, is it?" I said quietly, drawing their attention without raising my voice. "This is about something else."

Both heads swiveled toward me, momentarily united in their surprise.

"There's nothing—" Elijah began.

"Yeah, it's not—" Matt said simultaneously.

I held up my hand, cutting them both off. "Someone targeted this house. Targeted Crystal specifically. Crystal recognized the threat and mentioned a name change."

I turned my attention directly to Crystal, whose face had gone pale. "Either you tell us what's happening, or I start investigating you as deliberately endangering this family by withholding information."

Harsh, but necessary. Sometimes the truth needed to be forced to the surface.

Tears welled in Crystal's eyes, spilling silently down her cheeks. Still, she said nothing.

"You don't get to interrogate my grandmother," Elijah snapped, his protectiveness reaching new heights.

"She's not just your grandmother." Matt stepped forward again. "She's my mother. If she knows something that puts this family at risk—"

"This family?" Elijah laughed, a bitter sound with no humor. "Is that all you care about? Your new family? What about us? Huh? You didn't want us."

Matt recoiled as if slapped. "That's not what happened."

"Stop it." Crystal's voice, barely above a whisper, somehow cut through their argument. "Please, just stop."

The room fell silent. Crystal's hands trembled as she clutched the blanket still wrapped around her shoulders. She looked fragile in the morning light, older than her years.

"Our priority is keeping Crystal safe," I said, stepping into the center of the room. "Whatever secrets exist can be dealt with later. Right now, we need to secure her and investigate this intruder."

Neither Matt nor Elijah responded directly to me. They remained locked in silent confrontation, Matt's frustrated pacing resumed, Elijah's fists still clenched at his sides. Crystal's tears continued silently.

I watched them, this fractured unit that could hardly be called a family in this moment. Elijah, guarding more than just his grandmother. Matt, confused and hurt by his son's animosity. Crystal, the apparent center of it all, was keeping secrets that were now putting everyone at risk.

"The forensic team will be here soon," I said, taking control of the situation as both agent and the only apparently rational adult present. "Matt, call the office. You're not going in today. Elijah, help your grandmother get something to eat. She's staying with us, here, not a hotel, until we figure this out."

As they reluctantly moved to follow my instructions, I pulled out my phone to call Chief Annie. Whatever Crystal was hiding, whatever had caused this family to splinter apart under pressure, was connected to the silver-haired woman who had come through our window in the night.

And I was going to find out what it was, whether they wanted me to or not.

## Chapter 24



Will Johnson sat cross-legged on his bed, staring at his closet door with the kind of intensity only a ten-year-old convinced of monsters could muster. The door wasn't anything special—just ordinary white-painted wood with a brass knob that had lost its shine years ago—but lately, it had become the center of his universe. Something was wrong with that closet. And tonight, he was going to figure out what.

Moonlight filtered through his bedroom window, painting silver rectangles across his dinosaur-patterned rug. The shadows stretched long and thin, like fingers reaching across the floor toward his bed. His desk lamp cast a warm yellow glow that somehow made the darkness in the corners seem deeper, more secretive. Outside, the maple trees that gave Maplewood its name rustled in the evening breeze, their shadows dancing on his walls like puppet shows he couldn't quite follow.

Will's eyes darted to his shelf of action figures. There it was again—Captain America was standing beside Iron Man, when Will distinctly remembered putting him next to Thor before going to school that morning. This had been happening for weeks now. His Justice League comics, usually arranged by issue number, had been reshuffled twice. His favorite book had migrated from his desk to his bookshelf overnight. His mom blamed his "scatter-brain," but Will knew better. He was meticulous about his stuff.

"I'm not crazy," he whispered to himself, picking at a loose thread on his comforter. The words hung in the quiet room, a challenge to the universe.

Then he heard it—a soft rustling sound, like a plastic bag being carefully opened, coming from inside the closet. Will's heart lurched into his throat, pounding so hard he felt it might leap right out of his chest. The sound stopped, then started again. Not the house settling. Not the wind. Something—or someone—was in there.

A monster.

Will's hand fumbled under his bed, fingers wrapping around the smooth handle of his Little League baseball bat. The wood felt cool against his sweaty palm. He wasn't supposed to keep it in his room—his mom had rules about sports equipment—but lately, he'd felt better having it nearby.

His legs felt like they'd been filled with lead as he swung them over the edge of his bed. The floor creaked under his bare feet, and he winced at the sound, irrationally worried about alerting whatever lurked behind the closet door. Will's mouth had gone dry, his tongue sticking to the roof as if glued there. Part of him wanted to run straight to his mom's room, to dive under her covers like he used to do during thunderstorms when he was little.

But he wasn't little anymore. He was ten—double digits.

"Don't be a baby," Will mumbled to himself, gripping the bat tighter. He took one step, then another. The distance to the closet seemed to stretch, much farther than the actual eight feet it measured in daylight hours.

When he finally reached the door, he stood there frozen, bat raised awkwardly in front of him. His heart thumped wildly in his ears, drowning out everything but his own shallow breathing. Sweat beaded on his forehead despite the cool night air coming through his partially open window.

Will's hand trembled as he reached for the doorknob. The brass felt cold against his fingertips. He hesitated, then with a surge of courage that surprised even himself, yanked the door open in one swift motion, bat poised to swing.

Nothing lunged out at him. No monsters. No intruders. Just his hanging clothes, shoes scattered across the floor, and boxes of old toys his mom kept telling him to donate. The beam from his desk lamp illuminated only ordinary closet things. Will poked the bat among his hanging shirts, pushing them aside. He nudged a box of Legos with his foot. Nothing seemed out of place, yet the feeling of wrongness persisted.

"I know you're in here," he whispered, though he felt foolish saying it to an empty closet. After a minute of searching and finding nothing, Will backed away slowly, keeping his eyes fixed on the dark recesses of the closet until he bumped into his bed. He didn't close the door, preferring to keep watch from under his covers, bat clutched to his chest.

Deep within that same walk-in closet, tucked into a space Will hadn't thought to check, Ellie Thompson held her breath until her lungs burned. She was wedged between the back wall and a large storage box of winter clothes, knees pulled tight against her chest. The small fort she'd made from an old blanket was invisible unless someone specifically looked behind the boxes, which thankfully, Will hadn't.

Her heart hammered against her ribs like a trapped bird. She'd been so careful these past several weeks—only moving around when the house was empty, or everyone asleep, replacing everything exactly as she found it, collecting crumbs from the kitchen in the dead of night. But she'd gotten sloppy today, touching his stupid toys, shifting in her hiding spot when she should have remained perfectly still.

A bead of sweat trickled down her spine despite the cool air. Her green eyes, wide with fear, tracked the strip of light visible through the crack between the wall and the box. She'd seen Will's shadow pass by, heard his breathing, and felt the vibration of his footsteps. She'd bitten her lip so hard to keep quiet that she tasted blood.

Ellie clutched the worn friendship bracelet on her wrist—her talisman, her only constant possession through so many foster homes. She couldn't get caught. Not now. Not when she'd finally found a safe place to hide while she figured out her next move.

The floorboards creaked as Will settled back into bed. Ellie didn't move a muscle. She'd wait hours if necessary, until the boy was asleep and the house was silent once more. She was good at waiting. Good at being invisible. It was how she'd survived this long.

But a cold knot formed in her stomach as she realized her time in this hiding place was running out. The boy was suspicious now. She needed a new plan, and soon.

Morning sunlight streamed through the kitchen windows the next day, turning the Johnson family breakfast nook into a square of honey-gold warmth. Will sat hunched over a plate of scrambled eggs that had long since gone cold, pushing the yellow mounds into fortress-like shapes with his fork. Dark circles hung under his eyes like bruises, evidence of a night spent watching his closet door instead of sleeping.

The kitchen hummed with morning sounds—the coffee maker gurgling its last drops, the refrigerator's steady drone, the distant ticking of the antique wall clock his parents had received as a wedding gift from his grandparents. Everything seemed so normal, so ordinary in the light of day, making last night's fears seem almost foolish.

Almost.

His mom moved around the kitchen with practiced efficiency, her auburn hair tied in a bun that somehow never lost its charm. As she rinsed a coffee mug in the sink, she glanced over at her son, noticing his untouched breakfast.

"Earth to Will," she said, her voice gentle with just a hint of morning huskiness. "Those eggs aren't going to eat themselves, kiddo." She leaned against the counter, studying him with the careful attention that always made Will feel like she was reading his mind. "You look like you've been up all night. Bad dreams?"

Will stabbed at an egg clump, watching it fall apart under his fork. The memory of last night's rustling sounds echoed in his head. He'd spent hours staring at that closet, bat in hand, until exhaustion had finally pulled him into a fitful sleep.

"Mom," he started, then paused, suddenly aware of how childish his concerns might sound in the bright kitchen. He pushed his plate away and sat up straighter, trying to look as grown-up as possible. "I need to tell you something important."

His mom raised an eyebrow, pouring herself another cup of coffee from the carafe. "Sounds serious. Should I sit down for this?" The corners of her mouth twitched upward, but she slid into the chair across from him anyway, wrapping her hands around the warm mug.

Will took a deep breath. "Mom, I think there might be a monster in my closet." The words tumbled out in a rush, hanging awkwardly between them.

His mother's face softened into a smile that Will knew all too well—the one that meant she thought he was being cute but ridiculous.

"Sweetie, you're getting a bit old for monster stories, don't you think?" she said, reaching across the table to ruffle his already messy blond hair. "Next thing, you'll be telling me there's a dragon under your bed."

"I'm not making this up!" Will insisted, ducking away from her hand. "It's not monsters exactly, but… something's in there. My action figures keep moving around. My comics are all out of order. And last night, I heard noises—like somebody was in there, moving stuff around."

Kathy took a slow sip of her coffee, her green eyes studying him over the rim of her mug. "Will, honey, you're a boy with a very active imagination. It's one of the things I love most about you. But old houses make noises. Pipes knock, wood expands and contracts.

As for your toys—" She gave him a pointed look. "When was the last time you properly cleaned your room?"

"This is different," Will insisted. He could feel heat rising in his cheeks. Why couldn't she just believe him? "I know exactly where I put Captain America before school yesterday. And then last night, he was standing next to Iron Man instead of Thor."

"And the only possible explanation is… closet monsters?" His mom's voice was gentle, but Will could hear the amusement underneath. She stood up and carried her mug to the sink, then began loading the dishwasher with breakfast dishes.

"Not monsters," Will corrected, his jaw tightening with frustration. "Someone. Or something. I don't know what, but it's real, Mom. I know what I heard."

Will's mom wiped her hands on a dish towel and walked back to the table. She bent down and planted a kiss on his forehead. "Will, sometimes when we're tired or stressed, our minds play tricks on us. Remember last summer when you were convinced there was a ghost in the attic, and it turned out to be a squirrel that had found its way in?"

Will folded his arms across his chest. "This is different," he repeated, knowing it sounded weak even to his own ears.

"Tell you what," she said, collecting his untouched plate, "how about we clean your room today? Top to bottom. We'll organize everything, and then if things start moving around again, we'll have a better idea of what's happening."

"You don't believe me," Will said flatly.

His mom sighed, her shoulders dropping slightly. "I believe that you believe it, sweetie. But there are usually simple explanations for these things." She glanced at the clock. "I need to get some work done this morning. Those tax returns won't file themselves. Why don't you play outside for a while? It's beautiful out. Maybe call Derek to come over?"

Will pushed his chair back with more force than necessary. "I know what I heard, Mom. Something's in there."

"Will—" she started, but he was already heading for the stairs, shoulders hunched against her dismissal.

In his room, Will stood in the doorway, staring at the innocent-looking closet. In daylight, with sunshine streaming through his window, it was just a closet—nothing sinister or strange about it. But he couldn't shake the feeling that someone had been watching him last night, that someone was hiding among his winter coats and old toys.

He set his jaw with determination. If his mom wouldn't help him, he'd handle it himself. Tonight, he'd set a trap. Whatever—or whoever—was hiding in his closet wouldn't stay hidden for long.

## Chapter 25

THE RHYTHMIC CREAK of the porch swing carried through the night air as I stepped toward the back door. It had been a long day with the forensics team going through our house, and me trying to figure out what was what in this whole affair. I had called for a security company to come out and set up alarms and cameras, just to help us out and make us feel safe. I had told Crystal to go sleep in our bed upstairs, and Matt was watching some show on his laptop in the kitchen, trying to get his mind off things. The two youngest were asleep in their rooms. I just wanted some fresh air. Through the screen, I made out two silhouettes pressed close together, their whispered conversation punctuated by soft laughter—my daughter's laugh. I pushed the door open and watched Christine and Elijah spring apart like opposing magnets, their guilty expressions illuminated by the string lights hanging along the porch railing. Too close. They'd been sitting too close.

"Mom!" Christine's voice cracked on the single syllable. "We were just talking."

"At midnight?" I stepped onto the porch, letting the screen door shut behind me with a soft snap.

The night air hung heavy with humidity, carrying the distant roll of surf and the sweet scent of the jasmine climbing our trellis. Mosquitoes swarmed the porch light, casting erratic shadows across the wooden planks.

Elijah stared at his hands, his lanky frame hunched defensively. At thirteen, he seemed caught between boyhood and something not quite manhood—all sharp angles and uncertain boundaries. Christine, at seventeen, projected a confidence she didn't entirely possess, crossing her arms over her chest as if preparing for battle.

"We couldn't sleep," she said. "With everything going on."

I leaned against the porch railing, studying them both. "Understandable. It's been a difficult time for everyone."

A moth fluttered against the light, its wings casting giant shadows on the house siding. I watched it struggle, bang itself against the glass, retreat, then try again—some lessons we never learn.

Christine studied me, her expression softening slightly. "We're just… Elijah was sad. It helps to talk to someone who understands."

I nodded, understanding more than she realized. "It's late. You should head in."

She hesitated, glancing at Elijah. Some silent communication passed between them before she stood. "Don't interrogate him," she whispered as she passed me.

"Goodnight, Christine."

The screen door creaked, then slapped shut behind her. In the newly empty space, the swing's creaking seemed louder. Elijah remained seated, staring out into the darkness beyond our yard, his jaw set at a stubborn angle.

I took Christine's vacant spot, careful to leave space between us. The swing protested under our combined weight.

We swung in silence for several minutes, the rhythm hypnotic. A pair of headlights swept across the street, briefly illuminating our yard before plunging it back into darkness.

"I need to understand why you're so angry with your father," I said eventually.

His body tensed immediately. "I'm not angry."

"Elijah."

His fingers dug into the wooden armrest of the swing, knuckles whitening. "It doesn't matter."

"It matters to Matt. It matters to you. And that means it matters to me."

"He knows why." The words emerged clipped, each one bitten off.

"Tell me anyway."

He stared straight ahead, refusing to meet my eyes. The porch light caught the sharp edge of his profile, so like his father's, yet set with a hardness Matt's never had.

"He doesn't want me."

"What do you mean?" I asked.

"He's got you guys. A new child. A better family."

"That's not true," I said. "Elijah, look at me. Tell me you don't believe that."

"He told me he didn't want me back home," he said. "At your house."

"What? When was this?"

"When he lost his leg. He told me to go stay with Grandma, that he couldn't deal with me."

My shoulders slumped. Matt had always told me that it was Elijah's choice. Apparently, they weren't in agreement on that. But it made sense. Matt had been depressed, and it took some time for him to realize he could live a normal life without his leg, that there was still a place for him in this world. And at work.

"Then last year," he continued, his voice unnaturally flat, "my grandma was in the hospital. She had surgery. Dad promised he'd take me to see her that weekend. He promised." His jaw clenched. "Then he got called in to work. Some emergency that couldn't wait. He left me with a neighbor and said he'd be back in a few hours."

The swing creaked beneath us.

"He didn't come back until the next day." Elijah's voice dropped. "Crystal got very sick that night while he was gone. While I was sitting with the neighbor, eating mac and cheese and watching cartoons, not knowing…. She almost died that night, the doctor told us when we got there. She lost consciousness. Some internal bleeding or something. When she came back to life, she cried in pain, asking for me and him. She was all alone." His voice cracked. "He knew she was in danger. The doctors told him. But he still left."

"Oh, Elijah." My heart ached for them both—the boy who'd felt so alone, so lost, and afraid he might lose the only woman he remembers as a mom, but also the father who'd made an impossible choice and lived with the consequences.

"He chose his job over us." Elijah's hand ran through his hair, tugging at the roots. "He's done that over and over again. Either chosen the job or… you."

"Did you ever tell him how you felt?"

"What's the point? It won't change anything."

"It might change how you feel. How he feels."

Elijah shook his head. "It's easier just to be angry."

"Easier isn't always better."

He stood abruptly, the swing lurching with the sudden shift in weight. "I should go in."

I remained seated, looking up at him. "He loves you, you know. More than anything."

Elijah paused, his back to me, shoulders rigid under his over-sized hoodie. For a moment, I thought he might say something more. Instead, he gave a single sharp nod and walked away, the screen door closing quietly behind him.

I stayed on the swing, pushing it gently with my foot, listening to its rhythmic protest. Inside my home, my blended family lay frac-tured in different rooms, separated by walls both physical and emotional. But I'd seen it—that brief hesitation, that almost-imper-ceptible nod. A crack in the defensive wall. Not reconciliation, not yet. But a beginning. Maybe.

## Chapter 26



Will's fingers trembled slightly as he looped the thin string around the doorknob of his closet. Not from fear, though the thought of actually catching whatever had been rustling around in there at night did make his stomach flutter—but it was also from a strange feeling of excitement. Three nights in a row, he'd heard those strange sounds, and tonight, he was ready.

"You're not getting away this time," he whispered, carefully tying a knot in the string before stretching it across the narrow gap between his closet and bedroom wall.

His bedroom glowed in the soft blue light of his rocket ship nightlight, casting long shadows that danced whenever he moved too quickly. Outside, crickets chirped their endless summer song, occasionally punctuated by the distant bark of a neighbor's dog. The rest of the house sat quiet, his parents long since retired to their bedroom down the hall.

Will reached into his treasure box—actually just a shoebox decorated with superhero stickers—and pulled out three small silver bells he'd carefully removed from an old Christmas ornament. His mom would probably notice they were missing eventually, but by then, he'd have proof of the closet monster, and that would be worth any trouble he might get into.

"Perfect," he murmured, attaching the bells to the string at carefully calculated intervals. He'd seen a trap like this in a movie once, where the hero knew when bad guys were coming because they triggered a warning system just like this one.

Will stepped back to examine his handiwork. The string stretched invisibly in the dim light, the tiny bells hanging like silent sentinels. His trap wasn't just about catching the intruder—it was about knowing exactly when it emerged. The rest of his defenses lay hidden under his bed: a flashlight, a plastic sword, and his dad's old baseball mitt (just in case he needed to grab something icky).

He glanced at his bedside clock—10:45 p.m. His parents hadn't come to check on him. That was good. They might ruin everything with their grown-up logic about old houses and settling noises.

Will knew better. The sounds he'd heard weren't the random creaks of an aging home. There had been purpose in them, light footsteps and the subtle shifting of things in his closet. Yesterday, he'd found his toy dinosaur collection rearranged; the T-Rex had been moved from the top shelf to the middle one. His parents never touched his dinosaurs.

He climbed into bed, pulling his space-themed comforter up to his chin. The ceiling above him was dotted with glow-in-the-dark stars, arranged in constellations his dad had helped him place. The Big Dipper winked down at him as he settled against his pillow, trying to find a position that looked natural but still allowed him to keep one eye on the closet door.

"Just gotta stay awake," he told himself, though his body already fought against him, heavy with the day's activities. The baseball game at school had gone into extra innings, and he'd run more than usual, playing outfield where the action seldom reached him, but the requirement to remain vigilant never ceased.

Much like now, he thought with a smile.

As the minutes ticked by, Will's bedroom transformed in subtle ways. The shadows deepened, growing more substantial as moonlight replaced the fading evening glow. The house settled around him, occasional pops and groans from the heating system creating a comforting background rhythm. From down the hall came the faint sound of his father's snoring, a familiar, reassuring rumble.

Will's eyelids grew heavier. He blinked deliberately, forcing them back open each time they threatened to close. In his mind, he rehearsed the moment of discovery: the bells jingling, the closet door creaking open, and him sitting bolt upright, flashlight beam catching the culprit in its glaring spotlight.

Would it be a monster with purple fur and yellow eyes, like in his favorite storybook? Or maybe something with scales and a long tail? Part of him hoped it would be friendly, whatever it was. He'd read enough stories to know that not all monsters were bad—some were just misunderstood.

His thoughts grew fuzzier as sleep beckoned. The space between his blinks lengthened, the closet door blurring slightly in his vision. Will pinched his arm hard, wincing at the sharp pain but welcoming the renewed alertness it brought.

"Just a little longer," he promised himself, shifting to lie on his side with one arm tucked under his pillow. From this angle, he had a perfect view of his trap while still appearing to be asleep. The bells hung motionless in the dark, waiting.

As the night deepened around him, Will's determination waged a losing battle against his exhaustion. His breathing slowed, his thoughts scattered like leaves in a gentle breeze, and despite his best efforts, his eyes finally closed completely—his small body surrendering to sleep even as his mind clung to its mission.


The soft tinkling of bells pulled Will from the depths of sleep like a fish being reeled to the surface. His eyes snapped open, his body instantly alert in that way only children can manage, sleep shrugged off like an unwanted blanket. The trap. His trap had worked. Something—or someone—was coming out of his closet.

Will lay perfectly still, his breath caught somewhere between his lungs and his throat. The room was darker now, his nightlight casting just enough blue glow to transform familiar objects into mysterious shapes. The bells tinkled again—a delicate, almost musical sound that seemed impossibly loud in the night silence.

His heart hammered against his ribs, a wild creature seeking escape. This was the moment he'd been waiting for, yet now that it had arrived, a cold trickle of fear ran down his spine. What if it really was a monster? What if his childish defenses weren't enough?

The closet door moved, a fraction of an inch at first, then wider, its hinges releasing a low, protesting creak that stretched through the darkness. Will clutched his blanket, pulling it up to just below his eyes. Through narrowed lids, he watched as the string with its tiny bells swayed gently, evidence of disturbance.

A sliver of deeper darkness appeared in the gap between the door and the frame. Will held his breath. The door continued its agonizingly slow journey, revealing the shadowy interior of his closet inch by cautious inch. His imagination painted monstrous shapes in the darkness—claws, fangs, glowing eyes.

Then a hand appeared—a small, human hand—curling around the edge of the door. Will blinked, his fear momentarily replaced by confusion. The hand was followed by an arm, then a head peeking out with extreme caution.

It wasn't a monster at all.

A girl emerged from his closet, moving with the careful deliberation of someone walking on thin ice. Her curly brown hair stuck out in unruly directions, as if it had been compressed for too long and was now expanding in freedom. She wore a T-shirt that hung loosely on her small frame and shorts that had seen better days. Around her wrist was a worn, frayed friendship bracelet, its colors barely discernible in the dim light.

Will stared, recognition dawning slowly.

*Ellie!*

She moved like a shadow, each step carefully placed to avoid making noise. Her gaze swept past his bed without lingering, clearly assuming he was asleep. Will noticed how she carried herself—

shoulders slightly hunched, body tight like a coiled spring ready to flee at the slightest provocation.

In one hand, she clutched something small and dark that Will couldn't identify. With her other hand, she reached up to brush a tangle of curls from her face, revealing the spray of freckles across her nose and cheeks. Her movements held a strange mix of childish awkwardness and practiced stealth.

The moonlight filtering through his curtains caught her face as she turned, illuminating features pinched with worry. There was a smudge of something—dirt maybe—on her left cheek, and her lips were pressed together in concentration. She looked both younger and older than Will remembered from the party, vulnerability and determination battling across her expression.

She took another step, and the floorboard beneath her foot released a betraying creak. She froze, holding her breath, eyes darting to Will's bed. Will, in his excitement at finally seeing who had been hiding in his closet, had forgotten to maintain his sleeping facade. His eyes were fully open, staring directly at her.

Their gazes connected across the darkened room, and for a heartbeat, time seemed suspended between them—a shared moment of mutual discovery that crackled with the intensity of a lightning strike.

The girl's eyes widened, her pupils dilating until they nearly swallowed the green. The object she'd been holding—Will could now see it was a small stuffed animal, worn threadbare with love—dropped from her suddenly limp fingers. Her body went rigid, caught in the invisible headlights of discovery.

Will could see the pulse jumping in her throat, could almost hear her heart pounding to match his own. Her mouth opened slightly, but no sound emerged. She looked like a wild creature, poised between fight and flight, fear radiating from her in almost visible waves.

The moonlight caught a tremor in her hands, the slight shake of her shoulders. Her chest barely moved, breath held in that moment of terrible realization. The friendship bracelet on her wrist caught the dim light as her hand twitched involuntarily.

Will sat up slowly, the blanket falling away from his chest. The girl flinched at his movement, taking a half-step backward toward the sanctuary of the closet. Her eyes never left his face, tracking him with the desperate attention of prey watching a predator. In those wide green eyes, Will saw something beyond simple fear—he saw panic, desperation, and a terrible resignation, as if she'd always known this moment would come.

They stared at each other across the bedroom, two children caught in a midnight encounter neither had fully anticipated, connected by surprise and separated by the vast unknown reasons for her presence in his closet.

———————————————

# Chapter 27

———————————————

I'D BEEN WATCHING Matt slice tomatoes with the practiced ease of someone who finds peace in simple tasks when the alarm tore through the house—the new alarm that we had just gotten installed for protection. We both froze—his knife suspended mid-cut, my wine glass halfway to my lips—for that single heartbeat before training kicked in.

"Intruder," I said, already moving.

Matt dropped the knife with a clatter and followed me to the security panel mounted near the refrigerator. The small screen flashed zone six—the French doors leading to the backyard patio. Not a false alarm or a child sneaking out. Someone was out there. The motion-activated security light had been triggered.

"Kids?" Matt asked, his voice barely audible beneath the shrieking alarm.

"Upstairs with Crystal." I punched in the code to silence the alarm but left the system armed. We needed to know if other entry points were breached.

Matt crossed to the kitchen drawer—the one with the childproof lock—and retrieved his Glock. I grabbed my weapon that I hadn't put away since I had just gotten home from work. I had spent the day looking through the case files of Eleanor Blackwood, trying to figure out what the connection could be to my mother-in-law, but so far, I had found nothing. Crystal wasn't of much help, even though I showed her pictures of the woman who had been murdered recently. It was like she would rather get murdered herself than tell me the truth, and it annoyed me.

We moved without discussion, a silent choreography built from years of respective training. I pointed two fingers toward my eyes, then toward the living room, indicating my path. Matt nodded, gesturing that he would cover the direct approach to the back door. In the sudden quiet after the alarm, I heard footsteps overhead, then Elijah's voice.

"Dad? I heard the alarm go off. What's happening?"

Matt looked up toward the stairwell. "Stay up there," he called, firm but calm. "Keep the door closed. We're checking it out."

I pressed my back against the wall, using the kitchen entrance as cover while scanning the darkened living room. The digital clock on the cable box read 6:47 p.m. Early for a break-in. Bold. Desperate.

My eyes adjusted to the shadows. Nothing moved in the living room. I edged forward, staying low and using furniture for conceal-ment. I reached the window that overlooked the side yard and the path to Crystal's guest room.

That's when I saw her. A shadow among shadows, moving with deliberate steps across our backyard. She paused at the corner of the house, head turning toward Crystal's window.

The stance. The careful movements. The way she checked her surroundings. This wasn't some random burglar who'd picked the wrong house.

Matt appeared silently at my side, questioning eyes meeting mine.

"It's her," I whispered, my voice tight. "The killer's back."

His jaw tensed, but his hands remained steady on his weapon. We'd discussed this possibility—that the person hunting Crystal might escalate—but facing it now sent ice through my veins.

I pointed to myself, then to the side door that would let me circle behind the intruder. Matt nodded once, indicating he'd cover the kitchen door. He tapped his pocket where his phone was—a reminder that backup was a call away. I shook my head slightly. We needed to contain the situation first, especially with the children upstairs.

My heart hammered against my ribs, the familiar rush of adrenaline sharpening my senses. I cataloged escape routes, possible weapons, and distances between cover points—the automatic assessment of an agent entering a potentially lethal situation. But this was different. This wasn't some anonymous operation. This was my home. My family.

I slid toward the side entrance, keeping low beneath the windows. My fingertips brushed against the cool wall as I moved, using it to steady myself. The tactical part of my brain calculated angles and timing, while another part—the mother, the protector— screamed warnings I couldn't afford to hear.

Three seconds to the door. Two controlled breaths to center myself. One last glance at Matt, who had positioned himself perfectly to create a crossfire situation if the intruder entered. The coordination between us felt like a dangerous dance, with precise movements that carried lethal potential.

The sound of breaking glass shattered the night. I pivoted toward Crystal's room just as a gloved hand reached through the newly created opening to unlock her window from inside. The alarm system was set off and blared through the house. I didn't hesitate. Three quick steps and I was there, weapon extended in both hands, dropping into a shooter's stance.

"FBI! Freeze!" My voice rang with authority, even as my eyes took in the details of our intruder.

She was older than I'd expected—late seventies, with her silver hair pulled back so tightly it created unnatural tension in her face. Her thin frame belied the strength in her movements. I recognized her suddenly. It was the woman who had been next door to Crystal in the Airbnb. Had she kept Crystal there in that house all this time? While we were searching for her? So close by and we couldn't see it? The thought haunted me.

She whirled toward me, a hunting knife clutched in her right hand. The blade caught the light—six inches, serrated edge. Her eyes were fever-bright, pupils dilated with rage or adrenaline or both.

Behind her, Matt appeared, his weapon trained on her back. Perfect tactical positioning. Nowhere for her to run.

"Drop the weapon!" Matt's command was steady, controlled. "Now!"

The woman's head snapped between us, calculating odds with the cold precision of someone who'd planned for contingencies but hadn't expected this level of resistance. The knife remained clutched in her white-knuckled grip, but she took half a step back, finding the wall behind her.

"She killed my brother." Her voice cracked with decades of grief hardened into rage. "She has to pay."

I kept my aim centered on her chest. "Put down the knife, and we can talk about this."

"There's nothing to talk about." The woman's gaze flicked toward the ceiling, then back to me. "She's lived a lie her entire life while Will's been in the cold ground."

A floorboard creaked, followed by urgent whispers. I didn't dare look, but I sensed movement behind me.

"Let me talk to her." Crystal's voice was strained but composed.

"Go back upstairs!" Matt ordered, not taking his eyes off the intruder.

"No." Crystal's voice came closer. "This has been coming for a long time."

I heard another scuffle behind me—Elijah trying to hold his grandmother back. I maintained my position.

"Crystal, don't—" I started.

"It's all right, Eva." She moved beside me, her eyes fixed on the woman with the knife. "She's Carol. Will's sister."

The woman—Carol—let out a sound somewhere between a laugh and a sob. "You remember his name at least. How generous."

Crystal took another step forward. I shifted slightly to maintain a clear shot, but something in Crystal's posture told me she wasn't afraid of the knife.

Carol's face contorted. "You left him bleeding to death."

"I was nine years old." Crystal's words tumbled out faster now.

The knife in Carol's hand trembled. "You disappeared. Your clothes were found by the river. Everyone thought you drowned. But I always knew you were out there."

Crystal's shoulders slumped. "I panicked."

## Chapter 28

THEN:

"What are you doing in my closet?" Will whispered, his voice neither accusing nor frightened, just puzzled. The question hung in the air between them, simple words that carried the weight of all her secrets. Ellie remained frozen, her eyes wide pools of terror, her small shoulders rising and falling with rapid, shallow breaths.

Will watched as a tear formed at the corner of her eye, catching the faint blue glow of his nightlight before tracking a silvery path down her freckled cheek. Her body trembled visibly now, a leaf caught in an invisible wind. She opened her mouth to speak, but nothing came out except a small, choked sound.

Curiosity overcame caution as Will slowly pushed his blanket aside and swung his legs over the edge of the bed. The floor felt cool beneath his bare feet as he stood, careful to move deliberately, the way he approached stray cats in the neighborhood—with interest rather than threat.

"It's okay," he said, keeping his voice low. "I'm not mad. I just want to know why you're here." He took a small step toward her, then another, noticing how she tensed with each decrease in distance between them.

Her fingers worked nervously at the edges of her T-shirt, twisting the fabric into small, tight knots. Her gaze darted between Will and the closet door, measuring escape routes and possibilities. Her chest heaved with suppressed sobs, each breath a battle against the breakdown that threatened to overwhelm her.

Will stopped a few feet away, giving her space. "I haven't seen you since my birthday party," he said, recognition solidifying into certainty. "You ate three pieces of cake. I remember because my mom said it was nice to see someone enjoy her baking so much."

Something in his mundane observation seemed to crack her defenses. Her shoulders slumped, and the tears began flowing in earnest now, silent rivers that she wiped away with angry swipes of her hand.

"I have nowhere else to go," she finally whispered, her voice rough and small. Each word seemed to cost her something to produce. "Your house is nice. Your closet is big. I didn't take anything important. I was careful. I only came out when everyone was asleep."

Will tilted his head, processing this information with the straightforward logic of childhood. "But don't you have a home? Parents or somebody?"

The question unleashed something in her. Words began tumbling out, her voice still quiet but urgent now, as if a dam had broken.

"Foster homes. So many of them that I lost count." Her fingers unconsciously moved to the friendship bracelet on her wrist, twisting it round and round.

"The social worker doesn't believe me anymore. Says I'm 'difficult to place.'" She mimicked an adult voice with bitter accuracy. "At the last home, I heard them talking about sending me to a group facility, which is just a nice way of saying the place where they send the throwaway kids."

She looked down at the stuffed animal she'd dropped, a small, worn rabbit with one ear slightly longer than the other. "I ran away months ago. Been sleeping wherever I can. Till I came here." A ghost of a smile touched her lips. "It was the nicest day I've had in forever. And your house—it felt safe. That night, I just wanted to be somewhere warm for a little while."

Will took another careful step closer. "You've been living in my closet for that long?" He sounded more impressed than upset.

She nodded, wiping her nose with the back of her hand. "I'm careful. I only eat little bits of food, things nobody would notice. I use the bathroom when everyone's asleep or out of the house. I keep all my stuff neat in one corner of your closet." Pride flickered briefly across her tear-streaked face. "I'm good at being invisible."

"Aren't people looking for you?"

Ellie's face darkened. "Probably. But they won't be looking to help me. They'll just send me somewhere worse." Her voice cracked as she clasped her hands together in a gesture that was painfully adult. "Please, don't tell anyone. They'll make me go back. Please. I won't bother you. You won't even know I'm here."

The desperation in her plea hung between them, heavy and undeniable. Will stared at her, his expression cycling through confusion, concern, and something deeper—an understanding beyond his years. He chewed his bottom lip, a habit his mother always said meant he was thinking hard about something important.

Ellie stood perfectly still under his scrutiny, as if her fate rested entirely on what this boy decided in the next few moments. In many ways, it did.

"My dad says that everybody deserves a safe place," Will said finally, his voice quiet but firm. His small face was serious in the dim light, childhood and something older meeting in his eyes. "And my mom always tells me to help people when I can."

He picked up the stuffed rabbit from the floor and held it out to Ellie, an offering and a decision all at once. "I won't tell. It can be our secret."

Ellie's fingers brushed his as she took the rabbit, and they both felt a spark—not just the static from the dry air, but something more profound, a connection formed in this strange midnight moment.

Her eyes, still wet with tears, searched his face for any sign of deception, finding only solemn sincerity.

"Thank you," she whispered, clutching the rabbit to her chest like a shield.

Will nodded as if they'd just made the most important agreement of their lives. Perhaps they had. He glanced at his closet, seeing it with new eyes now—not a space for clothes and toys, but a sanctuary, a hiding place, a secret he'd now sworn to keep.

"Are you hungry?" he asked suddenly, practical concerns asserting themselves. "I could sneak some cookies up from the kitchen."

The question—so normal, so kind—brought fresh tears to Ellie's eyes, but these were different from before. She nodded, a small, cautious smile breaking through her fear like the first light of dawn.

## Chapter 29

THEN:

The Sunday afternoon quiet in the Johnson home shattered like a dropped plate when the pounding began. Three sharp, angry knocks that made the front door shudder in its frame. Kathy looked up from her book, the peaceful moment gone in an instant, replaced by the weight of unspoken dread.

"I'll get it," Henry said, folding his newspaper and rising from his armchair. But Kathy was already on her feet, a mother's intuition sparking in her chest.

"No, I've got it." Her voice was steady, but her fingers trembled slightly as she tucked her auburn hair behind her ear.

In the room upstairs, Will and Ellie sat cross-legged on the floor, a board game spread between them. Will noticed Ellie freeze at the sound of the knocking, her small hand tightening around a game piece until her knuckles turned white.

Kathy pulled open the front door to find Mr. Baker's flushed face, his thin lips twisted in anger. Behind him stood Mrs. Baker, her arms crossed tightly over her chest.

"Where is she?" Mr. Baker demanded, not waiting for an invitation, before shouldering his way into the foyer. His polished shoes clicked against the hardwood floor like impatient fingers on a tabletop.

"Excuse me?" Kathy stepped back, her shoulders bumping against the wall. "You can't just—"

"We know she's here." Mrs. Baker followed her husband in, her voice higher and thinner than his but no less accusatory. "We've been looking everywhere for months."

Henry appeared beside his wife, his stance widening slightly as he positioned himself between her and the intruders. "I think you both need to calm down. This isn't—"

"Don't tell us to calm down," Mr. Baker jabbed a finger in Henry's direction. "You're harboring our foster child illegally. Someone told another one of our children at school that she was here. Apparently, your son has been telling people he has her living in his closet. We could have the police here in five minutes."

Ellie's eyes met Will's. "I only told Peter. I swear. I made him promise he'd never tell anyone."

"But he did," Ellie said and stood, her shoulders slumped. "And now it's all over."

From around the corner of the hallway, Will peered out, Ellie's face visible just above his shoulder. Her green eyes were wide with a familiar fear that made Will's stomach hurt. He reached back without looking and found her hand, squeezing it the way his mom did when he was scared at the doctor's.

"Ellie!" Mrs. Baker spotted them and took a step forward. "Get your things. You're coming home right now."

Kathy moved. "What on earth is going on here, Will? Where did that girl come from?"

The air in the hallway seemed to thicken, making it hard to breathe and heavier than it should be. Will felt Ellie's fingers tremble in his.

"She… she's been here. Living in my closet."

"She has what?" Henry said. "What are you talking about, Will?"

"She's scared to go home."

"She's our foster child," Mr. Baker's voice rose, bouncing off the walls of the modest entryway. "And you've been keeping her illegally! Do you understand what that means?"

Mrs. Baker's thin shoulders hunched forward. "We could press kidnapping charges. Is that what you want? To go to jail?"

Henry cleared his throat, his lawyer's composure settling over him like a familiar coat. "We had no idea she was even here. I think we should contact social services and inform them of the situation. The girl is obviously afraid to go back to your home."

"What situation?" Mr. Baker's voice was dangerous and quiet. "The situation where you encouraged a child to run away? The situation where you've been filling her head with lies?"

Kathy's hands clenched at her sides. "Now listen here. We had no idea she was here, but the way it sounds, she is most welcome to stay. For as long as she wants."

Will watched his mother's face flush with color. He'd never heard her talk like this before, like her words were stones she was throwing.

"How dare you?" Mrs. Baker hissed. "We've taken in six foster children over the years. We know what we're doing."

"Clearly not," Henry said, his usual measured tone giving way to something harder.

Mr. Baker stepped closer, his height forcing Henry to tilt his chin up to maintain eye contact. "You have no right. No legal standing whatsoever."

"And you have no moral standing," Kathy countered.

The words ricocheted around the room, followed by shouted responses that tumbled over each other. Adult voices rising and falling like waves crashing against rocks, hands gesturing, fingers pointing. Will felt the fight washing over him, making his heart beat too fast.

He looked at Ellie and saw her face had gone still in that way it did sometimes, like she was trying to disappear while standing right there. Her eyes darted between the adults, between the front door and the stairs, calculating escapes the way Will calculated baseball scores.

Will's hands felt cold, but his chest burned with a tight, hot feeling he recognized as protective fury. Mr. Baker took another step forward, his shadow stretching across the floor toward them. "She is not going anywhere but with us," he said, each word precise as a hammer hitting a nail.

Ellie's fingers dug into Will's palm, her breathing shallow and quick. Will looked at the adults—his parents' faces flushed with righteous anger, the Bakers' tight with cold fury—and knew with absolute certainty that none of them were seeing what he saw: Ellie, disappearing a little more with each shouted accusation, her small body tensing like a spring about to release.

Will's mind raced faster than his heart as the adults' voices grew louder, sharper. He watched Ellie shrink against the wall, her eyes darting between the angry faces like a trapped animal. Something clicked into place inside him—a decision as clear as the lunch bell at school. They needed to run, now, before the grown-ups remembered they were there, before Mr. Baker's bony fingers could reach for Ellie's arm.

He tugged gently at her sleeve, pulling her back around the corner where the adults couldn't see them. The hallway stretched behind them, leading to the rarely-used back staircase.

"Come on," he whispered, his mouth close to her ear. "We can hide at my friend Jake's house. He lives three doors down, and his mom is nice. She makes the best cookies." He tried to sound confident, like this was just another adventure and not an escape.

Ellie's eyes, so green they reminded him of the marbles he collected, searched his face. Her teeth worried at her bottom lip, a habit he'd noticed appeared whenever she had to make a choice. For a moment, he thought she might refuse.

"They'll just find us," she whispered back, her voice barely audible beneath the shouting match in the foyer.

"No way. Jake has this awesome hideout in his backyard. We built it last summer. Nobody knows about it except us."

Ellie glanced back toward the voices, wincing as Mr. Baker's tone sharpened like a knife being whetted. Her small shoulders squared with decision. "Okay."

Their fingers intertwined, warm and slightly sweaty with nerves. They backed down the hallway, past the framed family photos that now seemed to belong to another life, one where the front door didn't shake with angry fists. Will led the way, walking backward to keep his eyes on Ellie, whose movements had gone silent as fog—a skill she'd explained came from not wanting to be noticed in bad homes.

The doorway was just ahead, its morning cheerfulness now feeling strangely abandoned. Beyond it lay the narrow back staircase that Mom always complained needed updating.

They were halfway across the hallway when Mr. Baker's voice cut through the house like a bullhorn.

"She's not going anywhere!"

Will turned to see the man's tall frame sprinting up the stairs and into the hallway, gaining on them, his wire-rimmed glasses flashing in the light. The stillness shattered. Will yanked Ellie's hand, and they broke into a run, sneakers squeaking against the floor.

"Will! Stop right now!" His mother's voice was high with panic.

But stopping wasn't an option anymore. They raced toward the staircase, its wooden steps rising steeply before them. Behind them came the thunder of adult footsteps, the chaos of reaching hands and raised voices.

"Quick, down the stairs!" Will gasped, pushing Ellie ahead of him. She took the first step, her small body already turning the corner of the narrow staircase.

Will followed, but something made him look back—some child's instinct to gauge the trouble he was in. Over his shoulder, he saw his father's worried face, his mother's outstretched hand, and Mr. Baker's red-faced fury as they all rushed toward him.

In that split second of distraction, Will's foot caught the edge of the top step. His sneaker—the one with the always-untied laces that his mom constantly reminded him about—betrayed him.

Time slowed. His expression shifted from determined to surprised, his eyes widening as balance deserted him. His hand, warm and certain in Ellie's grasp just seconds before, slipped away like a fish darting from reach. His stomach lurched with the horrible sensation of nothing beneath his feet, of falling forward into empty space.

"Will!" Ellie's scream seemed to come from very far away.

His body twisted awkwardly in the air, arms flailing for a railing that remained just beyond his grasp. The first impact came as a shock—his shoulder connecting with the edge of a step halfway down. Then his head snapped forward.

The sound was the worst part—a sickening thud that wasn't quite loud but somehow filled the entire house. Wood against skull, unforgiving and final. Will didn't feel the pain, just a strange confusion as the staircase became a tumbling blur around him.

He bounced twice more, each impact duller than the last as his body went strangely loose. The world spun, with ceiling, steps, and walls trading places in a dizzying carousel. A flash of Ellie's terrified face from above. His mother's scream stretched and distorted like taffy.

Then the final impact at the bottom—his small body crumpling into a heap of awkward angles on the hardwood floor. One arm twisted beneath him, the other flung outward. His legs tangled like discarded string. His head, the one his teacher had just last week called "full of wonderful, wild ideas," lay still against the floor, a thin trickle of red emerging from where it had met the unforgiving edge of the stair.

His eyes, usually bright with mischief or curiosity, remained closed. The shoelace that had started it all trailed beside him, finally, completely still.

The house held its breath. For one impossible moment after Will's body settled at the bottom of the stairs, not a single person moved or spoke. The angry words that had filled the air seconds before evaporated, leaving behind a silence so complete that it seemed to have weight, pressing down on their shoulders and filling their lungs with lead instead of air. Then, like a glass shattering in slow motion, the moment broke.

Ellie stood frozen, her hand still outstretched where Will's had been seconds before. Her mouth hung open, but no sound emerged —just the ghost of a scream trapped behind her teeth. Her freckles stood out in stark relief against her skin, which had suddenly turned as pale as paper. The world had tilted beneath her feet, leaving her unmoored in a nightmare she couldn't navigate.

Kathy was the first to move, a strangled cry tearing from her throat as maternal instinct overrode the paralysis of shock. She lunged forward, knocking against Henry's shoulder in her desperation to reach her son.

"Will! Baby, can you hear me?" Her voice cracked on his name as she dropped to her knees beside his crumpled form. The hardwood floor bit into her knees, but she didn't feel it. Her hands hovered over his body, afraid to touch, afraid not to touch. Finally, they settled on his shoulders with excruciating gentleness.

Henry followed, his movements stiff as though his joints had aged twenty years in those few seconds. He knelt beside his wife, the attorney's composure completely stripped away. His hands trembled as he reached toward his son, gently turning the small body onto its back.

"Will, buddy," he murmured, the words barely audible. The thin line of blood from Will's forehead tracked a crimson path across his temple, disappearing into his tousled blond hair.

Behind them, Mr. Baker stood with his mouth slightly open, the angry flush draining from his face. Mrs. Baker pressed a hand to her lips, her eyes wide with shock. The tension that had held their bodies rigid with righteous indignation dissolved, leaving them deflated and uncertain.

Mr. Baker moved to the phone with fingers that didn't seem to belong to him. They shook slightly as he dialed.

"We need an ambulance," he said when the operator answered, his voice suddenly subdued, the bark of authority gone. "A boy fell down the stairs. He's unconscious." He recited the address when prompted, his eyes never leaving the small body on the floor.

Each step creaked softly as Ellie descended the stairs, her movements slow and dreamlike. Her curly brown hair had come loose from its ponytail during the chaos, framing her face like a tangle of dark vines. Her thin shoulders curved inward as though trying to make herself smaller, less responsible. At the bottom step, she paused, barely breathing.

"Will?" The name emerged as a whisper, hanging in the air between them. None of the adults looked up, locked in their private horror as they were.

Kathy had gathered Will's head into her lap, her tears falling onto his still face. She stroked his hair with shaking fingers, careful to avoid the growing bruise at his temple. "Wake up, sweetheart. Please, wake up. Mommy's here." Her words stumbled over each other, prayers disguised as reassurances. "You're okay; you're going to be okay."

Henry pressed two fingers against the side of Will's neck, his own pulse pounding so hard he had to concentrate to separate it from his son's. The relief when he found the steady, if faint, rhythm nearly collapsed him.

"He's got a pulse," he said, his voice raw. "It's steady. Kathy, his pulse is steady."

Mrs. Baker had backed up against the wall, her arms wrapped around herself as though for warmth. Mr. Baker stood with the phone still in his hand, forgotten now that the call was complete. The rigid line of his back had softened, the bureaucrat temporarily overtaken by the human.

"The ambulance is coming," he said, the words oddly formal in the intimate disaster unfolding before him. "They said not to move him."

Ellie's small hands clenched and unclenched at her sides, uncertainty radiating from her thin frame. A tear tracked down her cheek, then another, silent witnesses to her guilt.

"I'm sorry," she whispered, though no one seemed to hear. "I'm so sorry."

Kathy continued her gentle stroking of Will's hair, her voice a constant stream of comfort. "Mommy's right here, Will. You're going to be fine. Just open your eyes for me, baby. Just open your eyes." Below the forced calm, hysteria lurked, held at bay by the thinnest thread of maternal strength.

Henry's hand found Kathy's shoulder, squeezing in wordless support even as his eyes remained fixed on his son's chest, counting each rise and fall as though his attention alone could maintain them.

In the distance, a siren wailed, growing steadily louder as it navigated the quiet streets of their neighborhood. The sound cut through the terrible stillness, a reminder that the outside world still existed, that help was coming. But inside the Johnson home, time had stopped, suspended in the moment between accident and consequence.

They remained frozen in their positions—Kathy cradling Will's head, Henry kneeling beside them, the Bakers standing awkwardly back, and Ellie half-hidden in the shadows of the stairwell.

The siren grew louder, insistent, promising help and answers. But for now, they waited in that terrible limbo, united in fear around the small, still body of a boy who had only wanted to protect his friend.

## Chapter 30

THE AIR THICKENED with the weight of decades of secrets and pain. I watched Crystal's rigid posture collapse inward, her shoulders curving as though the weight of her confession physically pressed upon her. Her hands—usually so controlled and precise—fluttered uncertainly before settling at her sides, palms open as if surrendering not just to Carol but to the truth itself.

A floorboard creaked behind me. Elijah was still there. For one paralyzing second, my focus split between the knife-wielding woman in front of me and the teenager now dangerously close to her reach.

"Grandma?" Elijah's voice cracked, raw with confusion.

Carol's eyes flashed. Her gaze locked on Elijah, then darted back to Crystal. Something calculated and terrible crossed her face.

"Is this your grandson?" she asked, her voice suddenly soft. "Family is precious, isn't it, Ellie?"

Then she moved. One second, she was backed against the wall; the next, she was lunging, not at Crystal, but at Elijah. The knife slashed through the air, where my gun couldn't follow without risking the boy.

Matt was faster than I'd ever seen him move. He launched

forward, a blur of determined motion, placing himself between the knife and his son. No hesitation. No thought. Pure instinct.

"Dad!" Elijah shouted.

The knife caught Matt's sleeve, tearing fabric but missing flesh. He twisted, using his momentum to knock Carol off-balance, but she was surprisingly nimble for her age. She pivoted, knife still extended.

What happened next unfolded in fragments of time too quick to process. Elijah grabbed the heavy ceramic lamp from the side table. He didn't throw it; instead, he thrust it in Carol's direction, the movement clumsy but effective. Her attention was divided for that crucial half-second.

Matt seized the opening. He dropped low and tackled her around the knees. They went down hard, the impact of bodies against hardwood echoing through the room. The knife skittered away, spinning across the floor like a deadly top before coming to a stop against the baseboard.

I moved in, weapon still drawn. "Don't move," I commanded, keeping my voice even despite the thundering of my heart. With one knee pressed carefully into Carol's back, I holstered my gun and retrieved my handcuffs.

"You're under arrest for breaking and entering, assault with a deadly weapon, and attempted murder." The words came automatically as I secured the cuffs around her thin wrists. "You have the right to remain silent. Anything you say can and will be used against you in a court of law...."

The fight had drained from her. Beneath me, Carol's body shook with sobs. Not the violent rage of before, but something deeper and more hopeless.

"He was only ten," she whispered. "My baby brother. Ten years old."

Crystal knelt beside us, her face streaked with tears. "I know," she said, her voice thick. "I've lived with that knowledge every day." She reached out a trembling hand, not quite touching Carol. "I've wanted to apologize for sixty years."

"Too late," Carol murmured, but the venom had leached from her voice.

The wail of sirens cut through the night, growing louder, closer. Christine must have called them from upstairs when the confrontation began.

"Eva Rae." Matt's voice pulled my attention away from the women. He stood a few feet away, breathing hard from the exertion. A thin line of blood marked his forearm where the knife had grazed him.

"You're hurt," I said.

He glanced down as if noticing the cut for the first time. "It's nothing."

Elijah appeared at his side with a kitchen towel. "Here," he said, offering it awkwardly. Matt took it, their fingers briefly connecting before Elijah pulled back.

"Thanks." Matt pressed the towel to his arm. "Quick thinking with the lamp."

Elijah shrugged, but I caught the flash of something in his eyes —pride, maybe. Or relief. "You moved pretty fast for an old guy."

A smile tugged at Matt's mouth. "Parental superpowers. Activate when needed."

The moment between them was fragile, new. They stood shoulder to shoulder, both still breathing heavily from the confrontation. For the first time since I'd known them, I saw no tension in Elijah's stance as he stood beside his father. No defensiveness. No practiced teenage disdain.

Blue lights flashed against the walls as police cars pulled into our driveway. I helped Carol to her feet, maintaining a firm grip on her arm.

"I'll handle this," I told Matt, nodding toward the door. "Get that cut looked at."

As I led Carol toward the arriving officers, I glanced back. Matt and Elijah hadn't moved. They stood in the aftermath of chaos— surrounded by broken glass, a toppled lamp, the lingering scent of fear—but something had shifted between them. I watched as Matt placed a cautious hand on Elijah's shoulder, and instead of shrugging it off, Elijah leaned into the touch, almost imperceptibly.

They had moved as one during the crisis—Matt diving to protect, Elijah creating the distraction that gave his father the advantage. Two people who had struggled to find common ground had found it in an instant when it mattered most. The connection was tenuous, a first step across damaged terrain, but it was real.

In the driveway, I transferred Carol to the custody of my colleagues, providing a brief explanation. But my attention kept returning to the house, to the tableau visible through the open door: a father and son standing together in the wreckage, building something from the broken pieces.

Part IV

## Chapter 31

ONCE CAROL WAS GONE, I walked back into the house and closed the door. I spotted Matt, perched on the edge of the sofa, his shoulders rigid as if he were bracing for impact. Elijah had left, and the tension shifted. Matt's mother stood across from him, pacing, her fingers working the edge of her shirt into a frayed mess. The air between them crackled with something more dangerous than tension—the truth about to break free after decades of captivity.

I should have backed away. This wasn't my conversation to witness. But my feet refused to move, and the FBI agent in me recognized a confession in progress. So, I stood there, silent as a shadow, watching the foundation of my partner's life crack beneath him.

"I've lived with this secret my entire life," Crystal said, her voice thin but steady. Her silver hair caught the sunlight streaming through the blinds, turning her into something ghostly. "After Will died—after the accident—I couldn't face what happened."

Matt's hands gripped his knees, knuckles white. "What exactly are you saying, Mom? This is all because of this Will?" Matt's voice broke.

Crystal stopped pacing abruptly. "Yes. No. It's complicated." She took a breath so deep I could see her shoulders rise from my hiding spot. "Will's death was… I was scared, so I ran. I put my previous life behind me."

"Previous life?" Matt stood up, the motion so sudden I nearly gasped. "So you did change your identity? Who the hell are you?"

"I'm your mother," she insisted, her voice cracking. "That has never been a lie."

"But everything else was?" Matt stepped toward her, then back, like his body couldn't decide between comfort and confrontation. "Christ, Mom. My entire life, years and years of—what? Playing pretend?"

Crystal moved to the window, her back to both of us. "I chose Cocoa Beach because it was far from Minnesota, and no one asks questions in Florida. Everyone's from somewhere else. The space program brings people from all over. It was anonymous. Safe."

"Safe for who?" Matt's voice had turned to ice. "Was I born before or after this grand identity switch?"

"After." She turned back to him, and her face had aged a decade in minutes. "You've only ever known me as Crystal."

Matt laughed, a hollow sound that made my skin crawl. "So, my birth certificate is fake too?"

"Technically, yes." Her shoulders slumped. "But you are mine, Matt. My son. That's not paperwork—that's blood and bone and every day of raising you."

The silence that followed stretched so tight I could almost hear it hum. I stood motionless, barely breathing. This was the kind of revelation that tore families apart, the kind we uncovered during investigations, not in our living rooms on ordinary Tuesdays.

Matt paced now, running his hand through his hair in the same gesture I'd seen from Elijah a hundred times. The inheritance of mannerism suddenly seemed like the only true thing in the room.

"Every story about your childhood." His voice was dangerously quiet. "Your parents. Where you grew up. All lies?"

"Not lies." Her voice strengthened. "Adaptations. I took what I could from my real life and adjusted the rest. I needed you to have a history that wouldn't unravel."

"What about my history?" Matt turned to face her fully. "Do you have any idea what this does to everything I thought I knew about myself?"

Another silence fell, heavier than the last. Crystal moved to the couch but didn't sit, her fingers tracing patterns on the cushion.

"I never meant to hurt you," she whispered. "I was protecting us both."

"From what?" Matt demanded.

"From who I used to be. From the mistakes I made." She looked up, her eyes clearing. "From the people who might still be looking for who I used to be. I had left my clothes in the river and stolen some new ones from a house nearby. I wanted people to believe I had drowned. But I made a mistake. I went to the funeral, to Will's funeral, or rather, I watched it from a distance, but Carol saw me. She started yelling that she would hunt me down for the murder of her brother. That she was never going to stop. I was terrified she'd find me. So, yes, I ran away and changed my name."

Matt staggered back slightly, like the sentence itself had physical weight.

I backed away silently, my heart pounding. Some truths weren't meant for witnesses. And Matt deserved privacy for whatever came next—rage or forgiveness or something in between. But as I retreated down the hallway, the FBI agent in me was already assembling the pieces, wondering what else Crystal might be hiding.

# Chapter 32

I KNOCKED on Christine's door the next day, then pushed it open without waiting for a response—a parental privilege I'd been reconsidering lately. She sat cross-legged in the center of her bed, surrounded by a semi-circle of college brochures like she was conducting some arcane ritual with glossy paper. Her dark hair was pulled into a messy bun that defied gravity, and her eyes flicked up to mine with that mixture of challenge and vulnerability that had become her default expression since turning seventeen.

"Planning your escape route?" I asked, nodding toward the brochures.

Her fingers stopped mid-page-turn. "Just exploring options." A defensive edge already sharpened her voice. We hadn't even started the conversation I'd come to have, and already the barricades were rising.

I moved into the room, noting the details with my trained eye— clothes folded neatly instead of her usual floor-based filing system, bed made with hospital corners, desk organized with mathematical precision. Christine cleaned when she was anxious. Her room looked like it had been prepared for a military inspection.

I perched on the edge of her desk chair. Not too close. Not too far. "We need to talk. About you and Elijah. I sense something is going on."

"Are we really doing this now?" She tossed a UCF brochure aside. "With everything else going on?"

"That's precisely why we need to talk about it." I kept my voice measured and professional. FBI Agent Eva Rae, not Panicking Mom Eva Rae. "Things are complicated right now. For everyone."

Christine's eyes hardened. "He's not my step-brother. We're not related."

"Technically, no."

"There's no 'technically' about it. Zero shared DNA." She began gathering the brochures, stacking them with sharp, angry movements. "And we're not little kids. I'm almost eighteen, and he's thirteen—"

"That's what concerns me," I interjected. "The age difference—"

"Dad was seven years older than you!"

The comparison stung, mainly because there was truth in it. I tried another angle. "Christine, you're living in the same house. You're part of a blended family that's already under enormous strain. Matt just found out his mother has been living under a false identity. Elijah is working through major abandonment issues with his father."

"And that's exactly why we understand each other." Her voice softened slightly, which somehow worried me more than her anger. "No one gets it like he does. How messed up everything is."

I leaned forward, hands clasped tightly together. "I'm not trying to control you, but I need you to understand the complications here." The words came out exactly as I'd rehearsed, measured and reasonable.

Christine's eyes met mine, suddenly clear and fierce. "You don't get it. When everything else is falling apart, he's the only one who makes sense."

That stopped me cold. I recognized the look on her face—I'd seen it in the mirror twenty years ago, when her father came into my life during another period of chaos. The realization made my stomach drop.

"How long has this been going on?" I asked quietly.

She looked down at her hands. "Nothing is going on, Mom. We've always had a connection. We just started talking more. Really talking. He sees me." Her voice grew stronger. "Not as Matt's girlfriend's daughter or as FBI agent Eva Rae's brilliant mini-me. Just me."

I tried to separate the threads of concern tangling in my mind. Was I worried about the age gap? The family complications? Or was I simply afraid of losing her—to college soon, and now emotionally to Elijah?

"What happens when you go to college in a few months?" I asked. "Long-distance relationships are hard even without family dynamics involved."

"What happens if Matt and his mom never reconcile? What happens if your next case puts you in danger?" She countered, eyes flashing. "Everything is uncertain. At least what Elijah and I have is real."

"And if it ends badly? We all still have to live together, Christine."

"So, we should just not care about each other or anything because it might get messy?" She shook her head. "That's not how you live your life. You chase killers for a living."

"That's different—"

"It's exactly the same. You take risks because some things matter more than being safe." She gathered the brochures into a neat stack.

I recognized the look in her eyes—the same determination I saw in the mirror every morning. And suddenly, I felt very tired. I stood up, knowing this battle wouldn't be won today.

"We'll talk more later."

"There's nothing more to say," she replied, turning back to her college materials, dismissing me with the casual cruelty only a daughter can perfect.

I stepped into the hallway and closed the door behind me. My legs felt suddenly weak, and I leaned against the wall, eyes closed, lungs struggling to fill completely. The house creaked around me, full of secrets and new wounds and complications I couldn't solve with a case board and evidence markers.

My FBI training urged me to analyze the situation objectively: Christine seeking stability in chaos. Elijah finding connection after abandonment. Both vulnerable, both using each other as emotional lifeboats. Probability of emotional fallout affecting family cohesion: high.

I pushed off from the wall and straightened my shoulders. This wasn't a case I could solve with evidence and deduction. This was family—messy, complicated, and utterly beyond my control. Even with all my training and experience, I had no protocol for this. Just the ache in my chest and the knowledge that whatever happened next would leave marks on all of us.

# Chapter 33

I WOKE to silence the next morning. Not the peaceful kind, but the hollow absence that raises the hairs on your neck. The house felt wrong. I slid from bed, careful not to wake Matt, and checked the time: 5:43 a.m. Too early for anyone to be up, too quiet even for sleep. I pulled on my robe and moved down the hallway, my bare feet soundless against the cool tile.

Christine's door was ajar. Strange. My daughter valued privacy like currency. I pushed it open, expecting to find her tangled in sheets, dark hair splayed across the pillow.

The bed was empty. Made neatly.

"Christine?" I called, stepping inside. My FBI training kicked in before maternal panic could take hold. I scanned the room methodically. Closet door open. Dresser drawers pulled out, contents disturbed. Weekend bag missing from its hook. Her phone—the one permanently attached to her hand—sat deliberately placed on her desk.

My stomach dropped.

Beneath the phone lay a folded piece of notebook paper. I snatched it up, recognizing Christine's angular handwriting:

"Mom, don't worry. Elijah and I need time alone. We'll be safe."

The words blurred. My fingers went cold. The note was too short, too vague—a hasty attempt to prevent immediate police involvement. My daughter knew exactly what to say to buy time.

I turned in a slow circle, cataloging details with forced professional detachment. Several favorite outfits were missing. Her toothbrush was gone from the bathroom caddy. No sign of struggle. A planned departure.

"Eva Rae?"

Matt's voice from the doorway shattered my analysis. He stood there in his worn gray T-shirt and sweatpants, his face a storm of emotions.

"Elijah's gone too." His voice cracked. "His backpack is missing and some clothes. The alarm had been shut off."

"They left together." I handed him the note, watching his eyes darken as he read.

"I can't believe this? They ran away…together?"

"Yes. And it's all my fault. I'm the one who pushed them away."

I couldn't argue with the physical evidence of my failure surrounding us—the drawers left open, clothes missing, Christine's phone deliberately abandoned to prevent tracking. Every detail pointed to the same conclusion: my daughter and Matt's son had chosen running away over living with our restrictions.

"It's not your fault," Matt said, placing a hand on my shoulder. "Please don't tell yourself that."

I turned to leave, then paused in the doorway. "But it is. And you know what the worst part is? They probably think they're in love. And instead of guiding them through those feelings, I made them feel their only option was to run. Some mother that makes me."

In the kitchen, I grabbed my phone while Matt paced like a caged animal. Seven steps from fridge to counter. Turn. Seven steps back. His bare feet slapped against the tile, a metronome of mounting anxiety. I scrolled through my contacts for Christine's friends. Cool logic was my refuge, my weapon. Matt's emotional tornado wouldn't help find our kids.

"What are you doing?" Matt stopped mid-pace, watching me pull Christine's class schedule from the refrigerator door.

"Creating a profile. Gathering information." I grabbed a notepad and jotted down Christine's friends, known hangouts, and recent behavior changes. "The first twenty-four hours are critical."

Matt ran his hands through his hair again, leaving it wilder than before. "Jesus, Eva Rae. They're not a case file."

"No, they're two teenagers with a head start if they left after we went to bed." My pen scratched against paper. "Christine withdrew two hundred dollars from her account yesterday. Did Elijah have access to money?"

Matt slammed his fist against the counter. The fruit bowl jumped. An apple rolled onto the floor.

"This is exactly what I meant. You're acting like they're suspects instead of scared kids."

I looked up from my notes. "I'm acting like someone who wants to find them before something bad happens."

"And I don't?" His voice cracked. The broken sound hit me harder than his shouting.

I dialed the police while Matt resumed pacing. Condensation beaded on the windows, Florida's morning humidity already promising another sweltering day. Outside, a neighbor's sprinkler system ticked on, marking time we didn't have.

"Cocoa Beach Police Department." The dispatcher's voice was professionally detached.

"This is Special Agent Eva Rae Thomas." My title slipped out automatically. "I need to report two missing teenagers."

I provided details systematically. Christine Thomas, seventeen. Elijah Miller, thirteen. Possible runaways, potentially romantically involved. Last seen at our home on Deleon Road. Description of both: Christine, five-foot-seven, athletic build, dark hair. Elijah, five-foot-ten, thin, dark hair. Possible clothing, known friends.

No history of drug use. No, no behavioral problems. Yes, we'd had a family disagreement about their relationship. No, no violence or threats.

Matt listened, his expression darkening with each factual detail I provided. When I hung up, he shook his head.

"You know as well as I that this is not of high priority." He leaned against the counter, defeat weighing on his shoulders. "They'll see it as two teenagers in love, not a real emergency. You heard her questions. They already think we're overreacting."

"They'll still search." I pulled up photos on my phone and sent recent images of both teens to the department. "And since it's us, two of their colleagues, I'm sure they'll take this seriously."

"Great. Now our kids will be in some database as troubled teens."

I opened my mouth to respond when movement at the doorway caught my attention.

Crystal stood there in her faded blue robe, hair in a tight silver braid instead of her usual perfect style. Her wire-rimmed glasses magnified red-rimmed eyes, from either sleep or worry. She didn't speak, just watched us with unsettling intensity.

"Mom." Matt straightened. "Did we wake you?"

"The children are gone." Not a question. Crystal stepped into the kitchen, her slippered feet silent on the tile. "Together."

"Christine left a note." I held it up, but Crystal didn't take it.

"I can help find them." Her voice was steady, matter-of-fact.

Matt and I exchanged glances.

"Mom, this isn't the time for—" Matt began.

"I've spent years hiding from people." Crystal cut him off, her hands trembling slightly despite her confident tone. "I know how runaways think, where they go, how they survive."

The kitchen fell silent except for the hum of the refrigerator. Crystal's words hung in the air like smoke, revealing glimpses of the past she'd never fully talked about.

Crystal waved her hand dismissively. "What matters is that I understand how people disappear. The police look in obvious places —bus stations, friends' houses. But smart runaways avoid those traps."

I studied her face, recognizing the calculation behind her eyes. Not the paranoia I'd previously dismissed, but something harder, earned through experience.

"How would you help?" I asked.

Matt turned to me, incredulous. "You're not taking this seriously?"

"I'm considering all resources." I met his gaze steadily. "And right now, we need every advantage."

Crystal's thin lips curved into what might have been a smile. "I'll show you. But we shouldn't waste time."

"These are children, Mom, not fugitives." Matt's voice held equal parts confusion and frustration. "I hardly think they're that clever. This isn't some spy game."

"No," Crystal agreed, her expression softening slightly. "But the principles are the same. People follow patterns when they run. They make predictable mistakes." Her fingers twisted the belt of her robe. "Let me help bring them home."

Our eyes met across the kitchen. For the first time, I saw beyond Crystal's prickly exterior to something unexpected—not just knowledge, but determination gained from whatever secrets she carried, whatever life she'd led before becoming the mother and grandmother we loved so dearly.

"Get dressed," I told her. "We'll start as soon as you're ready."

Matt looked between us, outnumbered. "This is insane."

"No," I said quietly. "This is family." The word felt strange in my mouth, applied to this fractured collection of people bound by choice rather than blood. But in that moment, with two missing children connecting us, it was the only word that fit.

Chapter 34

CRYSTAL TRANSFORMED our living room into a command center with military precision. She spread a map of Cocoa Beach across the coffee table, pushing aside Matt's fishing magazines and Christine's school books. Her thin fingers traced roads and side streets with practiced efficiency, nothing like the hesitant movements I'd come to associate with her. This wasn't the paranoid older woman who checked her locks twice before bed. This was someone else entirely—someone with purpose, with expertise in the art of disappearing.

"They'll avoid main roads," she said, uncapping a red marker with her teeth. "Too many cameras, too many police." She circled a cluster of budget motels on the outskirts of town. "They'll need somewhere to stay, but they're smart enough to avoid using credit cards. That's why they took out cash."

"What about friends?" I asked, sliding Christine's phone across the table. "The password is her birth date."

Crystal didn't touch it. "They won't go to known friends. That's the first place you'd check." She tapped three locations on the western edge of town. "Abandoned properties are another good choice. Kids think they're invisible there."

Matt stood apart from us, arms crossed tight over his chest, his body angled toward the door like he might bolt. He'd thrown on jeans and a rumpled T-shirt, his hair still chaotic, eyes bloodshot.

"This is ridiculous," he muttered. "We should be out looking, not playing with maps."

"Searching without strategy wastes time," Crystal replied without looking up. Her glasses slid down her nose as she marked another location. "You need to think like they think."

"And you're suddenly an expert on teenage runaways?" Matt's voice held an edge of cruelty I'd never heard before.

Crystal's hand paused, hovering over the map. She met her son's gaze with steady eyes. "I'm an expert on not being found."

The silence stretched between them, tight with unspoken history.

"Elijah needs money," Crystal said finally, returning to the map. "Does he have an account? Cash? Valuables he might sell?"

Matt uncrossed his arms, then crossed them again. "I don't know."

"What about friends who might lend him money?"

"I don't know."

"Places he goes when he's upset? Hideouts? Favorite spots?"

Matt's jaw tightened. "I don't know, Mom. Okay? I don't know. You know him best. He's been living with you, remember?"

Crystal didn't flinch at his outburst. "What about social media? Gaming friends? Online connections?"

"He plays those shooting games." Matt shrugged helplessly. "With people all over the country. I don't know their names or if they're even real people."

I watched this painful interrogation, seeing Matt's defenses crumble with each question he couldn't answer. The wall between father and son materialized in the room with us, built of awkward dinners and monosyllabic conversations, of Matt's attempts at connection met with teenage indifference.

"I feel like I barely know my son," he added.

She turned to me. "We should check downtown first, then the

motels and the abandoned properties. They have a head start, but they're amateurs. They'll make mistakes."

I nodded, grabbing my keys from the table. Professional Eva Rae was taking notes on Crystal's methods, filing away questions about her past for later investigation. But mother Eva Rae was simply grateful for any help that might bring the kids home.

We moved toward the door, an unlikely search party unified by crisis—the FBI agent, the disconnected father, and the mysterious grandmother with secrets in her eyes. Our personal grievances were temporarily set aside, replaced by something more urgent. More primal.

"What if we don't find them?" Matt asked as we reached the hallway.

"We will," Crystal said with certainty. "No one stays lost forever. Trust me on that."

I caught her gaze, seeing the weight of experience behind her words. Whatever Crystal Miller had been running from, whoever she had been before becoming the reclusive woman who worked at the space center and tended roses in her front yard, she was now our best hope for finding two teenagers who thought they'd found love.

We walked out into the Florida morning, the air thick with humidity and unspoken fears. The search for our children had begun, but I suspected we'd find more than just Christine and Elijah before this was over. Family secrets rarely stay buried once you start digging.

---

## Chapter 35

---

I GRIPPED the steering wheel tightly enough to leave impressions on my palms. The car cut through the humid air thick with salt and worry, through a stretch of A1A I'd driven a hundred times before —never like this. My daughter was out there. Many years in the FBI had taught me what happens to teenagers who disappear. Those same years had taught me not to think about it.

"Come on, Christine," I muttered, scanning each parking lot as I passed. "Where would you go?"

My phone buzzed with a text from Matt: Any sign?

I didn't answer. Couldn't. Each second spent typing was another second Christine and Elijah remained missing.

The clock on my dashboard read 1:17 p.m. They'd been gone at least eleven hours. Long enough to reach Georgia if they'd headed north. Long enough to reach the Keys if they'd gone south. But something in my gut said they were still nearby. First-time runaways rarely went far—they wanted the drama of disappearing without the complications of starting over somewhere truly unfamiliar.

I pulled into the parking lot of the Palmetto Inn, the fourth motel I'd checked today. The neon vacancy sign buzzed, letters flickering in a desperate bid for attention. Exactly the kind of place two teenagers with limited cash would choose—cheap, anonymous, no questions asked.

The manager barely looked up from his phone when I flashed my badge—he just slid the register across the counter, eyes glazed with boredom.

"No teenagers here," he said when I asked. "Just the usual—truckers and couples who don't want their spouses knowing."

I checked the names anyway. Nothing familiar.

Back in my car, I mentally recalibrated my search grid. Three more motels stretched along this section of A1A. The cheaper they got, the more likely Christine would choose them.

The Driftwood Motor Lodge was empty except for a tour bus crowd. The Pelican's Rest had a clerk too eager to help, raising my hackles. He hadn't seen anyone matching their description.

The Seaside Inn appeared like a forgotten prop from a 1970s film. Paint peeled from the wooden trim. The parking lot was cracked concrete with weeds forcing their way through. I drove past slowly, then circled back, parking across the street.

My eyes swept the row of doors—some with missing numbers, all with faded blue paint. Room 12's curtain was pulled shut, but a slice of light escaped where it didn't quite meet the window frame. Through that slim opening, I caught a glimpse of something that stopped my breath—Christine's purple backpack with the NASA patch, tossed carelessly beside a bed.

I approached the door, stopping to listen. Murmured voices—young, agitated. A laugh, quickly hushed.

I should text Matt.

I should—

I knocked three sharp raps against the door.

Silence fell inside, followed by urgent whispers and the sound of feet scuffling across the carpet. A shadow passed in front of the peephole.

"Mom?" Christine's voice was muffled through the door, equal parts question and accusation.

"Open up, Christine."

The door cracked open, revealing my daughter's face—defiant, exhausted, and unmistakably relieved despite her attempt to hide it. Her hair was pulled back in a messy ponytail.

"How did you find us?" she asked, not moving to let me in.

"I'm an FBI agent. It's what I do." I kept my voice neutral and professional. "Let me in, Christine."

She hesitated, then stepped back. Behind her stood Elijah, shoulders hunched under his oversized hoodie, his lanky frame tense like a cat ready to bolt. At thirteen, he was all angles and uncertainty, his face caught between childhood and something harder.

The room smelled of cheap takeout and cheaper soap. Fast food wrappers littered the nightstand. Two twin beds with faded floral spreads dominated the small space, one unmade, one still perfectly tucked. A duffel bag lay open on the floor, clothes spilling out as if they'd been searching for something in a hurry.

I closed the door behind me and took a slow breath.

"You scared the hell out of us," I said, my voice steadier than I felt. My hands trembled slightly—adrenaline or relief, I couldn't tell. Maybe both.

"We're fine," Christine said. "Obviously."

"Obviously." I echoed, gesturing at their surroundings—the peeling wallpaper, the water stain spreading across the ceiling like a dark continent. "This looks like an excellent life choice."

Elijah's eyes flicked between us, his body language screaming flight. His shoes were still on, laces tied tight.

I sat on the edge of the unmade bed, creating space between us. FBI training kicked in—establish a non-threatening presence, open body language, reduce the subject's anxiety.

But this wasn't an interrogation room, and these weren't suspects. This was my daughter and Matt's son, two kids who had decided running away was better than whatever they were facing at home.

"I'm not here to drag you back kicking and screaming," I said finally. "But we need to talk about what happens next."

Christine and Elijah exchanged a glance loaded with unspoken communication. They looked so young in that moment, so utterly unprepared for whatever they thought they were doing.

"How much trouble are we in?" Elijah asked, the first words he'd spoken since I arrived.

I met his eyes. "That depends on what you tell me in the next five minutes."

## Chapter 36

SILENCE FILLED the motel room like rising water. Outside, a car horn blared, then faded. The ancient air conditioner rattled in the window, pumping out air that smelled vaguely of mildew. Christine sat on the opposite bed, her fingers twisted together in her lap. Elijah remained standing, halfway between her and the bathroom, as if calculating his escape route. I waited. I'd interrogated cartel members and serial killers. I could outwait two teenagers.

Christine broke first.

She looked up, defiance flashing across her face. "We just needed a couple of days to…" She trailed off, searching for words.

"To breathe," Elijah finished for her. He moved closer to Christine, perching on the edge of her bed. Not touching, but close enough. His voice was quiet, but had a surprising steadiness. "Everything at home is just… suffocating."

"Suffocating," I repeated, keeping my tone neutral and letting them talk.

Christine nodded. "Everyone is watching us all the time. Everyone has opinions about everything we do." Her words rushed out faster now. "Dad and school and your job and his grandmother and—"

Their fingers brushed on the bedspread. Not holding hands, just a fleeting connection, but I caught it. Not much escapes an FBI agent trained in behavioral analysis. Especially not when it's happening right in front of you. Especially not when it involves your daughter.

"We just needed space to figure things out," Christine said. As if on cue, her hand found Elijah's, their fingers interlacing.

I took in the protective way Elijah positioned himself slightly in front of Christine, the way they seemed to communicate without words. I'd seen it before, in couples who'd survived trauma together, in partners who'd crossed lines they couldn't uncross.

"How long?" I kept my voice as steady as possible, even though my stomach was doing slow flips in anticipation of whatever answer would come. Christine's whole body snapped taut; she looked ready to duck and run, and if she'd still had her car keys, she might have.

"How long what?" she shot back, like maybe if she put a hole in the question before it fully formed, it wouldn't hurt as bad.

I pushed further, resisting the urge to let them off the hook. "How long have you two been… whatever this is?" I said. In the moment it left my mouth, I realized how little I understood the shape of their connection, and how much of my own fear and projection was leaking into the words. Christine got this wild, almost frightened look, like an animal caught between barbed wire and headlights. Elijah, though, just seemed to shut down: skin going ashen, eyes gone flat, jaw working in a rhythm I knew too well from Matt.

Elijah's lips parted, but what came out was less voice and more exhale. "What do you mean?"

I paused, trying to find the softest way to say it, and failed. "You don't need to explain it to me, but you should probably talk about it between yourselves. And if you're hiding something—if you're having—" I let the sentence trail because I saw in both of them a sudden bracing, as if I'd conjured a parent's worst-case scenario.

Christine's chin rose. "If you're asking if we're together, like dating—no. It's not that."

Elijah's whole face twisted, the muscle under his cheekbone

ticking like a metronome. "Oh, you think… You believe we're… together?" He sounded almost betrayed by the thought.

I held my hands up in a peacekeeping gesture. "The secrecy. The way you talk to each other, the weird coded looks—what am I supposed to think?"

Elijah spat out a laugh that was one part relief, two parts pure insult. "No. Ugh. Christine's basically my sister, okay? That's disgusting." He didn't even look at her as he said it, almost as if the words were meant to build a wall between them and whatever had actually happened.

Christine didn't answer right away. She glanced at Elijah, caught in some silent argument, then looked away and pressed her lips together so hard they blanched.

I pressed, "Then what is all this about?"

A long, silent time stretched, growing brittle with every second. For a moment, I thought Elijah might bolt, hurl himself through the sliding glass door, and sprint into the wet grass. Christine looked at him, then back at me, and in her eyes, I saw something that wasn't disgust but a deep, fractal sadness.

"Well…," Christine started, her voice threading in with the hush of the air conditioner and the low tide of surf beyond the windows, "something happened."

Elijah's shoulders tensed, and a flicker of emotion passed over his face before he schooled his features into a mask of indifference. Christine's eyes darted between us, her hands twisting together in her lap. The weight of her unspoken words hung heavy in the air, thick with tension.

I held my breath, waiting for one of them to break the suffocating silence that enveloped us like a shroud. When Christine finally spoke, her voice was barely above a whisper, as if she feared the truth would shatter the fragile peace we were clinging to.

"It was a mistake," she admitted, each word laden with guilt and regret. Elijah's gaze flickered to her, a mixture of surprise and resignation crossing his face before he looked away again.

"A mistake?" I repeated, my heart pounding in my chest. The

room felt too small, too stifling, as if the walls were closing in on us. "What kind of mistake?"

Christine swallowed hard and cast a fleeting glance at Elijah, who remained as still as a statue, his silence echoing louder than any words could. The confession hung in the air like a heavy fog, enveloping us in a suffocating embrace of tension and uncertainty.

"It was just one night," Christine finally confessed, her voice barely audible, laden with the weight of her guilt and regret. Her eyes flickered with a mix of emotions—shame, fear, and a hint of defiance. Elijah's jaw clenched, his fingers tapping an agitated rhythm on his knee.

I felt a surge of anger and disappointment rising within me, threatening to spill over. "One night?" I repeated, my voice edged with disbelief. The room seemed to constrict further around us, trapping us in this moment of revelation.

Christine's shoulders slumped as she braced herself for my reaction. "I made a mistake, Mom. It shouldn't have happened," she admitted, her words tinged with sorrow. "Please don't be mad. I'm… I'm pregnant."

I froze, the words hanging heavy in the air like a storm cloud about to burst. My mind raced, trying to process Christine's confession. The room felt charged with tension, every breath drawn in heavier than the last.

"Pregnant?" The word slipped out of my mouth, laden with shock and disbelief. I looked at Christine, at Elijah, searching for any sign that this was all some cruel joke. But their expressions mirrored my turmoil, reflecting the weight of the truth that lay between us.

Christine nodded, her eyes glistening with unshed tears. "I didn't mean for it to happen," she whispered, her voice barely audible over the pounding of my heart in my ears.

A surge of emotions washed over me: anger, betrayal, but underneath it all, a mother's instinct to protect and support. "How… how far along are you?" I managed to ask. "And who… who is he?"

"A boy from school. I don't think you know him. It was just a one-night thing… I wanted to try it. I had never… been with a boy."

I felt like the air had been sucked out of the room, leaving me gasping for breath. My mind raced, trying to process Christine's confession and the weight of the news she had just dropped on me.

Pregnant. My daughter was pregnant.

"Elijah was just trying to help me. He has been there for me through it all."

Elijah shifted, a mix of emotions flickering across his face—surprise, concern, and a hint of something I couldn't quite place. His gaze darted between me and Christine, as if trying to gauge our reactions before settling on a steely resolve.

The silence stretched between us, heavy with unspoken questions and the weight of this unexpected revelation. Every heartbeat echoed in my ears, a frantic rhythm underscoring the gravity of the situation.

Finally, I mustered the strength to speak, my voice barely above a whisper. "We'll figure this out. Together," I said, reaching out to grasp Christine's trembling hand. The bond between us felt fragile yet unbreakable in this moment of uncertainty and fear.

I pulled out my phone. "I need to let Matt know you're both safe."

Christine's eyes widened. "Are you taking us home now?"

I texted Matt their location, but added: Found them. They're safe.

His reply came immediately: On my way. Bringing Crystal.

I exhaled slowly. "Matt's coming. With Crystal."

I worried about what would happen when Matt and Crystal arrived.

I felt the weight of my badge in my pocket, the responsibility it represented. For years, I'd balanced being an agent and being a mother, compartmentalizing each role. But here, in this dingy motel room with its water-stained ceiling and flickering lamp, those worlds collided.

"It's not terrible to care about someone," I said finally. "But running away is never the solution. Trust me on that."

"We didn't know what else to do," Elijah said, his voice suddenly small.

The room grew quiet except for the persistent hum of the air conditioner and the distant sound of traffic. A car pulled into the parking lot. Not Matt's car—too early for that.

Both teenagers looked exhausted, their brief defiance crumbling into something closer to relief. Whatever they'd hoped to accomplish by running, reality was catching up.

Chapter 37

THE RAP on the door came like gunshots—three sharp knocks that made Christine jump. Matt didn't wait for anyone to answer. The door swung open, and he filled the frame, backlit by the parking lot lights, his shoulders tense and squared. Behind him, Crystal hovered like a shadow, her hands clutching her purse strap so tightly her knuckles shone white.

For a moment, nobody moved. The motel room shrank around us, walls closing in with each shallow breath. The fluorescent light buzzed overhead, casting harsh shadows beneath everyone's eyes, making us all look haunted.

Matt broke first, rushing toward Elijah. "Thank God," he breathed, pulling his son into a tight embrace.

Elijah's body went rigid. His arms hung at his sides, neither returning the hug nor pushing away. His eyes found mine over Matt's shoulder—panicked, pleading. I gave him a slight nod. It's okay.

Matt stepped back, hands still gripping Elijah's shoulders. Relief cracked across his face like ice breaking on a river, revealing something darker beneath. "What were you thinking?" His voice rose with each word. "Do you have any idea what you put us through? I thought—" He stopped, unable to finish the sentence.

I knew what he'd thought, what we'd both thought. Every missing child case I'd ever worked flashed through my mind like crime scene photos.

Crystal remained in the doorway, her face drawn into tight lines. Her eyes darted around the room, taking in details—the rumpled beds, the food wrappers, Christine's hand reaching for Elijah's. She looked exactly like someone cataloging evidence.

"It wasn't Elijah's idea," Christine stepped between them. "It was mine."

Matt turned to her, anger shifting targets. "You think that makes it better? You two disappear without a word, with no phones, while—"

"Matt," I interrupted. "Maybe you and Elijah should talk privately." I glanced around the crowded room. "Christine, Crystal, let's step outside."

Christine looked ready to argue, but caught my expression. She knew that look—the one that said this wasn't a negotiation. She brushed past Crystal without meeting her eyes.

The air hit us like a wet towel—hot, heavy with moisture. We walked to the railing overlooking the parking lot. Three cars sat in the cracked concrete expanse.

"You should have called us the minute you found them," Crystal said, her voice tight.

I turned to face her. "I needed to assess the situation first."

"Assess the situation?" She nearly spat the words, suddenly sounding just like her son. "They're not suspects, Eva Rae. They're children."

"Exactly." I kept my voice level. "So, I approached them like children, not like fugitives."

Christine leaned against the railing, deliberately looking away from both of us. Tension radiated from her body, her shoulders pulled up toward her ears.

Through the motel window, we could see Matt and Elijah. They stood facing each other, Matt's hands moving in short, choppy gestures, Elijah's arms crossed defensively across his chest. Their silhouettes were framed by the dingy curtains, like shadow puppets in some strange play.

The neon VACANCY sign flickered on and off.

"They think they're in love," Crystal said suddenly. Not a question. Her voice had dropped to barely above a whisper, as if saying it too loudly might make it more real.

Christine's head snapped toward her. "You don't know anything about it."

"I know more than you think," Crystal replied. Her hands smoothed invisible wrinkles from her slacks—a nervous gesture I'd noticed before. "I know how it feels to think the whole world is against you."

Inside the room, Matt had stopped gesturing. His hands hung at his sides now, his head slightly bowed. Elijah's posture had softened, too, arms unfolding gradually. The distance between them had decreased by half. Elijah had told him the truth.

The neon light flashed red again. Matt was speaking now, his words inaudible through the glass but his expression unmistakable—pain, not anger. Elijah's face remained in shadow, but I could see the slight tilt of his head as he listened.

"He's a good father," I said, more to Christine than to Crystal. "He loves Elijah."

"I know that," Christine snapped, but her voice lacked conviction.

Matt moved to sit on the edge of the bed—the same spot where I'd sat earlier. He patted the space beside him. After a moment's hesitation, Elijah joined him, leaving a careful gap between them.

Matt's hand moved to rest lightly on Elijah's shoulder. This time, Elijah didn't stiffen.

The three of us watched in silence as the distance between father and son gradually closed, an invisible current pulling them together against the undertow of teenage rebellion and parental fear. Matt said something that made Elijah's head drop forward, his hair falling across his face. Matt's arm circled his shoulders, and for the first time, Elijah leaned in.

For a moment, they looked like any father and son, the complicated layers of their relationship stripped away by simple human connection.

"We should give them more time," I said.

Behind us, Crystal turned away from the railing, her shoulders drawn up with tension. "I need to sit down," she said, moving toward a plastic chair tucked against the wall. She lowered herself carefully, like someone much older than her years, and buried her face in her hands.

# Chapter 38

THE PLASTIC CHAIR creaked as Crystal's weight shifted. Her shoulders shook with suppressed sobs—tiny, controlled tremors that seemed to travel through her entire body. I'd interviewed enough witnesses to recognize when someone's carefully constructed walls were crumbling. Christine stood frozen beside me, her expression caught between teenage disdain and reluctant concern.

"This is all my fault," Crystal whispered. Her voice sounded scraped raw. "Everything that's happened."

Christine shot me a look—part confusion, part alarm. I moved closer to Crystal, kneeling beside her chair. Professional instinct made me keep my distance and avoid touching her. Witness protocol. But this wasn't an interview room.

"What's your fault, Crystal?" I asked quietly.

She raised her head. Tears had carved pale tracks through her makeup, revealing the skin beneath—not just aged by years, but by something heavier. Her silver hair, always perfectly coiffed, hung limp around her face.

"My real name is Ellie," she said, her voice barely audible over the drone of passing cars and the distant crash of waves. "I should have told you this sooner, but didn't know how to. My name is not Crystal. It's Ellie—well, actually, it's Eleanor Blackwood."

Christine edged closer, her earlier defiance dissolving into wary curiosity.

"Will was everything to me. My protector. My family when I had none." Her voice broke on the word family. "We promised we'd always look out for each other."

A car pulled into the lot, and the engine was cut off. The sudden silence made Crystal's next words seem louder.

"He died because of me."

I didn't prompt her. Didn't push. Just waited, the way I'd waited through a hundred confessions before.

"It *was* an accident," she said, the words tumbling out faster now. "I know this in my heart. But it was my fault it happened."

Christine sank down to sit on the concrete walkway, her back against the railing. All her teenage cynicism had vanished, replaced by rapt attention.

Her voice dropped to a whisper. "He tried to save me. One minute he was there, laughing, and the next…"

A car horn blared somewhere down the street. Crystal flinched as if the sound had physically struck her.

I studied her face, not as an FBI agent but as someone who recognized the ravages of long-carried guilt.

"Eleanor Blackwood," I said, while the pieces fell into place. "She was murdered recently. Why did she have your name?"

"Because we switched identities. I met her many years ago. We were both living on the streets, up north, in upstate New York. We got to talking and realized we both needed a new identity. So, we switched. She was running from her parents, a stepdad who was abusive. I thought if he ever found me, then he'd realize I wasn't her when he saw me. I didn't… well, I should have thought about her safety, but I didn't. I thought Carol would look at her face and know it wasn't the right Eleanor Blackwood. But after all these years, I guess we look more alike now, perhaps. We switched social security cards and went our separate ways. I guess she, too, came to Florida. I had no idea until I saw on the news she had been murdered, and that's when I got scared. I knew I was going to be next. It was really me the killer was looking for. I feared that Eleanor would tell her the truth, and I guess she did, but was murdered anyway.

"Probably so she wouldn't go to the police," I said.

Crystal sighed while shaking her head. "Two people have died because of me."

Christine's eyes widened. "Matt doesn't know any of this, does he?"

"No one knows," Crystal said. She looked directly at Christine, something fierce burning through her tears. "That's why I understand why you ran. But trust me, it never solves anything. The past always catches up, one way or another."

Traffic noise filled the silence that followed. The motel sign buzzed and flickered.

"We need to tell Matt," I said finally.

Crystal's face crumpled. "He'll hate me. After everything I've kept from him—"

"He's your son," I said. "He deserves to know the whole truth."

I helped Crystal to her feet. She seemed smaller somehow, as if the confession had diminished her physically. Christine stood too, her face thoughtful in a way I rarely saw—the self-absorption of adolescence temporarily eclipsed by someone else's pain.

When we walked into the motel room, Matt and Elijah were sitting side by side on the bed. Not touching, but no longer straining away from each other. A fragile peace hung between them, tentative as a soap bubble.

They looked up as we entered. Matt's eyes immediately fixed on Crystal's tear-stained face, his expression shifting from confusion to concern.

"Mom? What's wrong?"

The word—mom—hung in the air between them. Simple, complicated, loaded with expectations. Crystal's hand found my arm, gripping it for support.

The time for running was over.

## Epilogue

THE WAITING room of the women's clinic was filled with the scent of antiseptic, mixed with artificial lavender—a blend meant to calm nerves with a false sense of peace. Christine sat next to me, her fingers nervously flipping through a glossy magazine that boasted "10 Easy Nursery DIYs!" in bright yellow letters. I observed her hands as they turned another page, a slight tremor revealing the anxiety beneath the confident front she had maintained during our drive there. Once upon a time, those hands were small enough to completely encircle my index finger.

It seemed like just yesterday.

"Anything interesting?" I asked, nodding toward the magazine.

"Just stupid stuff." Christine closed it with more force than necessary, sending a small puff of air against our faces. "Who has time to hand-stencil woodland creatures onto nursery walls?"

I smiled despite myself. "People with too much time and money."

"Not us," she murmured, reaching for another magazine from the side table.

Not us. The words lingered between us, loaded with implications. We'd spent the past two weeks recalibrating our lives around the reality of Christine's pregnancy. Her college acceptance to UCF —hard-won and celebrated—was now complicated by the life growing inside her. My career, my relationship with Matt, and our newly blended family were all shifting to accommodate this unplanned addition.

"Your name should be called soon," I said, checking my watch. "They're running about twenty minutes behind."

Christine nodded, unsurprised by my assessment. She didn't ask how I knew. After years of watching me work, she had come to understand my constant awareness of timing, movements, and patterns.

Across from us, a heavily pregnant woman shifted uncomfortably in her chair. Mid-thirties, wedding ring, designer handbag worn at the edges—suggesting financial comfort recently strained. Beside her, a man I presumed was her husband scrolled mindlessly on his phone, occasionally patting her knee without looking up.

To our left, a much younger woman sat alone, arms wrapped protectively around her middle, though her pregnancy barely showed. Her eyes darted nervously each time the door opened.

Christine followed my gaze. "Stop profiling everyone, Mom."

"Can't help it," I admitted, turning my attention back to her. "But I'm off the clock, I promise."

Her hands found another magazine—*Parenting*, this time. She opened it, then immediately closed it again. "How did you do it?" she asked suddenly. "With all of us. While working."

The question caught me off guard. Christine rarely asked about my early parenting years.

"Not easily," I answered honestly. "I made a lot of mistakes."

"But we turned out okay."

I raised an eyebrow. "Debatable."

That earned me a small laugh. Progress.

"I'm serious, Mom." Christine lowered her voice, though no one was paying us any attention. "How will I finish school with a baby? How will you manage with another kid?"

I placed my hand over hers, stilling the nervous tapping of her fingers against the magazine cover. Her skin felt cool despite the overheated waiting room.

"One day at a time," I said. "That's all anyone can do. We figure out childcare. We adjust schedules. We make it work."

"Just like that?"

"No, not 'just like that.' It'll be hard. Probably the hardest thing you've done." I kept my voice matter-of-fact. Christine had never responded well to sugar-coating. "But you're not alone in this. Even though the father has said he doesn't want anything to do with it. Matt and I will be here for you. We'll help you in any way we can. That's the difference."

She looked down at our hands—hers pale beneath my tanned fingers. "Does Matt hate me?"

"He doesn't hate you." I squeezed her hand gently. "He's processing. He and I promised each other we would take care of the baby while you focus on school. You can live with us with the baby and drive to classes in Orlando until you have your degree."

"He's barely spoken to me since I told you guys."

I considered my words carefully. "Matt's had a lot of change in his life. This is one more thing. It's a curveball for sure, but one we can deal with. Give him time."

Christine nodded, but didn't look convinced. She opened her mouth to say more, then closed it as the door to the examination rooms opened. A nurse in lavender scrubs appeared, clipboard in hand.

"Christine Thomas?"

Christine froze, her body suddenly rigid beside me. I felt her sharp intake of breath, saw the panic flash across her face—quick, but unmistakable. For a moment, she looked exactly as she had at seven, standing at the edge of the high diving board, desperate to jump but terrified of falling.

"That's me," she said, her voice smaller than I'd heard it in years.

We stood together. I gathered our purses while Christine smoothed her shirt over the slight swell of her stomach—a protective gesture she'd developed recently. The nurse smiled profession-ally, holding the door open as we approached.

Christine stopped abruptly at the threshold. "Will you come in with me?" she asked, turning to me with eyes that stripped away her carefully maintained independence. In that moment, she wasn't a college-bound adult or a soon-to-be mother. She was simply my daughter, scared and seeking reassurance.

My throat tightened. "Of course," I said, the words coming out rougher than intended. "Whatever you need."

Relief washed over her face. She nodded once, decisively, then turned to follow the nurse. I walked behind them, cataloging details automatically—the corridor's mint green walls, the spacing of examination room doors, the quiet beep of medical equipment somewhere unseen.

The nurse led us deeper into the clinic, her shoes squeaking slightly against the polished floor. Christine walked just ahead of me, her spine straight, shoulders squared. From behind, she looked so grown up, so determined. But I had seen her face when they called her name—had seen the fear she was trying to hide.

I quickened my pace until we walked side by side, my arm brushing against hers. She didn't look at me, but her hand sought mine, gripping it with surprising strength.

"I'm right here," I murmured as the nurse stopped at a door marked Exam Room 3.

"I know," Christine whispered back. "You always are."

Then she took a deep breath, released my hand, and stepped forward into the next phase of our new reality.

The examination room felt smaller than it was—white walls closing in like the pages of an unwritten future. I positioned myself near the wall, giving Christine space as she changed behind the thin privacy screen. The paper gown crinkled loudly as she pulled it on, the sound emphasizing her vulnerability in ways her voice couldn't. I studied the medical diagrams on the wall—female reproductive system, fetal development by week, proper nutrition during pregnancy—while trying not to catalog the thousand ways life could go wrong.

"You can turn around now," Christine said, settling onto the examination table. The paper covering it crackled beneath her weight. She tugged at the gown's edges, trying to maintain some dignity in the clinical exposure.

I moved to stand beside her, noticing how the harsh fluorescent lighting washed out her complexion. Under it, she looked younger, more fragile. The room smelled of disinfectant and hand sanitizer—odors I associated with crime scenes and hospitals, not beginnings.

"Cold in here," I remarked, noting the goosebumps on her arms.

"Everything's cold in these places." She glanced at the ultrasound machine in the corner, its screen dark and waiting. "What's taking so long?"

Before I could answer, three short knocks preceded the door opening. The ultrasound technician entered with efficient movements—a woman in her forties with dark hair pulled back in a practical ponytail and eyes that held the practiced warmth of someone who'd delivered both good and terrible news countless times.

"Christine Thomas?" she confirmed, glancing between us before settling her gaze on my daughter. I noted the wedding band, the sensible shoes, and the way she positioned herself to include both of us in her field of vision. Professional. Experienced. Kind but not overly familiar.

"Yes," Christine answered, her fingers plucking at the paper gown.

"I'm Marisol, your ultrasound technician today." She smiled, wheeling a stool closer to the examination table. "And you're mom?" she asked, looking at me.

"Yes," I said. "Eva Rae."

I stepped closer to Christine's head, unsure where to place myself. In interrogation rooms, I knew exactly where to stand for maximum effect. Here, I felt clumsy, oversized, unnecessary, yet essential.

"This gel will feel cold," Marisol warned, uncapping a bottle of blue gel. Christine flinched slightly as it hit her exposed skin. "Sorry about that. They never seem to make a warmer version."

Christine's eyes found mine, wide with something between fear and anticipation. I reached for her hand without thinking, and she gripped my fingers with surprising strength.

"Okay, let's see what we've got here." Marisol pressed the transducer against Christine's abdomen, moving it with practiced precision. The screen flickered with gray and black shadows, meaningless to my untrained eye.

Then, a sound filled the room. Fast, rhythmic, like distant horses galloping.

"That's your baby's heartbeat," Marisol said, her voice gentling. "Good and strong at 150 beats per minute."

Christine's breath caught audibly. I felt her fingers tighten around mine as my chest constricted. The sound penetrated every defense, every professional detachment I'd cultivated over the years of law enforcement. This rapid, insistent rhythm belonged to my grandchild.

"Is that… normal?" Christine asked, her voice barely above a whisper.

"Completely normal," Marisol assured her. "Baby's heartbeat is typically faster than ours." She adjusted something on the machine, and the image on the screen shifted. "And there's your little one."

I squinted at the screen, trying to make sense of the grainy, black-and-white shapes. Marisol pointed with her free hand.

"Here's the head," she said, tracing a curved outline. "And the spine, see how it curves here? Those are little arms, and—oh!—looks like baby's waving at us."

Christine's eyes filled suddenly, tears spilling over without warning. I brushed them away with my thumb, my own vision blurring.

"Everything looks perfect," Marisol continued, moving the transducer to different angles. "Good fluid levels, placenta looks healthy, baby's measuring right on track."

She took several measurements, clicking and typing periodically. The room filled with the steady whoosh-whoosh-whoosh of the heartbeat. I found myself breathing in rhythm with it, my own heart adjusting to match its pace.

"Would you like to know the sex?" Marisol asked, looking up from the screen. "I've got a clear view if you want to know."

Christine's eyes met mine, questioning. We hadn't discussed whether she wanted to find out.

"It's your choice," I said softly. "Whatever you want."

She nodded slowly. "Yes. I want to know."

Marisol smiled, adjusting the transducer slightly. "Well, I'm seeing three white lines here, which is what we look for to identify female anatomy. Congratulations, you're having a little girl."

A girl. Christine was having a daughter.

The very thought brought me to tears.

My baby was having a baby.

Christine's hand shot out to grab mine, her grip almost painful. Our eyes locked in a moment of shared recognition—a lineage continuing, women raising women raising women. Something primitive and profound passed between us, transcending the complications of our situation.

"A girl," she repeated, as if testing how the word felt in her mouth. Her free hand moved to rest protectively over her gel-covered stomach. "She's real."

"Very real," Marisol confirmed, her smile knowing. "Would you like some pictures to take home?"

Christine nodded, unable to speak. I found myself equally mute, watching as Marisol captured several images from different angles. The technician gently wiped the gel from Christine's abdomen, then handed her a strip of black and white photos.

"I'll give you a minute," she said, standing. "The doctor will be in shortly to discuss the results, but everything looks perfect from my perspective." She paused at the door. "Congratulations to you both." Then she was gone, leaving us alone with the echo of the heartbeat still ringing in our ears.

Christine stared at the photos, her fingers tracing the outline of the tiny profile. "She has your nose," she whispered, attempting a joke through her tears.

I laughed softly, my own emotions threatening to overwhelm me. "Poor kid."

"A daughter," Christine said, the word heavy with meaning. "I'm having a daughter." Her voice caught on the last word, breaking into something between a laugh and a sob.

I sat carefully on the edge of the examination table and pulled her against me, paper gown crinkling between us. She buried her face in my shoulder, her body shaking with silent tears. I held her, my hand stroking her hair as I had when she was small.

"It's okay," I murmured, though I wasn't sure what exactly I meant was okay—the pregnancy, her tears, our future? All of it seemed simultaneously overwhelming and manageable in the aftermath of seeing that tiny heartbeat, those waving hands.

"What am I going to do?" she whispered against my shoulder.

I pulled back enough to see her face. "We," I corrected gently. "What are we going to do? And the answer is: whatever needs to be done."

She nodded, looking down at the ultrasound photos again. "A girl," she repeated softly, and this time, beneath the fear, I heard a note of wonder.

# Epilogue

THE CAR FELT like a confessional booth—private, contained, safe for the truths we'd been avoiding. Neither of us reached for the ignition. The ultrasound printouts lay between us on the console, black and white evidence of a future reshaping itself around us. Christine picked one up, her fingertip tracing the curve of a spine, the round of a skull no bigger than a plum. I watched her face, searching for regret or resolve, finding both in the tightness around her eyes.

Outside, life continued with oblivious normalcy. A young couple loaded groceries into their trunk. An elderly man walked a tiny dog that stopped to investigate every parking space marker. The Florida sun beat down on the windshield, turning the car into a greenhouse despite the shade I'd parked in.

"She has hands," Christine finally said, her voice barely audible. "Tiny, perfect hands."

I nodded, unsure how to respond to the wonder in her voice. "And feet. Did you see those toes?"

"Five on each foot." A smile ghosted across her face before fading. "I'm scared, Mom."

The words hung between us, honest and raw. I'd heard similar confessions from criminals in interrogation rooms, from victims in hospital beds, from colleagues facing impossible choices. Never had they hit me with such force.

"I know," I said, because there was no point denying what we both knew. "It's scary."

"Not just about the birth." Christine set the photo down, her hands moving to rest on her stomach. The small bump was barely visible beneath her loose shirt, but her palms cupped it protectively. "Everything after. How am I supposed to go to college with a newborn? How are you going to manage another kid when you already have enough and work and—"

"One problem at a time," I cut in, using the same voice that had talked jumpers off ledges and hostage-takers into surrender. "College has daycare facilities. We can make it work with your schedule. As for me, I've raised four kids. I can handle a fifth."

"It's not the same." Her eyes met mine, challenging. "You were younger then. And they were your kids, not your grandkid."

"She's family," I said simply. "That's all that matters."

Christine's eyes filled suddenly. She blinked rapidly, looking away. "What about the father?"

"What about him?" I kept my voice neutral, though the thought of the nameless, faceless boy who'd participated in creating this situation and then vanished made my jaw tighten. "You said he doesn't want involvement."

"He doesn't." She fiddled with the edge of an ultrasound photo. "But is that fair? To the baby? To not even know her father?"

I chose my words carefully. "Many children grow up without knowing one parent. Look at Elijah—he didn't meet Matt until he was eight. It's not ideal, but it's also not insurmountable."

"And look how well that turned out," Christine muttered.

"Elijah is adjusting," I said, a defensive edge creeping into my voice. "He's making progress. Living back with us again and being around his father is what is best for him. But it's a lot for him."

"Life is a lot for anyone to take in." She looked down at the ultrasound photos again. "Sometimes I still can't believe it's real."

"The heartbeat makes it real," I said softly, remembering the galloping rhythm that had filled the examination room, how it had seemed to reverberate through my chest, changing something fundamental inside me.

Christine nodded. "I keep thinking about everything I had planned. Dorms. Classes. Normal college stuff." Her hand moved in small circles over her stomach. "Now, everything's different."

"Not everything," I countered. "You're still going to college. You'll still take those classes. Some things will be harder, yes, but the fundamentals haven't changed."

"Mom." Her voice held a note of exasperation. "I'm having a baby. Everything has changed."

I couldn't argue with that. Instead, I reached across the console and took her hand. "What are you thinking about right now? Beyond the logistics, beyond the fears. When you look at these pictures, what do you feel?"

She was quiet for so long that I thought she might not answer. When she did, her voice had dropped to a whisper. "I feel like I know her already. Is that crazy? I've only seen these blurry photos, but I feel like I've met her before."

The confession hit me with unexpected force. I remembered that sensation—the strange recognition of someone I'd never seen. With each of my children, I'd experienced that peculiar *déjà vu*, as if they'd always existed somewhere in my consciousness.

"It's not crazy," I assured her. "It's biology. It's connection."

"I want to do right by her." Christine's eyes met mine, fierce and determined despite the tears threatening to spill over. "I want to finish school and make something of myself so she can be proud of me someday."

"She will be," I said, certainty threading through my voice. "And so will I."

The moment stretched between us, heavy with promises neither of us was sure we could keep, but both of us were determined to try.

Finally, Christine took a deep breath. "We should go. I have that bio lab report due tomorrow."

The mundane reminder of ordinary life—homework, deadlines, routine—felt jarring against the weight of what we'd just experienced. Yet it was also reassuring. Life would go on. It would change shape, adjust its boundaries, but continue forward.

I started the engine, and the car's air conditioning quickly chased away the accumulated heat. As I backed out of the parking space, I looked at Christine. She was looking at the ultrasound photos again, her expression a complex mixture of fear and wonder.

"We should stop for lunch," I suggested, watching the clinic recede in my mirrors. "You need to eat."

"I'm not really hungry."

"Wasn't asking," I said mildly. "You're eating for two now."

She groaned, but I saw the small smile tugging at her lips. "You're going to be insufferable about this, aren't you?"

"Oh, I haven't even started," I warned her, feeling my smile emerge. "Just wait until I start buying tiny clothes."

We drove in comfortable silence for several blocks, the ultrasound photos now safely tucked into Christine's purse. At a red light, I glanced over at her.

"What?" she asked, catching my look.

"Just thinking," I said, "about how much your life can change in a single moment."

Her hand moved to her stomach again in that now-familiar protective gesture. "For better or worse?"

The light turned green. I accelerated smoothly, considering her question. "Both, usually. But we adapt. We survive. We find the joy where we can."

Christine nodded, turning to look out the window. "A daughter," she said softly, testing the word again. "My daughter. Your granddaughter."

I gripped the steering wheel tighter, the weight of this new responsibility settling into my bones, becoming part of me. Behind the practical concerns, the logistics, the worries about Elijah and Matt and our complicated family—behind all that was a simple, undeniable truth: another child was coming into our lives. Not as I'd expected, not as I'd planned, but coming nonetheless.

And despite everything, I felt a flicker of something unexpected.

Not just determination or resolve, but anticipation. Another chance. Another beginning.

"Your daughter," I agreed. "My granddaughter." The words felt strange and right all at once. "We've got this."

Christine didn't answer, but her hand found mine on the console, squeezing once before letting go.

It was enough.


**THE END**

# Afterword

Dear Reader,

Thank you for reading *The Girl in the Closet*. I hope you enjoyed it. I've had the idea for this book with me for a long time.

Ever since my children were young and scared of monsters in the closet or under the bed.

I kept thinking, what if someone actually decided to hide in the closet and live in your house without anyone knowing? And just like that, the story was born.

I'm so happy that I finally got the chance to write it.

I hope you enjoyed it and will take a moment to leave a review, if possible. It means so much to me.

Take care,

*Willow*

# About the Author

Willow Rose is a multi-million-copy best-selling Author and an Amazon ALL-star Author of more than 100 novels.

Several of her books have reached the top 10 of ALL books in the Amazon store in the US, UK, and Canada.

She has sold more than six million books that are translated into many languages.

Willow's books are fast-paced, nail-biting pageturners with twists you won't see coming.

That's why her fans call her The Queen of Plot Twists.

Willow lives on Florida's Space Coast. When she is not writing or reading, you will find her surfing and watching the dolphins play in the waves of the Atlantic Ocean.

**To be the first to hear about new releases and bargains from Willow Rose, sign up below to be on the VIP List.** (I promise not to share your email with anyone else, and I won't clutter your inbox.)

# Books by the Author

## HARRY HUNTER MYSTERY SERIES

- ALL THE GOOD GIRLS
- RUN GIRL RUN
- NO OTHER WAY
- NEVER WALK ALONE

## MARY MILLS MYSTERY SERIES

- WHAT HURTS THE MOST
- YOU CAN RUN
- YOU CAN'T HIDE
- CAREFUL LITTLE EYES

## EVA RAE THOMAS MYSTERY SERIES

- SO WE LIE
- DON'T LIE TO ME
- WHAT YOU DID
- NEVER EVER
- SAY YOU LOVE ME
- LET ME GO
- IT'S NOT OVER
- NOT DEAD YET
- TO DIE FOR
- SUCH A GOOD GIRL
- LITTLE DID SHE KNOW
- YOU BETTER RUN
- SAY IT ISN'T SO
- TOO PRETTY TO DIE
- TILL DEATH DO US PART
- REST IN PEACE
- DARK LITTLE SECRETS
- NOT MY DAUGHTER
- THE GIRL IN THE CLOSET

## EMMA FROST SERIES

- Itsy Bitsy Spider
- Miss Dolly had a Dolly
- Run, Run as Fast as You Can
- Cross Your Heart and Hope to Die
- Peek-a-Boo I See You
- Tweedledum and Tweedledee
- Easy as One, Two, Three
- There's No Place like Home
- Slenderman
- Where the Wild Roses Grow
- Waltzing Mathilda
- Drip Drop Dead
- Black Frost

## JACK RYDER SERIES

- Hit the Road Jack
- Slip out the Back Jack
- The House that Jack Built
- Black Jack
- Girl Next Door
- Her Final Word
- Don't Tell

## REBEKKA FRANCK SERIES

- One, Two…He is Coming for You
- Three, Four…Better Lock Your Door
- Five, Six…Grab your Crucifix
- Seven, Eight…Gonna Stay up Late
- Nine, Ten…Never Sleep Again
- Eleven, Twelve…Dig and Delve
- Thirteen, Fourteen…Little Boy Unseen
- Better Not Cry
- Ten Little Girls
- It Ends Here

## MYSTERY/THRILLER/HORROR NOVELS

- Sorry Can't Save You
- In One Fell Swoop
- Umbrella Man
- Blackbird Fly
- To Hell in a Handbasket
- Edwina

## HORROR SHORT-STORIES

- Mommy Dearest
- The Bird
- Better watch out
- Eenie, Meenie
- Rock-a-Bye Baby
- Nibble, Nibble, Crunch
- Humpty Dumpty
- Chain Letter

## PARANORMAL SUSPENSE/ROMANCE NOVELS

- In Cold Blood
- The Surge
- Girl Divided

## THE VAMPIRES OF SHADOW HILLS SERIES

- FLESH AND BLOOD
- BLOOD AND FIRE
- FIRE AND BEAUTY
- BEAUTY AND BEASTS
- BEASTS AND MAGIC
- MAGIC AND WITCHCRAFT
- WITCHCRAFT AND WAR
- WAR AND ORDER
- ORDER AND CHAOS
- CHAOS AND COURAGE

## THE AFTERLIFE SERIES

- BEYOND
- SERENITY
- ENDURANCE
- COURAGEOUS

## THE WOLFBOY CHRONICLES

- A GYPSY SONG
- I AM WOLF

## DAUGHTERS OF THE JAGUAR

- SAVAGE
- BROKEN

Cover design by Juan Villar Padron,
https://www.juanjpadron.com

Special thanks to my editor Janell Parque
http://janellparque.blogspot.com/